THE FIRST BREACH

Relief was the first emotion that Elspeth felt when she avoided by a hair's breadth the seduction so skillfully planned by the poetically persuasive Mr. Francis Treyford. Elspeth sent that eloquently amorous young man away with strict instructions never to be alone with her again.

But Elspeth's next and even stronger emotion was dread. For she had no doubt that her absent husband, Lord Greywell, would ultimately hear of her near-fall from the position of impregnable maidenly modesty she so zealously had clung to.

Elspeth trembled to think what her husband-in-name-only would think of her then. And she trembled still more to think what he would feel quite free to do. . . .

Lord Greywell's
Dilemma

Lord Greywell's Dilemma

Laura Matthews

For Sue and Albert Walker
with Love

NAL BOOKS ARE AVAILABLE AT QUANTITY DISCOUNTS WHEN USED TO PROMOTE PRODUCTS OR SERVICES. FOR INFORMATION PLEASE WRITE TO PREMIUM MARKETING DIVISION, THE NEW AMERICAN LIBRARY, INC., 1633 BROADWAY, NEW YORK, NEW YORK 10019.

SIGNET, SIGNET CLASSICS, MENTOR, PLUME, MERIDIAN and NAL BOOKS are published by The New American Library, Inc.,
1633 Broadway, New York, New York 10019

First Printing, June, 1983

1 2 3 4 5 6 7 8 9

PRINTED IN THE UNITED STATES OF AMERICA

Chapter One

"She's going to drive me to Bedlam," Sir Edward insisted, his blue eyes scowling beneath bushy brown eyebrows. "You have no idea, Hampden. From the time I get up in the morning until the time I go to bed at night I can feel her watching me, and you may be sure it's not with approval. Why the devil doesn't she get married? She's had opportunities enough! There was Knedlington back when she was only seventeen, but I didn't think anything of it when she turned him off. Seventeen is still a flighty age, though she's never been what you'd call frivolous."

His companion surreptitiously pushed an encroaching dog away with one booted foot. "She's not a bad-looking woman. Handsome in a prim sort of way. Not a beauty, of course, but there's nothing in her countenance to give a fellow a disgust of her. How old is she now?"

Sir Edward allowed his eyes to flick exasperatedly toward the ceiling of the one room at Lyndhurst from which his daughter was most decidedly excluded, his study. Not a very appropriate name for it, he thought. "Five and twenty, for God's sake. Can you believe she's still here at five and twenty? Knedlington wasn't the only one, you know. Somerville came around when she was eighteen, and Prestbury when she was nineteen or twenty, I forget which. And it's not as if they were old men like you and me," he said, not really believing himself old, but willing to concede the point that his daughter was a great deal younger. "When Chastleton showed some interest, I warned him off. He must be my age if he's a day. Probably older."

"Yes, Chastleton has to be almost sixty." Hampden Winterbourne stretched his legs toward the warm fire in the grate, thinking rather dolefully that it was nice to know a few people who were older than oneself and still alive. "Why *doesn't* she marry?" he asked, curious.

"How the hell should I know? To spite me, more than likely. She says she has to keep an eye on my bastards, since I won't do it."

Hampden choked on the sip of brandy he'd just taken. After a fit of coughing he ran a finger under his neckcloth before speaking. "Does she call them bastards?"

"No," Sir Edward admitted. "Elspeth is far too puritanical to use such offensive language. She calls them 'love children,' with the most obnoxious emphasis on 'love.' I've tried to induce her to simply refer to them as illegitimate, but she won't have anything to do with the term, as it in no way links them so thoroughly to me. Imagine, Hampden, having a daughter who is forever harping on one's responsibility to a string of snotty brats. They probably aren't even all mine! The whole neighborhood knows what she is. Any woman without a husband comes running to her, insisting I'm the father, and Elspeth provides her with money. My money! She makes a weekly round of them, you know, seeing that they all have food and medical attention. And whenever she returns from one of her Good Samaritan jaunts, she's out of patience with me and expects me to take some interest in their welfare. Now I ask you!"

Hampden studied his companion for a moment. Who would have thought a fifty-five-year-old man would have such astonishing luck with the women? Sir Edward's full head of hair was beginning to gray and his waistline had thickened somewhat since Hampden had first encountered him in London more than thirty years previously. But the charm was still there, apparently, as it had been when he'd courted Elspeth's mother. Mary was the granddaughter of an earl and could probably have looked considerably higher than Sir Edward, but, no, one look into his lively blue eyes, one evening spent in his intoxicating company, and she never had eyes for anyone else.

A pity she'd died, really. More than ten years ago now, it

must have been. She'd always kept a firm rein on Edward, and he hadn't seemed to mind, but look at the way he'd behaved since then. Odd how grief took some people. Edward had sworn he'd never remarry, though there were women who'd eagerly have had him then, at forty-five, possibly even now. Instead of settling for the comfort of one woman who'd take care of him, he gallivanted about like a man less than half his age, unconcerned with the proprieties and totally lacking in a sense of responsibility to the women he impregnated. Hampden knew a moment's sympathy for Elspeth Parkstone.

He ran a hand through his grizzled hair, shrugging. "You can't expect her to appreciate your providing her with a lot of unrecognized half brothers and sisters, Edward. They must be a great embarrassment to her."

"Not a bit of it! She dotes on them. You've never seen such a mother hen. When one of them is sick, she frets herself to flinders. She knows more about caring for sick children than anyone else in the vicinity, including the doctor. *He* comes to *her* for advice. It's disgusting. And when is it going to end, if she won't even consider marriage? Hinchwick hung around for two months last summer. I know it's hard to believe, when she's already a spinster, but he'd have had her if she'd given him the least encouragement. I threatened to turn her out of the house if she wouldn't accept, and she merely laughed at me. Her own father! Something *must* be done about her."

There weren't many opportunities for Sir Edward to complain about his daughter. His neighbors to a man (and woman) considered her nothing short of a saint (with himself cast as sinner). It was only on those rare occasions when a visitor came from outside the area that he grasped the chance to let off a little spleen. Hampden had been visiting a nephew in Warwickshire for some time and was only making a short stop on his way through to London. Edward didn't expect his old friend to be of any real assistance; he didn't, in fact, feel there was any possibility of his situation changing. Elspeth was going to remain at Lyndhurst for the rest of her life, his nemesis right up to the day he drew his last breath. Perhaps he wouldn't have minded so much if under her austere gray gowns and severely drawn-back hair she hadn't reminded him so thoroughly of his dead wife. It was like having Mary there to witness his dissipation, except that

Mary wasn't there, and he wouldn't be at such loose ends if she were.

His glass was empty, and he rose to pour himself another from the bottle of his best brandy which stood close by. He could hear movement in the hall but relaxed in the knowledge no one would interrupt him. If Elspeth was still up, she wouldn't even bother to put her head in the door to say goodnight. She had learned, some time ago, and rather drastically, not to take such a chance. Edward smiled at the memory. Though it was not without its embarrassment, it had served a most useful purpose. Lifting a brow toward Hampden, who nodded, he refilled his friend's glass.

"She walked in on me once," he explained, though Hampden's preoccupation was not so much with the mysterious smile as with his own thoughts. "I'd warned her that the study was my private sanctuary, but when she's full of zeal she tends to forget ordinary politeness. It was late, about eleven I suppose, and I thought she'd gone off to her room. I'd slipped Fanny in through the side door. You have to do that on account of the servants, of course, though why a man can't do whatever he wants in his own home is beyond me. Anyhow, we were on the sofa over there, naked as the day we were born, when Elspeth walked in without a by-your-leave. I didn't notice, being a bit excited at the time, but Fanny kept poking me in the chest and opening and closing her mouth like a fish out of water.

"Elspeth was standing there with her eyes bulging out of her face, as pale as a ghost. It was rather dark in the room, fortunately. Fanny moaned and covered her face, but I'm sure Elspeth had already seen who she was. I couldn't very well get up without exposing more of myself than was absolutely necessary, and Elspeth kept standing there as if frozen to the spot. Finally I roared at her to get out, and she bolted, dropping some list she'd brought to show me and not stopping to pick it up. She didn't talk to me for a week."

"No wonder."

"Well, it was her own fault. Hell, it would be a lot more convenient to take them to my own room, where I have a perfectly comfortable bed. It's all for her sake that I use the study sometimes, in a pinch. I've been very indulgent with her, when you come to think of it. Maybe if I just paraded them around the house she'd be more eager to marry and leave home," he mused, a thoughtful light appearing in his vivid blue eyes. "I'd never considered that before. Desperate times demand desperate measures."

"No, no," Hampden protested, agitatedly waving a pudgy hand. "You're a gentleman, Edward. One doesn't do that sort of thing."

"What do I care what other people do?" Edward grumbled. "I have a right to some peace in my own house, and I'm not going to get it until I get rid of my daughter. *She* has no intention of leaving. I've told her it's her duty to marry and raise a family; she tells me she's not interested in a life of the flesh. The impudence! It's these demmed religious fellows casting aspersions on anyone who isn't as holy as they are. They just can't abide seeing someone having a good time. And Elspeth's around them all day long, organizing clothing drives and knitting scarves for orphans, running the autumn fete and the spring fete and the summer fete. I thought for a while she must be interested in the rector, though he's a sorry dog with a cadaverous body and greasy black hair. No such luck! Even a bishop wouldn't be good enough for her."

The late October night was becoming more chill, and Edward got up to put another log on the fire. Hampden drew his chair a little closer and allowed the dog to lie on his feet after all. One of the candles guttered, but neither of the men paid the least attention. They sat staring moodily into the flames for a while before Hampden spoke. It had occurred to him it was time he changed the subject.

"I've been with my nephew for some time, you know. Very sad situation. Poor fellow's wife died in childbirth. Fond of her, he was." Hampden sighed and reached down to stroke the dog in an excess of sympathy. "The child lived, but it's sickly, which is a great pity, since it's a son and heir. David's at his wits' end, mourning his wife, worrying that the child will die, plagued by Castlereagh to join him at Vienna for the Congress. You've met David, haven't you? Lord Greywell?"

"Some years ago," Edward answered absently. "Nice-looking fellow, tall, an avid angler?"

"That's him. He's also a superb diplomat." This was said with some pride, though rather offhandedly. "Castlereagh swears he can't pull the Congress off without David, and I'm convinced he'd do better to go, if only to get his mind off his personal troubles. But he won't leave the child there with his household staff when it's so fragile. Though what good he thinks he can do, heaven only knows."

"No man should ever set foot in a nursery," Edward declared with great firmness. "*I* never did."

"No, but you had Mary to oversee things there for you. David has no one, unfortunately. If he had a sister or some female relative . . ."

Edward had been rolling the brandy glass between his hands, not paying as much attention as he ought. He was still obsessed with getting rid of Elspeth. His eyes narrowed now, looking almost black in the dimly lit room. "You say he hasn't anyone at all he can call on?"

"Not a soul. He's the last of the Foxcotts, except for the new son, who might not live. This wasn't the first time his wife had conceived, I gather, but the first time she'd produced a living child. Might have been better if she hadn't tried again, knowing the end result. But there it is. Nothing to be done about it now."

"What he needs is another wife," Edward remarked with an abruptness that startled his companion.

"Another wife? How can you even think it? His poor lady hasn't been in her grave three months yet. Maybe I didn't make that clear."

"Oh, it's clear enough. Greywell should go off to the Congress and leave his new wife with the infant. Of course, he'd need to choose someone with a tender heart, who would look after the child as though it were her own. Someone who knew a bit about the care of sick babes, don't you know. And even then he wouldn't want to settle for just anyone. He's a viscount, after all, and could expect to marry—say, a baronet's daughter who was the great-granddaughter of an earl. Perfectly suitable, I should think."

Hampden was regarding him with a horrified expression. "You can't mean it! He's in mourning, for God's sake! And if your Elspeth wouldn't take Knedlington or Somerville or any of those others you mentioned, why would she consider Greywell?"

"Because," Edward reminded him, "she has a very soft heart for children. The story of the dying child will wrench her to the very soul. Wouldn't it be her Christian duty to save the poor child? Won't she be distraught to hear of a poor young woman dying at such a time? None of my bastards' mothers ever die," he said morosely. "And the children are always obscenely healthy when they're born, though according to Elspeth they have their share of childhood diseases. I tell you, she's just the wife for him."

"He doesn't want a wife," Hampden insisted.

"He doesn't know he wants a wife *yet*. It's the perfect solution to both of our problems." His eyes glazed over with satisfaction as he leaned back in his chair and took a sip of the brandy. "I think the thing for you to do is return to Warwickshire immediately and bring him here. Will he leave the child for a few days?"

"Edward, I think your wits have gone begging. Why would Greywell listen to such a crackbrained scheme? He's still grieving over his wife. He's not likely to dishonor her by marrying again so soon."

"Hmm. Here's what you can tell him. His wife gave her life to present him with a son, his heir, and it's his duty to see that the babe lives to perpetuate her memory. Yes, yes. That's exactly how it should be. No one is going to criticize him when he marries for the sake of his child. They'll understand the necessity and admire him for his courage in seeming to flaunt convention. Did his wife have family?"

"Only a maiden aunt in Yorkshire, who was too ill to journey to Ashfield. She raised the girl and had a friend bring her out in London, where David met her. Look, Edward, it's not the family who're going to oppose your scheme; it's David himself." Hampden swirled the remaining brandy in his glass with more vigor than necessary. "From his point of view, a new wife wouldn't have a vested interest in keeping the child alive, would she? A new wife would want to present him with an heir of her own, to solidify the match."

Edward's brows drew together in a prodigious frown. "I doubt if even Greywell could conceive of a woman's allowing a child to die because she wanted to present him with his heir. It's too monstrous to contemplate," he added self-righteously. "You know Elspeth better than that, and I'm sure you can convince your nephew of her rectitude. No one who's ever met Elspeth doubts her rectitude."

Hampden finished off his brandy in a gulp and set his glass on the table nearest him with a decided thump. "I'm due in London.

You'll have to excuse me from going back to Warwickshire, Edward."

Seeing the futility of urging that particular plan, Edward wisely backed off from it. "Of course, of course. You're a busy man, and you've already allotted a generous amount of time to your nephew. It was unconscionable of me to suggest such a scheme. A letter would be much the better idea, in any case. That would give Greywell a chance to mull over the proposal. He's likely, as you have, to reject it out of hand at first sight, but its merits may appeal to him after a little consideration. Well, of course they will, because it's an eminently suitable arrangement for everyone involved. Write him that he must come to stay with me and meet her before he makes up his mind."

"And what of Elspeth?"

"I can handle Elspeth," Edward assured him, with ungrounded optimism. "You have only to do your part and the thing is as good as done."

Hampden and Elspeth sat across the breakfast table from each other in the morning after Sir Edward had been called away to settle an urgent estate matter. No mention had been made of Lord Greywell and his sickly son. Elspeth was calmly buttering a muffin while she spoke of her parish activities. Her gray wool dress did not completely disguise her attractive figure, but went a good way toward doing so, and the style in which she wore her hair, pulled starkly back from her face, did litttle to soften the strong features with which she'd been endowed.

Her eyes were more hazel than green and were given to observing one in a disconcerting way, as though she had no patience with circumspection. Her high cheekbones and straight nose were emphasized by the scalped coiffeur she affected, and would have been greatly softened by some ringlets about her face. There was no way to conceal the soft, full lips other than keeping them in a prim line, which she attempted for the most part to do. When she smiled they curved slightly, but Hampden wasn't honored by a laugh.

Not the way she'd been as a child, he thought unhappily, when her lips were forever curling with delight, and her luscious laughter had bubbled forth without a moment's thought. Her golden-brown hair had more often than not been slightly disarrayed then, from her youthful exertions; still, that was a great deal more attractive than the matronly knot she wore now at the back of her head. Hampden remembered Elspeth as a spirited child, running almost wild over the estate, to the consternation of her mother and the delight of her father. The change in her had come about shortly after her mother's death, he thought, and the mischievousness that had so endeared her to the childless Winterbournes had never returned.

Hampden's wife had been Elspeth's godmother, and had looked forward after Mary died to bringing Elspeth out in London, but even that hope had faded as her own health deteriorated. Elspeth had insisted it made no difference; her letter had been full of concern for Mrs. Winterbourne, and had just mentioned that the frivolity of London was not, after all, just the sort of setting to which she was accustomed. Hampden had always thought it might have made all the difference, induced her out of her narrow life. But that chance was gone.

"You seem to keep quite busy," he remarked as he added cream to his coffee.

"Oh, there's always more to be done than there's time for," she said, giving him one of her halfhearted smiles. "The rector is a great one for putting idle hands to work. Things run so smoothly at Lyndhurst I rarely have to spend more than an hour or two a day on my household duties. I'm afraid we didn't give you much of a treat last night," she apologized, remembering the rumpsteak-and-kidney pudding, and the curried fowl. "If you'll stay over another night I'll plan something special—fricasseed sweetbreads or savory rissoles, with a second course of sirloin of beef and roast partridges. Papa didn't expect you until today."

"Can't stay, I'm afraid, my dear. I have business in London, and then I must go off to Kent as soon as may be. I long for my own bed, and my own things around me. You must understand how it is."

"Well, no," she admitted. "Actually, I've seldom been away from Lyndhurst since I was a child. The only times I've spent a night other than in my own bed were when I was nursing a sick child elsewhere, or was forced by inclement weather to spend the night at a neighbor's."

"Would you like to travel a bit?"

Elspeth looked surprised. "Travel? How should I do that? No, no, there is no chance of it, and I'm content to do my wanderings in the books I read. I'm needed in the parish, you know.

These are difficult times for the poor folk. They make so little for their piecework, with the manufactories producing so much at such low cost. Not that I approve of how they treat their workers! You mustn't think that. The conditions and the hours are quite appalling. I hear of the hardships. Whole families have moved to Manchester and Birmingham in hopes of making a better living, and they find themselves little if any better off than they were in the village. Often worse." She sighed and set down the remaining bite of her muffin. "We have so much compared to them."

"Yes, well, that's only to be expected, isn't it?" Hampden asked rhetorically. Such discussions made him uncomfortable.

"But we live in complete idleness and comfort while these people work and starve," Elspeth protested. About to let herself get carried away, she noticed that his expression was pained, and she abruptly reined in her enthusiasm. Too often that glazed look had come into her father's eyes, indicating the hopelessness of further expostulation. She picked up the last bite of muffin and asked, "Will there be decent hunting in Kent this winter?"

Relieved, Hampden set down his coffee cup to eye her with approval. Smart woman, to know when she'd gone past the bounds of pleasing. While he extolled the merits of his pack of foxhounds and his various hunters, he was turning over in his mind the possibility that Edward's plan might not be so far-fetched after all. Elspeth was a good listener, asking the right questions, and making the right comments. Her sympathy with the downtrodden was evidence of her kind heart, and if there was one thing David needed just at the moment, it was someone with a concern for the weak. Maybe he would just write that letter before he set off for London after all. What harm could it do?

"Too bad Hampden couldn't stay longer," Sir Edward muttered as he watched the traveling carriage disappear at the end of the drive. "We don't see much of him these days."

"No," Elspeth said absently. "A pity. Maybe you could visit him in Kent sometime. I gather he was only up this way to see his nephew."

Edward studied her face as she rearranged the candlesticks on a hall table. "Poor fellow, Greywell. I suppose Hampden told you about his misfortunes."

"About his wife's dying in childbirth? Yes. How dreadfully sad."

"And he mentioned the baby, and how sickly it is?"

"Yes. I told him he should write his nephew and suggest a different wet nurse. Sometimes one's milk won't agree with the child."

Edward didn't want to think about things like that. The thought of childbirth and nursing babies was almost (but not quite) enough to put him off lovemaking for good. "I'm sure it's more than that. The child obviously needs constant care, and no village girl is going to know how to give the proper attention. Certainly Lord Greywell doesn't know a thing about it. He needs someone capable to come in and take charge for him."

His insistence on the topic caused Elspeth to glance at him sharply. "If he wants the child to live, I'm sure he'll think of that."

"How could he not want the child to live?" demanded her father. "It's his heir, for God's sake. He's the fourth viscount, and he's not going to want to see the title lost after his time."

"I dare say," Elspeth rejoined indifferently. "If you'll excuse me, Papa, I should check the kitchen garden. There's going to be a frost tonight."

"Don't you *care* if the child dies? You who spend your entire life fussing over those . . . children in the village? Doesn't Greywell's plight affect you in the least?"

Elspeth paused at the doorway, frowning slightly. "But there's nothing I can do about it, Papa. It's very sad, of course, and I shall remember the poor child in my prayers. Don't forget you promised you'd go around to Mr. Knowle's this afternoon to see the gray mare." With a slight nod, she disappeared through the door.

The kitchen garden was protected by a stone wall covered with deep-red ivy at this time of year, as were all the buildings at Lyndhurst. Elspeth grew various herbs there, for cooking and medicinal purposes, and she planned to gather any lingering growth before the first real frost rendered the plants useless. It was only an excuse, though, to leave her father. She could have picked them at any time during the day, and even if she'd forgotten, there wouldn't have been much lost.

Why had Sir Edward suddenly taken an interest in Hampden

Winterbourne's nephew and his sickly child? Her father, charming but callous, had never shown the least concern for his own love children, sick or well, and she was highly suspicious of this sudden charity in him. Elspeth speculated that he might want her to go off to Coventry and take care of the child, leaving him in peace, but he must know as well as she did that such a scheme was totally ineligible. With no relationship between them, she couldn't very well live in the same house with Greywell, even if he had a dozen housekeepers to chaperon them. Besides, she didn't know the viscount; had never met him in her life.

As she mused over this mystery, the garden gate swung open to admit the Reverend Mr. Blockley, smiling in that fatuous way he had. "Beeton told me I'd find you here," he intoned in his deep, dramatic voice. That was perhaps Blockley's only really appealing quality, his voice. And issuing from his cadaverous body it had more a melancholy tint than one of holy reverence. Still, he was dramatic enough in appearance to hold the villagers' attention during services on Sundays, though his learning was slight and his breath often bad.

Mr. Blockley had recently latched onto the idea that Elspeth had conceived a passion for him, and had coyly courted her for several months before she put a stop to his absurd declaration. Though things had been awkward between them for a few weeks, Elspeth hoped she had weathered his scowls and attempts to find fault with her parish endeavors. She was by now accustomed to the moods of men, and had developed a sort of pious blanket which their barbs could not penetrate without greater malevolence than most of them were willing to expend on her.

"You look charming," he said, quite untruthfully, since he didn't approve of her low-necked gray wool gown, though it was worn with a lace tucker.

The dress was actually one of Elspeth's best daytime gowns. She had worn it expressly because Hampden Winterbourne was visiting and seemed to merit some special effort on her part. Unaware that he thought it dowdy, she was even less interested in Blockley's opinion, which she rightly guessed to be quite opposite from his remark. "We've had a visitor," she said, wandering over to the herbs and beginning to pluck and put them in her basket. "An old friend of my parents'. He's just left. He only stopped over on his way back to London."

"You didn't mention expecting anyone. I'd have been happy to call."

"He only spent the night. I wasn't expecting him until today, actually. There was no need for you to call."

Mr. Blockley was offended. Only on account of Elspeth's visitor's taking such a very short stay was he able to forgive her for not notifying him of the occasion. The fact that her visitor had come a day early was totally irrelevant.

The few sprigs left in the garden found their way to her basket, and Elspeth realized she had no option but to invite Mr. Blockley to tea with her. He invariably acted as though there were some unspoken significance in the gesture. "Won't you join me for tea?" she asked now, already heading toward the house. "Papa may still be here, though he's supposed to go to the Knowles' this afternoon."

"I'd be honored," the rector replied, a smirk twisting his lips. "If Sir Edward is still at home, of course I'd wish to pay my respects to him."

But Sir Edward had left, or at any event had hidden himself so well Beeton was unable to locate him, and Elspeth led Mr. Blockley to the Gold Saloon resigned to entertaining him by herself. She was careful to choose one of the Queen Anne chairs, because if she sat on the sofa he would certainly place his emaciated body as close to hers as he dared.

Until the tea tray was brought in, his eyes wandered about the room, lighting on those objects he most admired—the sleigh-shaped settee in the corner, the pair of rosewood card tables inlaid with brass marquetry, the ormolu clock depicting a boat navigated by Time and Youth, the pair of French candelabra in the form of Cupid drawing a bow, the half-dozen *famille rose* Chinese vases. Elspeth herself found little to admire in the room besides the Queen Anne chairs. Her taste was much less ornate than that of either her late mother or her father, and she would have been content to consign most of the elaborate pieces to the attics, or donated them to one of the church fetes as prizes.

"Mrs. Beeton has done herself proud," Mr. Blockley announced, eagerly eyeing the plates piled with cakes and biscuits. "I wonder if she knew who it was who was joining you."

"I'm sure she must have," Elspeth said, "since Beeton himself carried word to her when he carried my basket to the kitchen."

"Lord Knedlington swears he wouldn't have a woman cook in his house. I'm sure I've heard him say it half a dozen times."

"Yes, Lord Knedlington does have a habit of repeating himself," Elspeth agreed. "The meals I've partaken at Mundham haven't been anything out of the ordinary, however. Mrs. Beeton does very well for our purposes."

"Quite, quite." He downed one of the small cakes in two bites and wiped his fingers fastidiously on a napkin. "Sir Edward is not fond of entertaining, I believe."

"Only when I urge the necessity on him," Elspeth said, wondering how many times they'd covered this ground. Mr. Blockley was not an outstanding conversationalist. His interests were narrow and his opinions were legion.

"I came by today especially to speak with you," he said now, drawing his chair a little nearer to hers. "It has come to my attention that you've spoken with Jane Berwick, promising to give her support for her child. Really, Miss Parkstone, it won't do!"

Elspeth stared at him in surprise. "Why ever not? You know I've made similar arrangements with several . . . others in the neighborhood. Since my father doesn't see fit to do so, I have no choice but to attend to the matter myself."

"But Jane Berwick isn't a member of the church, my dear! One can't be doling out charity to a heathen. It's quite obvious she isn't properly penitent."

"I see. She and her babe are to starve because they don't fall within your purview. I've never heard such nonsense, Mr. Blockley," she declared, setting down her teacup and frowning at him. "Perhaps you think my father is penitent? If there is error here, it is as much on his side as hers, and I certainly can't recall when last he attended church. Really, I'm surprised at you."

His sunken cheeks swelled with indignation. "My dear Miss Parkstone, you are no judge of the matters involved here. Do you presume to tell me how to conduct the spiritual business of this parish? Sir Edward's behavior is not for you to criticize. I thought I had made that perfectly clear to you years ago. He is your father, and you owe him a proper respect. I am the rector of your church, and you owe me no less. These are concerns in which I am highly educated, ordained to carry out for the Church of England. No one has ever questioned my authority in the parish, least of all a woman of your age. I think you owe me an apology."

Elspeth considered his mottled face for a few moments before rising from her chair to pace about the room. "I don't question your authority in spiritual matters, Mr. Blockley," she murmured with her back to him. "But I question anyone's right to allow a woman and child to starve for any reason, least of all a Christian one. My father got Jane Berwick with child, and—"

"Ah, but he didn't," the rector interrupted triumphantly. "Or if he did, it was the merest chance. Everyone knows the Berwick woman had been keeping company with that n'er-do-well Odiham, who was forever throwing himself on the parish to support. Well, he's in the workhouse now, having refused to marry her, and she's simply looking for someone to support her. What an easy mark you proved! How foolish you will look supporting her and her child, when everyone knows the babe is not Sir Edward's. She's a loose woman, Miss Parkstone, with an eye for any advantage to herself. How your neighbors will laugh at you! And when I come to warn you of the disaster, you rip up at me like the veriest shrew." He straightened his neckcloth with a smugness that grated on Elspeth's nerves, and when he lifted one eyebrow to state, "It is most fortunate you and I never formed a closer connection," she almost walked from the room.

"Most fortunate," she said in a flat voice. Her interview with Jane Berwick had been almost as trying as this one, and she had only agreed to provide for the woman and her child out of a sense of duty, and because the woman's full-blown figure was just the sort that seemed most to attract Sir Edward. If what Blockley said were true . . . well, it wouldn't really have mattered, since the parish was in no position to take care of the woman, and she really couldn't be allowed to starve, could she? It was true Jane had spent a great deal of time with the man Odiham, and it had made Elspeth wonder, but there had seemed nothing else she could do. She had been firm in not allowing the woman to bargain for more money than Elspeth ordinarily awarded to Sir Edward's love children.

"You will, of course, excuse me," Mr. Blockley said now, rising and smoothing down his sleeves. "I think this must be a good lesson to you, Miss Parkstone, on the errors of self-conceit. It does not become a young woman to think so highly of herself that she sets herself in opposition to her father and her pastor. Good day."

There were a great many things Elspeth would have liked to say to him, but she didn't. She was not a docile woman by nature, and his goading infuriated her so she could scarce sit down when he had withdrawn from the room. Instead she grabbed up a queen cake remaining on the plate (there was only one left, since he had eaten four of them) and ran with it to the window overlooking the drive he must ride down as he took his departure. Years had passed since she had aimed a projectile at anything, least of all a man's hat, but she silently opened the window and waited for his tall, lean figure to pass beneath her on horseback. Taking careful aim, she sailed the cake downward at the beaver he wore, and felt a great deal of satisfaction as it smacked the hat from his greasy black locks. She quickly hid behind the draperies to one side of the window and listened to the very ungenteel language he spouted.

"Where are you, scoundrel?" he yelled. "How dare you knock the hat from a man of the cloth? Have you no respect? Demme, you have not heard the last of this." There were sounds of scuffling on the drive, and Elspeth peeked out to see him attempting to regain his horse, which was loath to stand still while Mr. Blockley tried to put his foot in the stirrup. His hat, already muddy from its first fall, tumbled from his head again and was trampled under the horse's hooves and permanently ruined. With another muffled oath the rector grabbed hold of the reins with a violent tug, and the bay balked, releasing himself, and cantered off down the drive.

Mr. Blockley stared after his horse and then threw one last, scathing glance about him to discover the perpetrator of this foul deed. It did not occur to him for even a moment that it was Elspeth Parkstone. The queen cake had disintegrated on impact. Any urchin might have done it, he decided. Possibly one of the stable lads whom he'd reproved for their laziness when he'd left his horse before joining Miss Parkstone in the kitchen garden.

As he stomped down the drive, meditating on the two-mile walk he had ahead of him, Elspeth stood at the window and made a face at his retreating back. It was the first time she'd behaved in such a fashion since her mother's death, and she felt surprisingly good about it, all things considered.

Chapter Two

David Foxcott, Fourth Viscount Greywell, read Hampton Winterbourne's letter with mounting astonishment. His uncle had always seemed a sensible, if rather prosaic, gentleman, and his kindness in coming to stay with Greywell during the last few months had been more than welcome. There was great relief in having someone lift him even temporarily out of his solitary grief. That his Uncle Hampden had been unable to provide him with any answers to his dilemma was only expected. To have him suddenly propose a most outrageous solution was enough to make Greywell toss the letter angrily from him onto the growing pile of condolence letters.

The draperies had been drawn against the gathering gloom outside and a lamp burned at the corner of his desk, but he closed his eyes against even the flickering images of the furniture around him. He was still in his riding clothes, his topboots dusty from the long, exhausting gallop he'd made that afternoon. Always he hoped for some cessation of the pain he felt, hardly believing that this nightmare wouldn't end and everything be as it had four months previously. But nothing changed. When he returned to the manor Caroline wasn't there, his child was still feebly clinging to life but showing no improvement, his servants went around with hushed voices and soft treads. He had no appetite for the meal which would soon be announced, and could scarcely remember what Mrs. Green had planned to tempt him, though she had, as always, taken the trouble to consult him that morning.

Several times Greywell had told himself he must get hold of his life, take a firm grip on the reins once again and move forward. But there was no direction in which he chose to go. If circumstances had permitted, he would have gone to Vienna, knowing that his services might be useful. The involvement in diplomatic bargaining would have brought some release from tormenting thoughts of his wife. Poor Caroline, so young, so vital, now laid to rest in the churchyard with the unweathered marble tombstone. He had stopped visiting her grave regularly, since people stared at him so, and there was really no purpose served. He thought of her no less often in the house, or out riding, or even by the river where he had attempted to fish once or twice since her death. Was there no end to this regret?

Apparently the doctor had warned Caroline that it would be a difficult delivery, but she'd not told Greywell, until the pains started. In fact, she had confessed then that the doctor had told her it wouldn't be safe to try for another child after her two disastrous miscarriages. Why hadn't Wellow told him? But Greywell knew. The doctor had assumed Caroline would tell him, and she hadn't. She was young and spirited and prone to think of herself as invulnerable. Greywell remembered she had said, shortly after the second miscarriage, that doctors didn't know everything. Sometimes Greywell wondered if she'd worried during the time she carried the child, but he'd never seen any evidence of it, and he could almost believe she'd forgotten the doctor's warning. She had been good at forgetting things she didn't wish to remember.

It was not her fault, really, that she'd developed a rather self-centered view of life. Her parents' only child, she had been petted from the moment of her birth, and when her parents had died, her aunt had cosseted her out of infinite pity for her loss. The wonder was, rather, that even given her tendency to think first of herself, she had been such a delightful young woman. Her iron will had not made her any less outgoing, or any less desirable. She had reminded Greywell of a Greek goddess—beautiful, imperious, and yet intelligent and carelessly generous. It was her vitality, her intoxication with life, that had first attracted him to her. He had seen her at Lady Rossmore's ball, surrounded by half a dozen gentlemen, her eyes sparkling with excitement and good humor, and he had immediately begged an introduction. While the other fellows hesitated, fingering their cravats and their quizzing glasses, he had walked away with her for the first quadrille of the evening, and he'd never regretted his determination.

Caroline had been too young at the time, not quite eighteen, to have given much thought to marriage. Her life consisted of a swirling round of balls and parties, breakfasts and picnics, rides and drives in Hyde Park. Greywell had not rushed her. It had been his tactic to watch from the sidelines, occasionally escorting her and her aunt's friend (who had introduced her to London) to some entertainment, but never making a fool of himself as some of her youthful admirers did with their histrionics. He was her most elusive suitor, always elegant, always polite, always an amusing companion, but never quite declaring himself as the others were wont to do. Whether this appealed to her as a challenge or whether she merely became accustomed to his steady regard, Greywell never exactly knew, but she turned to him in the end, during her second season in London.

Perhaps it was an acknowledgment of her need for a stabilizing influence in her life, a solid core around which she could revolve at will and return to with relief. Even after they were married she continued to attend half a dozen entertainments each week, but she seemed to appreciate a quiet evening at home with him as well, where they would sit in front of the fire, with him reading aloud from some novel he thought she'd enjoy, or explaining to her the intricacies of foreign policy. She would sit beside him on the sofa in the London house, her blond hair spilling over his shoulder, her head nestled against his cheek . . .

Greywell was rudely wrested from this revery by a tap at the window. Frowning, he rose to pull back the curtains, knowing even before he revealed his caller who it would be. No one in the entire length of his thirty-two years had been given to tapping at his window to gain his attention except Abigail Waltham. She peered at him now, myopically, through the glass, her wispy gray hair tossed by the slight breeze, her features indistinguishable in the gathering dusk. Greywell had never understood why she didn't come to the front door, a much more appropriate form of entry, but he smiled now, with faint welcome, and motioned her toward the library, where doors opened out onto the terrace.

Abigail wore only a thin shawl against the cool October evening, and he brought her back to the study where the fire would warm her.

"You really shouldn't come out so ill prepared for the weather," he chided as she huddled into the chair he set by the hearth. There was no use mentioning the length of her walk, or the lateness of the hour. He seated himself opposite, regarding her with rueful gray eyes.

"I don't feel the cold so much," she insisted, toasting her hands and feet at the blaze. "The exercise is good for me."

"Would you care for a glass of wine or brandy?"

Mrs. Waltham kept no spirits or wine in her house. Despite the appearance of her ancient clothing, it was a very handsome house, and she had a very handsome income on which to live since her husband's death a dozen years previously. She drank beer at home, as her servants did, perhaps out of economy, perhaps out of conviction. But when she was abroad (and sometimes Greywell thought it the reason she went abroad) she was easily induced to imbibe a little something against the cold, or against the length of her return walk home.

"I don't mind if I do," she said now, and watched as Greywell gave a tug on the pull.

"Perhaps you'll join me for dinner."

"No, no, I couldn't do that. The cats expect me at dinnertime. They wouldn't approve of my being out."

Greywell nodded, never surprised at any answer she might give. Sometimes it was the cats, sometimes the servants who expected her. Occasionally she slipped into the past and thought it was her husband. When Selsey entered to his summons, the viscount instructed him to bring the best brandy, since he knew Abigail was particularly fond of it.

"I came because you needed to talk to me," Abigail informed him when Selsey had bowed himself out the door.

"I see." Greywell allowed no hint of surprise or amusement to filter into his voice. "I appreciate your thoughtfulness, Abigail. Did you . . . perhaps know what it was I wished to discuss?"

She pursed her lips thoughtfully and regarded him with her small, sharp eyes. "You would be the one to know, wouldn't you? I'm not a reader of minds."

This was probably true, as Greywell had not consciously determined to speak to anyone, about anything. It was as good an excuse as any for her to come by and have a glass of brandy, but it seemed rather a long walk for so simple a pleasure. Finding it incumbent on him to look for a matter to discuss, he happened to notice his uncle's letter on top of the stack on his desk. "I've had a letter from Hampden Winterbourne," he said.

Abigail nodded. "An upsetting letter," she surmised.

"Not exactly." When she looked disappointed he corrected himself. "I suppose it would be upsetting, if one took it seriously."

"But you didn't."

"Actually, I dismissed it." Greywell was finding this rather hard going. He ran a hand through his straight brown hair and decided to simply tell her his uncle's suggestion. He was on the point of doing so when Selsey returned with a bottle of brandy and two glasses on a small silver tray.

Abigail watched with interest as Selsey poured a proper amount of brandy into each of the glasses and offered her one on the elegant tray. Her chapped hands, with their stubby fingers, looked slightly incongruous as she gripped the fragile crystal tightly and took a sip of the fiery liquid before Greywell was even offered his glass. "Good stuff," she murmured, to Selsey's disapproval and Greywell's amusement. "Your father put it down, you told me once."

"Yes, he always kept the cellars well stocked. It's not as easy to replenish them with such a superior spirit."

"I suppose not," she admitted, rolling the glass between her hands and gazing into the tawny liquid. "Your father always did the proper thing."

Unsure whether this was meant as a compliment or a criticism, Greywell decided it was best to ignore the remark. "I was telling you about the letter I had from my uncle."

"So you were." She sounded a little bored as she waved the glass under her nose. Her nose, he noticed, seemed to twitch from the strong fumes. "I've known Hampden Winterbourne for more than twenty years. A well-meaning man."

Greywell flicked the letter with an impatient finger. "He may mean well, but he doesn't always use his head. The long and short of this letter is a suggestion that I remarry immediately."

Her drooping eyelids shot up over her small brown eyes. "That doesn't sound like Winterbourne to me. He's every bit as proper as your father was, and he's just been staying with you. Knows the lay of the land. There must be some mistake."

"Apparently he stopped the night with an old friend of his, Sir Edward Parkstone. I've met the man a few times. Not at all proper," he informed her, with a hint of mockery in his tone. Abigail had a distracting habit of dividing the world into those who were proper and those who weren't, in spite of her own bizarre behavior. Presumably she respected people who did the right thing, behaved in the accepted manner, but Greywell had his doubts. "Ever since Sir Edward's wife died, he's led the life of a rake, though he must be in his mid-fifties. Sometimes I think Hampden envies him."

There was no comment from Abigail. It was impossible to tell if she was even listening, since her whole concentration appeared to be on the glass of brandy and the comfort of her large chair near the fire. Greywell continued.

"Sir Edward has a daughter, Elspeth, a twenty-five-year-old spinster, who is, in Hampden's words, an 'Angel of Mercy.' She provides for her father's illegitimate offspring and generally wanders about the countryside, I gather, doing good works. Hampden assures me she isn't unmarried from want of suitors, but neither does he explain why she hasn't married one of these eligible fellows. I am told," he said, referring to the letter now, "that she is a 'handsome woman,' not at all given to excesses of adornment on her person. Do you suppose that means she's a shabby dresser?"

Abigail frowned on his levity. "An Angel of Mercy," she muttered, nodding intently. "Indeed she is."

"You know her?" Greywell asked, surprised.

"Of course I know her. A heart of pure gold. The disposition of an angel. Handsome, did he call her? Yes, that suits. There's a subtle elegance to her bearing which one would not describe as beauty, since it hasn't the capriciousness gentlemen attribute to women with standard looks. Ah, the poor child. Think of the burden she suffers with such a father! To be caught in a small community where everyone knows exactly what's going on! I wonder why she hasn't married. Perhaps I could just have another small sip of this brandy."

Greywell refilled her empty glass. He'd hardly touched his own, since he wasn't in the habit of taking brandy before dinner. To his certain knowledge Abigail hadn't been farther than Coventry in the last three years, which made him highly skeptical about her rhapsodies on Elspeth Parkstone. How could she have met the young woman? Well, perhaps young was not precisely the right word. Of course, Caroline had been twenty-two when she died, and she had seemed very young to him still. When he had replaced the brandy on the tray, he asked, "Have you known Miss Parkstone long?"

"Long?" she repeated, her voice a trifle hazy. "I've lived a long time; I've met a great number of people, my dear Greywell. Why, I remember you when you were swaddled. A very ugly baby you were, too, with a red face and no hair. You had the most piercing cry. When your sweet mother (a very proper woman she was) first brought me to the nursery to see you I thought I should like very much to have a child of my own. Until you started crying. Lord, there was never such a racket! Your mother confessed to me that you quite gave her the headache. Small wonder. You could go on for hours at a time, and there was hardly a place in Ashfield where you couldn't be heard. Your father used to shut himself up here, but it wasn't far enough from the nursery and he got in the habit of leaving the house for a ride every time you started in. Of course, that was only when you were very small. Later you were given to temper tantrums where you stomped your feet."

His lordship took these reminiscences in good part, only once using his booted foot to kick the logs in the grate. "I dare say you haven't known Miss Parkstone quite as long, or as intimately, as you have known me," he pressed, his voice remarkably pleasant.

"One wouldn't have thought such a small child could have made the house shake so when he stomped his feet. I remember having tea with your mother in the Long Gallery when the whole place began to tremble. One of her best vases rocked on the mantel so I was sure it would fall and smash to smithereens. It was as though the earth itself quivered. There was an earthquake in London once, you know. From what I was told of it, I was quite sure that was what was happening. 'An earthquake,' I cried, jumping to my feet. But she assured me it was only you, dear boy, having one of your tantrums. Your father soon put a stop to *that*!"

There are those who remember the good things about their parents, and those who remember the bad, and Greywell was decidedly of the former group. He did, however, remember two occasions on which he had been firmly chastised by his long-suffering father for unacceptable behavior. He had never cherished the illusion that his progenitor was a wicked, unjust man in the distribution of punishment. The third viscount had been a reasonable man, neither dotingly indulgent nor overly strict in his management of his only child. Greywell was not, however, particularly pleased to be reminded of these episodes, since they cast his early character in a somewhat dubious light.

"Miss Parkstone was not given to crying and tantrums when she was a child, I take it," he offered, in a decidedly cooler tone, as he absently flicked a snuffbox open and closed.

"Certainly not! Haven't I told you she has the disposition of an angel? Just so it has always been, from the very moment of her birth. A better-natured person has never walked the face of the earth. You are more than fortunate she would consider your suit, when she could have anyone she chose."

"She isn't considering my suit! There is no suit!" No wonder the woman usually drank beer, Greywell silently fumed; she got everything confused when she had something the least bit stronger. He stifled his desire to remove the brandy glass from her roughened hands and toss it into the fireplace. In a few minutes he could send her home in his carriage, but first he made some effort to clarify her mind. It would do no good for her to be "just mentioning" to the neighborhood folks that he had offered for one Elspeth Parkstone, whom he'd never met and had no intention of meeting.

"The letter, Abigail," he reminded her. "It was Hampden's letter that suggested she would make me a good wife."

"And so she would."

"Yes," he said patiently, "but I'm not looking for a wife. Caroline has only just died and I have no intention of remarrying."

"Then why did your uncle suggest it? He must have gotten the idea somewhere," Abigail replied, as though it were perfectly reasonable to assume so. Her head rested against the chairback at a birdlike angle, her eyes observing him with quick, blinking glances.

"It seems Hampden felt Miss Parkstone would be the solution to some of my problems. He's aware, of course, of little Andrew's sickly constitution, and Miss Parkstone has dealt a great deal with children, despite her unmarried state. There was the suggestion that if I married her, I would be free to go off to Vienna, where I am needed, and leave the child in her capable hands."

"An excellent plan."

"I hardly see it that way, myself," he retorted, but her eyes had closed and her head listed to the side. He felt as though he were speaking to a bundle of rags. In a moment a gentle snore issued from them, her face now lost from sight behind the chair wing. Raising his voice to rouse her, he said, "I'll ring for my carriage."

Abigail straightened abruptly. "Are you going somewhere?" she asked, querulous.

"Your cats are expecting you."

"Not yet, not yet," she insisted. Her hands still gripped the glass with its few remaining sips of brandy. "I understand now why you wanted to see me. It's a slightly tricky problem, to be sure, but I can help you. Just what poor Caroline would have wished," she said shrewdly, as she lifted the glass to her lips. "She was determined to have that child, and she would see how fitting it is for you to find a woman with a heart of gold to care for it. Not just any woman would do, you know. There are women who wouldn't be willing to care for it as though it were their own. But not Elizabeth."

"Elspeth," he corrected, a frown forming between his brows.

She waved one hand to indicate the negligibility of this point. "Yes, yes, Elspeth. A nickname, I imagine. Certainly of the same derivation as Elizabeth. The problem, my dear boy, is not the woman, but in the parish," she announced with some vigor. Drawing the shawl a little more closely about her hunched shoulders, she leaned toward him, reaching to tap one short finger on his knee. "There will be astonishment at your marrying again so soon, but I'm just the one to take care of *that* sort of thing. I need only make the situation perfectly clear, spread the word among the gentry and the working folk. Oh, they'll listen to me. Never doubt it."

"I don't," he murmured.

"Let's see. I shan't call it a marriage of convenience; that has overtones of money and position, and marrying for personal advantage. I could call it a marriage of practicality, but that sounds far too mundane. Not quite the sort of thing such an angelic young woman would ordinarily do, if you see what I mean. But of course! I shall call it a Marriage of Mercy. Perfect, my dear Greywell, absolutely perfect. They'll all understand; see if they don't. You won't stay with her here, of course, and she will need to have the parish folk on her side, willing to lend her a hand. What could be more fitting for our purpose than to call it a Marriage of Mercy?"

"What indeed?"

She blinked uncertainly at his ironic tone. Her brandy was gone and he didn't offer to refill her glass, so she set it aside with a gesture of supreme indifference. "Your grief has disordered your mind, Greywell. Nothing could be more injurious to our plan than for you to marry and stay at Ashfield with her."

"I hadn't intended to."

"Ah, well, good. She'll do very well on her own, better than you could. I haven't the slightest doubt she'll wheedle the little lad back into health in no time."

"Haven't you?" he demanded. "What could this Angel of Mercy do that I haven't done, or the wet nurse, or the nursery maid? We're at our wits' ends trying to find a way to strengthen him. The doctor is of no use; how could Miss Parkstone be?"

Abigail looked surprised at his anger, and slightly offended. "But I *know* she will restore him to health. That's what I'm telling you, Greywell. That's why I came."

Exasperation, mixed with a great deal of nervous energy and a tiny drop of superstitious belief, propelled him to his feet. In times of severe stress such as Lord Greywell was suffering during his grief and his waning hope for his son, one is likely to grasp at the merest straw in the wind. Greywell knew this and refused to be taken in by her mysterious air of precognition. She was nothing but a crazy old woman—a longtime and dear friend, of course, but still . . .

"Abigail," he said sternly, "you can't *know* anything of the sort. You came for a visit and for . . . a little refreshment."

"Would I go out on a day like this, without a proper wrap, just for a neighborly visit? You haven't been the most congenial companion these last months, Greywell, as you must know very well. It was this matter of Elizabeth that brought me."

"Elspeth."

"Have it your own way," she snapped, rising unsteadily to her feet. "No one ever wants to listen to older, wiser heads. The young always think they know what's best. And your parents were both very proper," she added with a sniff as she turned toward the door.

"I'll send you home in the carriage, Abigail."

"There's no need," she said, but she stopped where she was while he gave a sharp tug to the pull. Selsey entered almost immediately with word that the carriage, anticipated, would be at the door in five minutes.

"Please sit down while you wait," Greywell urged. "You must understand, dear ma'am, that it would be most irregular for me to even consider marriage so soon after Caroline's death." He ran a hand through his brown hair, shaking his head dispiritedly. "It would be disrespectful, even if it served a purpose, which I cannot believe it would. I simply haven't the heart for it."

"It's not for your own sake that you would be doing it, but for poor Caroline and her child. Sometimes sacrifices are required of us, Greywell." She dropped back onto the cozy chair, regarding him intently. "You would be doing the young woman a service, too, you know, getting her away from all her father's bastards. A very uncomfortable position for a young woman to be in."

"If she wished to be out of it, she's apparently had the opportunity."

Abigail cocked her head at him. "By marrying one of the young men in the neighborhood? What good would that do? She would still be there, and possibly an embarrassment to her husband. No, she's very wisely avoided making a connection there. What she needs is to be a great distance away from all that. At Ashfield she'd have enough responsibility to keep her occupied while you were away in Venice."

"Vienna."

"I prefer Venice myself, but these government people never have any taste. Would you be away long?"

"Probably a few months. Negotiations always take longer than you expect."

She bobbed her head up and down. "Excellent. The longer you're away the better."

"I can't like to be away from Andrew that long. If he were to . . ."

"Don't worry about that. Eliz . . . Elspeth will have him robust by the time you return." Abigail shifted slightly in her chair so she could better face him. "What alternative do you have, my dear fellow? If you stay here, there's not a thing you can do about the babe. You will just mope about the house, casting gloom over everything. But if you bring the young woman here, with her sunny disposition she'll straighten things out in short order. Thank your lucky stars this excellent scheme has been put forward by your uncle. I never credited him with such sense."

Greywell regarded her ruefully. "You make the absurd sound reasonable, ma'am. I wish I had your confidence in the plan's utility and propriety. Frankly, I don't wish to consider it at all. It would be wrong for me to marry again so soon, and I cannot think why Miss Parkstone would wish to marry me, even if she's not perfectly comfortable in her neighborhood."

"Wrong?" Abigail snorted. "It's what's in your heart that determines what's right and what's wrong, Greywell, not the appearance that smallminded folk may take to gossiping about. It's between you and your conscience. And if you know you've done nothing of which to be ashamed, you can look anyone in the eye. As to the young lady . . . well, perhaps she wouldn't be interested. But you can't know unless you ask her, can you?"

Selsey entered to announce that the carriage was at the door before Greywell could answer her. With profound relief, he dropped the subject, walking with her to the carriage and handing her in himself. "Thank you for coming, Abigail. I hope you won't take a chill."

"I never take a chill," she asserted as she settled back against the squabs. "And the sooner you take care of this business, the sooner you will be able to get on with your life. That's the responsibility the living have to the dead, Greywell, getting on with life."

His murmur was neither consent nor disagreement. He closed the carriage door firmly and nodded to the coachman to start. Inside the carriage Abigail had her eyes closed again, and he watched the vehicle draw away with a troubled frown before he hunched his shoulders against the cold and took the stairs two at a time back into the house. Selsey inquired if he was ready for his dinner, which had been waiting these twenty minutes past.

"Very well. I'll just have a look in at the nursery first."

His habit of checking on his son just before each meal was not conducive to leaving him in good appetite, but then that wasn't why he went. If he went after his meals, he felt guilty looking down at the pale, undernourished child who seemed unable to gain weight despite the wet nurse's assurance that he suckled reasonably well. What was the matter with Andrew? The question was never far from his mind, though the doctor told him some children were simply born with weak constitutions and there was nothing he or anyone else could do to make the child healthy.

Greywell watched the small bundle that was his son, tightly wrapped and sleeping in the beautiful, lacy cradle Caroline had prepared for him. The baby's tiny lips were in motion even as he slept, making sucking noises accompanied by an occasional whimper. Andrew slept a great deal, and when he was awake he seldom cried. Instead he lay quietly, his dark eyes looking enormous in his pallid face, gazing about the small area his vision covered. The room was kept in semidarkness, as though a perpetual sickroom, and a disagreeable odor of burned pastilles frequently greeted Greywell's nostrils as he entered.

He touched the soft skin of his son's cheek now, almost wishing he would wake. If the child's eyes were open Greywell felt some special kinship with him when their gazes met. And when Andrew was awake, he would talk to him, awkwardly urging him to grow strong. Sometimes he would tell the uncomprehending babe about his mother and how much she had wanted to have him. Sometimes he would speak of the pleasures that awaited Andrew when he was older—the angling and horseback riding and cricket and dozens of other activities he himself had enjoyed when he was a boy. The child watched him when he spoke, the large eyes almost unblinking.

When he visited the nursery, Greywell always sent the wet nurse and the nursery maid from the room. Things were difficult enough without their curious, pitying stares. He wished one or the other of them would take more interest in his son, would feel the kind of devotion a mother might have given the lad. But they did their jobs, and assumed the child would die because they had seen it happen before. It was the strong who survived, not the puny, sickly ones like Andrew.

Even the housekeeper, Mrs. Green, who had been at Ashfield for twenty years, showed less interest in the babe than he would have expected. They were all convinced the child would die, and they weren't going to invest any special emotion in a lost cause. Their unspoken but clearly entrenched fatalism disturbed him so much he was tempted to send them all packing, despite Mrs. Green's years of devoted service to his family.

The sleeping baby turned his head restlessly as Greywell gazed down at him. The very helplessness of the infant overwhelmed him, and his own impotence made him feel nervously restless. Was there truly something he could be doing for the child that he wasn't? Abigail was undoubtedly a little loose in the haft, but she had seemed so *sure* about the Parkstone girl. Would someone with a sympathetic heart make a difference in his household? Nonsense. There was no saying the woman would be any more sympathetic to his son than all the others. If she entered the nursery, wouldn't she be as infected by despair as all the others?

Did he owe it to his son to at least meet Elspeth Parkstone?

Chapter Three

A hard frost had set in at Lyndhurst. The trees were almost bare of leaves and dark branches stood stark against the wintry sky. It was early yet for snow, but Elspeth wouldn't have been surprised to see the odd flurry of flakes descend as she hurried toward the house thumping her gloved hands against her sides to keep them warm. The ground was hard under her booted feet, and her toes felt numb from her ride. Her mare had needed exercising, but it had been too cold to stay out long, the icy wind whipping through her hair and turning her nose red. The fact that her appearance was totally disheveled didn't bother her in the least. Her only intention now was to head for the Gold Saloon, where a fire would be blazing.

If Elspeth had taken the mare into the stable, she would have noticed the extra horses and the extra men, but her groom had met her in the stableyard and led Minstrel straight in to be rubbed down. The lad was more interested in caring for her horse than in gossiping about the visitor who had arrived, which ordinarily would have pleased Elspeth. Grooms, she had noticed, were frequently less interested in people than they were in horses, and consequently it was not usually in the stable that rumor and gossip abounded. On this particular occasion she would have appreciated a warning, but Tommy had no way of knowing that, and had merely said, "Cold as an icehouse this afternoon, ain't it?"

Which had led her to think about icehouses and the possibility of serving ices at the summer fete as a special treat. They'd never tried it before and it would certainly provide an interesting novelty which the fetes under Mr. Blockley's direction frequently lacked. As a footman opened the door to her she was wondering where she should jot down the idea so she would be sure to remember it when next summer came.

"Is my father in?" she asked.

"In the Gold Saloon, Miss Parkstone. He asked that you join him there." The footman did not add that Sir Edward had a visitor, since Sir Edward had strictly instructed him not to.

Elspeth thanked him and stripped her gloves from her cold hands. The footman relieved her of them, and her rumpled bonnet, and preceded her to the parlor, where he elaborately flung open the door. Elspeth didn't notice this uncharacteristic gesture of elegance, since she was in the process of tucking her hair back under the pins which had come loose. She stopped abruptly on the threshold, her fingers twined in her windblown tresses, when she realized her father was not alone in the room.

Beside him, rising now from one of the Queen Anne chairs, was an unfamiliar gentleman whose height alone reminded her of Mr. Blockley. Nothing else about him bore the slightest resemblance. He had dark hair, brushed forward in the fashionable mode à la Brutus, and on him it looked natural. Elspeth had seen a half-dozen of the younger blades in Aylesbury on whom it looked perfectly ridiculous. This fellow, too, wore a starched cravat with delicate, intricate folds, and a well-cut black coat of superfine, but rather than projecting an air of high fashion, he somehow struck her as terribly sad. It was probably his face that gave the impression, she thought.

Though he was no more than a half-dozen years older than she, Elspeth guessed, his countenance had a careworn quality, with lines etched about his eyes and his mouth. Only the prominent, strong chin and the finely chiseled nose retrieved his appearance from being grim. He studied her now with melancholy eyes whose color she could not determine across the room, and his mouth never curved into a smile when he acknowledged her introduction. His voice, rather solemn in its deep timbre, nonetheless affected her with its gentleness.

But any favorable impression she might have received was shattered when her father announced, "Elspeth, this is Lord Greywell, Hampden's nephew, you know."

Certainly she should have known. Not that he bore any resemblance to the rather florid Winterbourne, but simply because he was here. She made no further effort to straighten her hair, instead dropping her hands listlessly to her sides and nodding a greeting to him. Despite her annoyance with her father and Hampden Winterbourne, she could not entirely bring herself to be unkind to this obviously grief-stricken gentleman.

"Mr. Winterbourne told me of your sad loss," she said as she crossed the room to join them. "You have my deepest sympathy."

"Thank you. It was good of Hampden to stay at Ashfield with me for so long." Greywell waited for her to seat herself before disposing himself in the chair he'd risen from. Sir Edward was regarding his daughter's disheveled appearance with chagrin tempered by the necessity to say nothing in front of their guest. And she *was* rather unkempt, Greywell thought, with her touseled hair, her red nose, and her dusty boots. Apparently no one had told her there was a visitor and she'd come straight from a ride—she wore an attractive navy-blue riding habit—straight to the parlor to warm herself. It was bitterly cold outdoors; Greywell could hear the wind beating against the windows of the room. Not exactly the sort of day a young woman usually chose to ride out for pleasure. Perhaps she'd gone on some mission of mercy to one of the families in the neighborhood. The thought encouraged him somehow.

There was a moment's silence before Elspeth turned to her father to ask, "Have you rung for refreshment for Lord Greywell?"

Sir Edward, who had entirely forgotten, said, "We were waiting for you, my dear."

"Would you prefer tea, or something stronger?" Elspeth asked their visitor as she rang for the footman. His eyes were gray, she decided as their gazes met. A rather interesting color, and unusual in their intensity.

"Tea will be fine, thank you."

Her father usually had Madeira at any time past three in the afternoon, but he said smoothly now, "That will be fine for me, too, dear."

Elspeth lifted her brows briefly in surprise, but did no more than relay her instructions to the footman. Tea, in Sir Edward's oft-expressed opinion, was the worst-tasting beverage ever invented by man. He didn't consider it redeemable, either, by adding a dollop of spirits. When visitors of whatever description came, it was his invariable rule to have his Madeira brought in with the tea, and Elspeth hadn't considered it even necessary to ask him. The footman gave no sign that there was anything unusual in her order as he withdrew his bland countenance from the room.

Again there was a silence, with Lord Greywell and Sir Edward both watching her expectantly, as though she were responsible for the conversation which would ensue. Elspeth felt her irritation grow. There was nothing the matter with either of their tongues, and she didn't want them staring at her disordered hair and crumpled riding habit that way. If someone had bothered to inform her they had a guest, she would have made herself presentable and not felt quite so much like an object of curiosity. She didn't choose to think about why Lord Greywell had come.

"Hampden said your son was not very stout, Lord Greywell," Elspeth finally stated. "I hope he's stronger now."

"I'm afraid not. He continues rather sickly despite our best efforts to strengthen him." Greywell's eyes were hooded for a moment, and one hand tightened against the chair arm where it rested. "The doctor in our neighborhood, Dr. Wellow, says there are some infants who simply have a difficult time. He doesn't know what the problem is."

"Have you considered changing his wet nurse? Her milk may not agree with the child." Elspeth ignored her father's frown.

"Wellow doesn't seem to think that's the problem. He's content to let matters rest as they are."

Elspeth grimaced. "But then, the child isn't his, Lord Greywell. Even the best of our doctors are not as knowledgeable as one might wish. If the child isn't thriving after this length of time, surely some change should be made in its routine to seek a better solution. One cannot blindly continue to follow a path which is leading nowhere."

Sir Edward interrupted sharply. "I'm sure Lord Greywell doesn't follow any path blindly, Elspeth. He's acting on the recommendation of his physician."

His daughter said nothing as the tea tray was brought in. Mrs. Hinton had seen that Cook included Scotch shortbread and queen cakes and seed biscuits as well as bread and butter in honor of their distinguished visitor. As usual, Elspeth poured, inquiring of the viscount whether he took cream and sugar and passing the plate of cakes to him first. She prepared her father's tea exactly as his lordship's, since she assumed Sir Edward wouldn't bother drinking it anyhow. And then, smiling blandly at the two of them, she rose, excused herself, and left the room.

Sir Edward stared after her retreating form, too astonished to protest until she had silently closed the door behind her. "I say," he sputtered, awkwardly trying to dispose of the fragile cup so he could rise to follow her. Tea sloshed onto the saucer and dripped over the edge onto his previously immaculate pantaloons. As he dabbed at the moisture with a napkin from the tea tray, he growled, "Where the devil has she gone? She's too fanciful by half, that girl!"

"Perhaps a call of nature," Greywell suggested. Though he looked unperturbed, he was no less startled than Sir Edward by her sudden disappearance. It was not the sort of thing a well-bred young woman did, suddenly leaving a room where she was entertaining a distinguished visitor. And he *was* a distinguished visitor, if for no other reason than his title. She hadn't indicated an intention to return.

"I don't know what's come over her," Edward insisted. He pushed his teacup well out of reach and wished he'd had the Madeira brought as usual. It would look foolish for him to ring again, either for the Madeira or for his daughter, and he momentarily forgot his intention of palming Elspeth off on Greywell in his recollection of an earlier event she'd confessed. "This is the second time in a week she's behaved so strangely. It was amusing, her knocking Blockley's hat off with a queen cake, but you must admit it was odd. She's such a damned paragon of every virtue, it really makes me wonder if she's not suffering from a brain fever."

"She looks perfectly healthy."

"Oh, she's always been healthy as a horse. It's in here I wonder about," Sir Edward said, tapping his head with a finger. "They get strange when they've never been married, you know. Take all sorts of notions about religion and doing good works and frowning on wickedness. Of course," he added hastily, recollecting to whom he was speaking, "Elspeth's a good woman. What she needs is a husband and an establishment of her own to distract her from all this morbid virtuousness. After all, what is there to occupy her in my house but a few small tasks each day? She turns her mind to the parish work, but it's hardly enough for a woman of her generosity and stamina, don't you know. And she's very good with children, very good indeed. Just the sort of woman one would want overseeing one's nursery."

Greywell regarded him with a noncommittal expression. When he had written to Sir Edward he had merely stated that he would be in Aylesbury for a day or two and asked if he might call on him. Sir Edward had written back that he would be honored to have Greywell stay at Lyndhurst for the duration of his business in the area. There had been no hint in either man's letter as to the nature of the "business." And it was apparent to Greywell now that Miss Parkstone had not been advised of his coming at all. She would not have entered the parlor as she had, nor been introduced in the manner Sir Edward had chosen, if he were a guest she had expected.

On the other hand, she had known who he was. Through Hampden, of course. But her odd behavior indicated she guessed more than that. Her sympathy for his plight was evident enough in her questions, but her eyes had remained wary. She seemed a little too brusque and opinionated to fill the role of Angel of Mercy in which everyone was inclined to place her. All in all, she didn't strike him in the least as a young woman who was willing to sacrifice her future to marrying him and devoting her life to his son.

When Elspeth did not rejoin them for tea, Sir Edward fidgeted in his chair while Greywell made polite conversation. It was not at all the sort of visit Greywell had expected, and he was irritated he'd left little Andrew at Ashfield to come all this way only to find himself discussing estate management with Sir Edward Parkstone, who wasn't even interested in it. What he should do was leave now, before any additional significance attached to his visit. But he found himself curious about Elspeth. Her looks were passable, he supposed, but mostly he was intrigued by her behavior. What was it Sir Edward had said about her knocking some fellow's hat off with a queen cake? That kind of hoydenish behavior did not mesh well with her seriousness when she discussed Andrew's illness, or her evident diligence in doing parish work and dealing with Sir Edward's ill-begotten offspring.

The more Greywell spoke with his host, the more he realized Sir Edward was a hedonist of the most inveterate kind. His pleasures were his first priority, and one which came well before his responsibilities as a landholder or father. He denied himself nothing, and expected the community to accept his peccadilloes with equanimity. Yet, in spite of that, he was an amusing rogue, drawing one into his conspiracy of debauchery with a wide grin and an almost boyish delight in his mischief.

"You wouldn't believe the strategems I go through to avoid the local rector," he said now with a laugh. "He's a skeletal fellow and sits at his upstairs window at the rectory on the edge of town just trying to catch a glimpse of me. Sometimes he doesn't even have a candle lit, but you can catch the gleam of his clerical collar if you look straight up at the spot where he always sits. It's unfortunate, of course, that he can overlook the whole village. Knows who's gone to the Bar and Bell every night, or who's slipped into whose house. One might expect that kind of spying from some old lady who hasn't anything better to do with her time, but the rector! I ask you. So I've devised a route that takes me behind the village and through the orchard. Never meet a soul, which is a bit odd, if you think about it. After all, I'm not the only one out and about at night. Do you supose they have even less of a care for his good opinion than I do?"

"I can't imagine." Greywell helped himself to a pinch of snuff.

"Blockley has a habit of preaching sermons about the evils of temptation, and he always manages to stare at any offenders during the course of it. I swear it's like being in grammar school, where you have black marks put against your name for any misdeeds during the week, and are called upon to confess to them before your classmates."

"This Mr. Blockley is the same one whose hat your daughter knocked off with a queen cake?" Greywell asked, fascinated.

"The very same. He was sweet on her for a while, but she'd have none of him. Not that I blame her. It wouldn't suit me to have a man of the cloth for a son-in-law. I can't think how he came to annoy her, and she wouldn't explain to me. She's not a gossip, mind you! Very closemouthed she is, probably because she thinks it's a sin to speak ill of other people. Almost everything is a sin in Elspeth's book," he informed the viscount, a melancholy light in his eyes. "I can't imagine how she came to be that way. She was quite spirited as a child."

"You don't think perhaps she developed her . . . piety to offset your profligacy?" Greywell wondered with a wry smile.

Sir Edward pursed his lips. "I shouldn't think so. What good would that do?"

"It wouldn't necessarily *do* any good, but it might seem appropriate to Miss Parkstone."

His companion considered this in silence. "Would she do it as an example for me, or in order to save my soul?"

"I haven't the slightest idea. It was just a thought," Greywell said dimissively. He had no idea why he'd put it forward in the first place. If he had done it to shame the baronet, he was far out in his calculations. Though Sir Edward was intrigued by the idea, the insinuation of his wrongdoing left him totally unaffected. If anything, he appeared rather proud of his exploits.

"You may be right. Yes, I'm bound to think you are. And you know what that means, don't you?" Sir Edward asked with obvious enthusiasm.

"I'm afraid I don't," Greywell apologized.

"Why, when she marries and moves away from here, there will be no reason why she shouldn't become an ordinary mortal again. None of this holier-than-thou stuff; there would be no reason for it." A nostalgic gleam appeared in his eyes. "I should like to see her as she was a few years ago, you know. My wife used to worry about her, but, Lord, she was a charmer, full of mischief and cute as a button. There wasn't a girl in the neighborhood to touch her—to my mind. Mary thought her a bit of a hoyden, but there, anyone with a little spirit is bound to be looked on askance. I've seen it happen all my life. When you get to be my age, you stop worrying about what other people think, though. It's a great relief."

"I dare say."

"All her mother's money was settled on her; she came into it when she reached one and twenty. And of course she'll have Lyndhurst when I die, though I shouldn't think I'll do that very soon. Still, you never know, do you? So she's a bit of an heiress. Nothing excessive, but a good ten thousand in the funds. I'm not sure it wasn't her money Somerville was most interested in. His family is always in the suds. But Knedlington doesn't need to marry for a few guineas, and Tom Prestbury had known her since she was a child. She wouldn't have any of them." Sir Edward eyed him thoughtfully. "You're a fine figure of a man,

Greywell, but no better than Somerville, and your title won't appeal to her if Knedlington's didn't."

"I've hardly met Miss Parkstone," Greywell demurred. "And I've just lost my wife."

A shadow of pained recollection passed over Sir Edward's face. "I know how it is, believe me. A part of me died with Mary. The best part, perhaps. That must be how Elspeth sees it." He sighed and shrugged off his gloom. "But you go on living, even if it isn't your choice. You're fortunate to have several good reasons to continue, sir. There's your heir to be raised, and your obligation to the government at the peace negotiations. I had little incentive. Elspeth was nearly grown, and there was nothing to involve my attention. Estate management has always bored me, more's the pity. You don't suffer from that problem, I gather."

"No."

"Well, you will find that Elspeth knows a great deal about it. She would be able to manage while you were away."

"Sir Edward, by all means let us be frank. I did come to meet your daughter, though I'm not quite sure what possessed me to consider the scheme. It's patently absurd in spite of its practicality. I can see it would be of as much benefit to you as it would be to me, and yet those are not necessarily its main facets. There is your daughter to be considered. Apparently she has no intention of marrying, if she's turned down the gentlemen you've mentioned. I can't offer her any advantage almost any of them couldn't."

"Ah, but you can. That's what makes the scheme, as you call it, so eminently suitable. You can offer her a purpose, an outlet for her abundance of charity. I don't think she wishes to marry, it's true, but she really should. It will do her nothing but harm to dwindle into a bitter old woman. She's uncomfortable living here with me, and she certainly cramps my freedom. How much better off she'd be at your home, taking care of your child. Elspeth would have the advantage of a home of her own without even the bother of a husband."

Greywell raised one elegant brow. "I did intend to return to Ashfield one day, Sir Edward."

"Yes, well, these things drag on, you know. And by the time you returned, she'd be perfectly well established and probably not mind at all your being around."

"The ideal marriage, in fact."

"My dear sir, you have already had the ideal marriage, by all accounts. You cannot expect to duplicate that sort of arrangement, and in the meantime you would have a responsible woman looking after your interests." Edward leaned forward, his forehead furrowed. "You believe it is only my own comfort of which I think, and perhaps, for the most part, it is. But Elspeth is a good woman and she deserves to have a life of her own. She wouldn't resent raising another woman's child. She wouldn't pine for being left alone the majority of the time. You would be free to pursue your own interests in London or elsewhere, discreetly. I'm not discreet, and I tend to leave a trail of brats behind me. They're an embarrassment to her. She'd be better off out of the neighborhood entirely."

"Even if that's true, your daughter may not see it in the same light as you do. You couldn't very well force her to marry."

"No, nor would I be inclined to do so. But you're a presentable young man, with exactly the right qualifications to appeal to her." Edward stroked his chin with one short, square hand, studying Greywell absently. "You would have to convince her of the benefits of such a marriage. She suspects what's afoot and she doesn't like it."

"Who can blame her? I wouldn't at all appreciate it if someone were trying to arrange my life for me."

"We're not arranging her life, we're offering her an opportunity," Sir Edward said airily, and then added, "You may be sure, if it doesn't meet with her approval, she'll have nothing to do with it. She has a most decided mind of her own. Now, if you will excuse me, I want to have a look at the new mare before I dress for dinner. Please make yourself comfortable."

"Will Miss Parkstone be joining us for dinner?"

Sir Edward looked startled. "Well, of course she will. Elspeth isn't one to let a little difference of opinion deter her from her duty as hostess."

"She didn't stay to tea."

"No, but she poured for us. I'm sure she'll come to dinner."

"Please don't insist upon it."

Sir Edward snorted. "It wouldn't do the least good if I did," he muttered as he left the room.

Chapter Four

When Sir Edward and Elspeth were dining alone, they dressed a little less formally than when they had company, but they did dress for dinner. It was a habit of long standing with them, and one Elspeth's mother would never have thought to question. Elspeth found it rather irksome, and was wont to wear one of two different gowns alternately. She did, of course, possess an adequate assortment of evening dresses, because she was frequently invited to one of the neighboring homes to dine.

As she surveyed the contents of her closet with her maid at her elbow, she was tempted to wear either the beige round dress or the rose sarsnet as usual, but Sadie immediately fingered the blue crepe over white sarsnet, saying, "You'll want this for his lordship, Miss Elspeth. It's only been worn twice, and it's very becoming to you. You can wear the necklace in the Grecian style, as you did to the Linchmeres."

Elspeth considered the dress for a moment before reluctantly agreeing. From the moment she'd gotten it home, she'd realized there was something frivolous about the three-quarter-length crepe apron which fell from the bust and had tassels at each end of the bottom. Why she'd let Mrs. Padworth talk her into having it made up for her she would never know. It was too low around the bust, and even wearing a jet necklace wide over the shoulders hardly made up for the amount of bosom it exposed. And

Sadie always insisted on dressing her hair differently when she wore it, as though the dress demanded something more exotic than the rather severe coiffure she ordinarily wore. But she submitted patiently to Sadie's ministrations, wondering the while whether her father had actually persuaded Lord Greywell to come and offer for her, or whether he had merely somehow managed to induce the viscount to visit them in the hope he could achieve his purpose once Greywell was in residence.

Poor Papa! Elspeth was aware her father insisted on believing that half the young men in the neighborhood had, at one time or another, courted her, though how he had come by that impression was beyond her powers of imagination. It was true that occasionally a gentleman had called a few times and perhaps with a little encouragement would have called more frequently, but the encouragement was not forthcoming. Lord Knedlington had been such a boring fellow, and Mr. Somerville had heard she was an heiress. Tom Prestbury had shared her interest in music, and Chastleton was a lecherous old man, only intrigued by her nubile (in those days) charms. Which was reason enough to show him the door, as far as Elspeth was concerned.

Since the day she had found her father and Fanny Heyshott on the sofa in his study, she had determined to have nothing to do with men. As though it weren't enough to ask a woman to abandon her home, give over her fortune, and risk her life producing progeny, a man apparently also found it necessary to inflict pain on a woman whenever the whim took him. For Fanny had most certainly been in pain. Her eyes were glazed with it, and her hands clutched frantically in paroxysms of agony. Had she not cried out in the most pitiful voice, "Oh, God, oh, God"? Had her body not contorted with waves of shuddering affliction? It was a bitter scene to behold, Sir Edward in no small pain himself, to judge by his groans.

Why did they do it? Elspeth could only see the sense in such mortification if one was intent on producing a child, and since there wasn't the slightest reason why either Sir Edward or Fanny Heyshott should desire a child, she thought them quite crazed to indulge in such ludicrous behavior. There was no dignity in it, surely. Animals suffered it with patience, as she well knew from being raised in the country. Elspeth assumed they were driven by instinct to procreate, but adult men and women who hadn't that excuse should be ashamed of themselves. Not only, as in Sir

Edward and Fanny's cases, was it against the religious teachings of the church (they being unmarried), but it was against all logic for two people to willfully engage in an activity so obviously painful. It seemed perfectly reasonable to Elspeth that two people who wished to create a third might make the sacrifice, a sort of trial by fire, but for them to do it otherwise . . .

Sadie had arranged curls on either side of her face, and Elspeth studied herself dispassionately in the glass. Her honey-brown tresses were usually pulled straight back, giving her a fine, austere look, she thought, making her eyes look not a murky greenish-brown, but a clear and devoted hazel. When the curls softened her countenance, she realized her eyes looked rather sultry. It was not the sort of effect she was interested in achieving. People paid her respect when she looked pious; they paid her attention when she looked fetching. A worldly sort of attention that made her feel corrupted. Men's eyes became speculative, and women spoke to her of trivial matters like fashion. Elspeth far preferred the kind of high-minded conversation that ensued when she looked serious and saintly. Not that she thought of herself as a saint, exactly; she felt sure no saintly women decked themselves out for parties with fancy gowns and crimped hair. Elspeth had spent some time considering this matter, and she was convinced that dressing well was less of a sin than embarrassing one's father and one's neighbors. The sacrifice was not too great for one of her inclinations to make.

So she accepted Sadie's ministrations without demur, allowing the girl to powder her wind-reddened nose and arrange a jet armlet below the very full, very short sleeve of the dress. That her bare arms and shoulders showed to advantage in their soft whiteness she did not deign to recognize. Lord Greywell would have seen a great deal of shoulders and arms, and her father would be pleased to see her garbed in something "decent" for a change.

Ordinarily Sir Edward was waiting for her in the saloon when she descended, since he always took a little something before his meals. When Beeton ushered her into the room, however, she found only Lord Greywell, standing by the fireplace staring moodily into the flames. He turned as he heard her light tred on the carpet, momentarily surprised at her appearance. Somehow he had expected her to wear something awful in protest at his being there.

"You look lovely, Miss Parkstone," he said politely. "I'm afraid Sir Edward hasn't come down yet."

"I might have known," she replied with a wry smile that barely curved her lips. There was no speculative gleam in his eyes, which immediately made her feel more comfortable. She seated herself on the white damask-covered settee and followed him with her gaze as he retreated once again to the fireplace. This time he stood facing her, waiting to see if she would speak first.

"We hadn't seen Hampden in some time before he visited last week," she said conversationally. "His wife was my godmother, and a great friend of my mother's. They'd grown up near one another."

"You've visited Kent, then?"

"Several times, when I was much younger. Papa hasn't traveled much since Mama died. He seems content to remain at Lyndhurst."

Since it was obvious she wasn't going to snub him, Greywell moved to take a chair opposite the settee. "Have you been to London, Miss Parkstone?" he asked as he smoothed his breeches. His evening clothes were impeccable: a fresh, starched cravat, with black waistcoat and coat and knee breeches. If they made him look somewhat somber, they also set off his figure to advantage.

"Only on the visits to Kent," she admitted. "My mother took me to some of the shops and the Tower and St. Paul's. She had intended that I come out there, but that wasn't to be. My godmother would have done it, but she too fell ill. I can't say that I mind. London, by all accounts, is a veritable den of iniquity." But she smiled slightly when she said it, as though at a private joke she had no intention of sharing.

"Any city that size is bound to harbor every evil known to mankind," he agreed. "And yet, London has its attractions. The theater, the opera, the shops, the entertainments. You would probably find some things there worthy of your interest."

"No doubt." Her brow puckered slightly as she mused, "Sometimes it surprises me that Papa has no interest in going. Not that he would take me if he did, but a city of that size . . . One would think the anonymity, the very range of possibilities, the sheer numbers of . . . people would attract him. Here, well, everyone knows him."

"Maybe he likes it that way," Greywell suggested, catching her drift. "Here he's on his own territory."

"Would you care for a glass of wine?"

"Thank you, no. My uncle mentioned you're active in parish work, Miss Parkstone. Does it take up a great deal of your time?"

"Not an excessive amount, except around the times when we're planning a fete." Elspeth had returned her gaze to him, and now admitted, "It's not a very large parish, and there are half a dozen of us who vie for the honor of doing the most work. I'm sure you'd consider it perverse of us; Papa does. Why is it we'd want to prove our mettle to people who already know exactly what we're capable of?"

"Maybe it's not a matter of proving yourselves, but of doing your share."

"Perhaps." She seemed dissatisfied with his response but allowed the subject to drop. Long ago she'd discovered other people weren't as curious as she was about what motivated people to do things, and it seemed discourteous to press any subject which held no appeal for her companion. His halfhearted attempt to make a reply was almost worse than not saying anything at all. There was little that irritated Elspeth more than not being taken seriously, but she was unaware of the small expression of annoyance that came and went on her face. No one had ever bothered (or been quite brave enough) to tell her how expressive her face was of exactly what she was thinking, so she assumed she wore as efficient a mask as any other woman bred to country society.

Lord Greywell was a reasonably acute absterver, and the flicker of annoyance did not escape his notice. When Sir Edward joined them the viscount was beginning to wonder whether he should have come to Lyndhurst at all.

"Ah, good," the baronet announced, rubbing his hands together happily, "the two of you have had a chance to get acquainted."

"Indeed," Elsepth said dryly. "Lord Greywell has shared several fascinating perceptions with me.".

Goaded, Greywell retorted, "And Miss Parkstone has illustrated a most interesting turn of mind."

Sir Edward beamed on them. "Excellent, excellent. I knew

the two of you would have a great deal in common. It stands to reason."

"Why?" Elspeth inquired. "Because you wanted us to?"

"Of course not." He frowned slightly at her but turned to smile at Greywell. "Because you are opposite sides of the coin. I should have thought you'd see that, Elspeth. Lord Greywell has a problem to which you are the solution. And you have a problem to which Lord Greywell is the solution. What could be more perfect?"

"What indeed?" Greywell retorted, smiling sardonically past the baronet at the outraged Elspeth.

"I was not aware I had a problem," she stated flatly, ignoring Greywell altogether, though she knew exactly what sort of look appeared on his countenance.

"Well, you do," her father informed her succinctly. "In fact, you *are* a problem, my dear. It's not that I don't appreciate your companionship or your usefulness around Lyndhurst, but you need an establishment of your own. What is the value in your being here doing what my housekeeper could accomplish, when you could be employing your talents much more profitably elsewhere?"

"This is my home. And Mrs. Hinton could *not* accomplish the same things I do here."

"She could accomplish as many of them as need doing." Sir Edward ran one hand through his graying hair. "Lord, Elspeth, how did you become so stubborn?"

"Mama said I took after you."

There was a snort of amusement from Greywell, and Sir Edward leveled a haughty gaze in his direction just as Beeton entered to announce dinner.

"Not a moment too soon," Elspeth murmured, rising.

Greywell offered her his arm, the amusement gone from his mouth, though a trace of it lingered in his eyes. Elspeth could feel her chin come up as she laid her hand so lightly on the black cloth she could scarcely feel his arm beneath her fingers. What did he find so amusing in the situation, anyhow? His future was as much under discussion as her own. And it was a wonder Sir Edward had not come right out and said the two of them should be married. Elspeth very much doubted her father would show that amount of restraint for long.

The dining room at Lyndhurst was large, and there was a

mahogany table that spread down three-quarters of the length of the room, but Elspeth routinely chose convenience over formality. The three place settings were grouped together at one end, and Greywell held a chair for her on the right-hand side before rounding the table to seat himself opposite her. Sir Edward began a systematic questioning of their visitor as to the extent of his estate, what crops and livestock it supported, the neighboring towns and villages, and any acquaintance he might have with the local gentry.

"Coventry, eh?" he said, narrowing his eyes in thought. "I was there once, as I recall. Has a considerable woolen manufacture and a dozen handsome gates left from the old wall enclosure. Ah, and I remember something else," he said, his eyes switching to his daughter with suppressed jocularity. "Elspeth, you will dote on Coventry, I promise you. They have a procession on the first day of the Trinity Week fair in honor of Lady Godiva, when the figure of a naked woman is carried on horseback through the town."

Elspeth gave him a scathing look and said nothing.

"It's true," Greywell interjected, drawing her attention. "The first lord of Coventry, who died during the reign of Edward the Confessor, was married to Godiva. When Leofric was offended with the people of the city, he burdened them with extra taxes, and his lady, a woman of exemplary virtue and piety, solicited him to ease their burden. Thinking her modesty too great to allow her compliance, he offered to remove the new duties if she would ride through the most frequented parts of the town naked, in daylight. But she was moved by the distress of the city and gave orders to the citizens that all doors and windows should be shut and no one attempt to look on her under pain of death. Then she rode naked through the streets on horseback, with her long hair hanging loose and covering her down to her legs. There's a legend that a tailor couldn't resist looking out, and that he was struck blind for his folly. The window from which he looked is still shown with an effigy of the 'Peeping Tom' newly dressed on the anniversary of the procession."

"So during Lady Godiva's ride the townspeople didn't look upon her nakedness," Elspeth summarized, "and now, in the procession, everyone for miles around looks on the figure of a naked woman instead. That speaks very well for the town's morals, Lord Greywell."

His lordship cast a helpless glance at Sir Edward, who shrugged and said, "That's the way Elspeth sees things, my dear fellow. I shouldn't let it bother me, if I were you. After all, it's the sort of thing any religious man might declaim against from the pulpit, save its being a tradition. Tradition, especially such a delightful tradition, is the one thing the church doesn't seem ready to take a stand against. It's a great pity, in some ways. Sermons would be a great deal livelier if some vicar would take on the habits of the past. They're willing enough to rant against harmless folklore, of course, but not against anything of substance. I'd love to see Blockley get up there and wave his skeletal arms while he declaimed the injustice of rotten boroughs or spendthrift ways in high places. By God, I might even attend his services if he'd talk about something of interest."

Elspeth listened with grudging admiration as her father adroitly changed the subject, but she would not hear Mr. Blockley denigrated without a word in his defense. "Mr. Blockley's sermons are well above the average, Papa, as you would know if you ever bothered to listen to one of them. He expects Christian behavior from the rich and the poor alike. In fact, if anything, he expects the highborn to set an example for their less fortunate neighbors."

"He expects a great deal too much," Sir Edward retorted, helping himself to another serving of the saddle of mutton. Turning to Greywell, he asked, "What sort of fellow do you have in your parish? Do you have the living in your gift?"

"Yes. We have an older man, a gentle soul, not given to ranting about anything at all." He surveyed the crimped cod with oyster sauce before tentatively taking a bite of it. "Very nice. My cook isn't much of a hand at crimped cod."

"Elspeth can bring the receipt," Sir Edward generously offered.

Greywell met her eyes over the low arrangement of flowers between them and smiled his sympathy. He was finding it difficult to know which of them to feel in charity with, since the conversation took so many unexpected turns. When she failed to acknowledge his commiseration, he returned his gaze to his plate and took another bite of the cod. The best thing he could do, he decided, was leave Lyndhurst first thing in the morning. That would alleviate Miss Parkstone's discomfort, and put him out of range of Sir Edward's dubious plotting.

"Well, I'm off," Sir Edward announced suddenly, standing abruptly and waving Greywell to remain seated. "Elspeth will entertain you, my lord. She's quite proficient at the pianoforte." And without another word, though carefully avoiding his daughter's eyes, he left the room.

Greywell stared after him, uncomprehending. Slowly his eyes moved back to Miss Parkstone, who sat rigid in her chair, a deep flush having invaded her cheeks. Her chin was high, all the same, and she addressed him with a calm born of something like desperation. "My father doesn't find it necessary to abide by normal rules for polite society, Lord Greywell. I hope you will forgive his . . . unusual departure. No doubt he has some urgent business which takes him off at such a time."

"Hogwash! His intention is perfectly clear. He's leaving us alone to get better 'acquainted.' The man is a menace to society."

"He means well."

"Is this the sort of thing he does often?"

Elspeth met his angry gaze. "No. Generally his behavior is unexceptionable . . . at home. Or at least, with company. Oh, you know what I mean. He doesn't give much weight to other people's opinions of him, but as a matter of course he behaves as one would expect. Please don't feel constrained to remain here with me. It's but a short ride into Aylesbury, where there is diversion to be found. You might wish to finish your meal first."

"I have every intention of finishing my meal." Greywell could not recall a previous occasion on which he'd felt so entirely disgruntled. His companion, however, seemed to be taking the matter in stride now, forking a bite of mutton as the high color faded from her cheeks. What would it be like to be in her position, living with a ramshackle fellow like Sir Edward? It was a wonder to him that she appeared to wish to stay here. He would have expected her to welcome himself (or any one of the alleged suitors) with open arms, for the sake of being rescued from a life of confusion, embarrassment, and downright neglect. Maybe she was as perverse as she had previously hinted.

The third course came with an apple custard and a cabinet pudding after the jugged hare. Greywell noticed that his companion had nothing but a tablespoonful of the custard with a minuscule glob of whipped cream, which she barely tasted before sitting back in her chair and nodding to the waiting footman to remove her plate. There was nothing wrong with the custard, he found; in fact, it was superb. Apparently Miss Parkstone had made a decision, because she regarded him thoughtfully for a moment, dismissed the servants, and said, "It's obviously of no use pretending you are an ordinary visitor, Lord Greywell. I cannot imagine how my father has induced you to come here, but, as you see, it's for the purpose of marrying me off to you. Were you aware of that before you came?"

Her frankness intrigued him. If they were going to endure an evening together it was best that all the cards be placed on the table so they both knew what was going forward. Sir Edward had already effectively overset propriety, leaving them nothing but honesty to deal with, if they were going to communicate at all.

"My uncle wrote me about you. His suggestion that you would make me a good wife seemed preposterous." Greywell flicked a finger negligently, to indicate he was not criticizing her in any way, but merely the situation. "My wife died only a few months ago; I wasn't looking for another. It's true that I am in despair over my son's health, and that if circumstances were otherwise I would be headed for the Congress of Vienna at this very moment. But those circumstances are real, and I couldn't see that adding a wife to the concoction would be of the least assistance."

Greywell was remembering the letter and how he had produced it for his neighbor. A wry smile twisted his lips as he shook his head in exasperation. "Abigail Waltham happened to visit me just after I'd read Hampden's letter, and, to my surprise, she concurred with his advice. She appeared to know you, or of you, and also thought you would be a splendid solution to my problems. She agreed you were an Angel of Mercy."

"Abigail Waltham?" Elspeth's brow wrinkled. "The name is not familiar to me." But she was pleased that someone so far away had heard of her. To think of her praises being sung by people she didn't even know! Elspeth was flattered and said modestly, "I'm afraid the term 'Angel of Mercy' is an exaggeration."

"It doesn't matter," he said, amused as he watched the struggle to overcome pleasure with humility pass across her face. "What mattered was that both of them thought so highly of you. And, of course, that they both assumed you would be willing to marry me for the sake of my child."

His voice held a note of query now, but Elspeth ignored it. "So you wrote to Papa?" she prompted.

"I merely wrote Sir Edward that I would be in the area and hoped to call on him. He wrote back and graciously invited me to stay at Lyndhurst. I accepted. Neither of us made mention of you in our letters."

"I see." Elspeth studied the floral arrangement between them for a moment. This would be the last of the autumn flowers, she supposed, and for the duration of the winter she would have to provide dried plants to decorate the table. They had come to the sticky part of the discussion, and her mind would not concentrate on how to broach the next question. Would it be better to ascertain how he felt about the arrangement now that he was here, or to state her own aversion to marriage straightaway?

"Which brings us to the present situation," he concluded, unnecessarily, but trying to give each of them a little time to think. "We are, as your father so succinctly put it, in similar predicaments. No, perhaps that's not altogether true. Neither of us *has* to do anything. I can remain at Ashfield with Andrew, but I will still be unable to change matters there. You can remain at Lyndhurst, and perhaps you have no wish to change matters here. Your position doesn't look very glamorous from where I sit," he admitted, shrugging, "but it may be entirely to your liking."

"Setting aside my position here," she said a bit stiffly, "you must realize, Lord Greywell, that there would be no reason my coming to Ashfield, as your wife or in any other way, would make a difference to the child. It's possible a different wet nurse might help him, but by no means certain. Having a substitute parent for him might ease *your* fears on his behalf, but it's really not at all likely there is anything I could do that hasn't already been done."

He listened carefully to what she had to say, accepting the truth of it, and yet not accepting it as the whole truth. "What you must understand," he said finally, "is that they've all given up on him. Everyone is convinced Andrew will die, as his mother did. Sometimes I feel as though I'm fighting their fatalism as much as anything else. Right now I don't seem to have enough influence to change that attitude. I'm too melancholy myself to force an optimism on them that they don't share.

Perhaps I don't even feel it myself. I'm too numb to feel much of anything, Miss Parkstone."

Against her will, Elspeth felt a surge of sympathy for him. And also for the poor child. She had wished to stay at one remove from both of them, keeping her involvement to some practical advice and some strong encouragement. Greywell's eyes, when he talked, developed a haunted quality, a power to move her that she hadn't expected. "It's not unusual to see that sort of fatalism in country people," she admitted. "It's a way of shielding themselves from more disappointments than they're able to bear. You mustn't think it's that they value human life any less than the gentry do; in fact, I almost think they value it more. But they're in a position of seeing more of their families die, without the proper care, and they've come to accept that in a way I don't think I ever could."

Greywell wouldn't have minded a glass of port, but she'd dismissed the servants, and he refrained from glancing toward the mahogany sideboard where the bottle had already been set out. "There is, of course, such a thing as unwarranted optimism," he said. "The child's health has been feeble since birth. I suppose those more knowledgeable than I have seen babies of his weakness die in large numbers. The odds may be against his survival."

"If I were you, I wouldn't be interested in the odds. I would only be interested in keeping him alive until he's old enough to gain strength." Elspeth glanced behind her to see if the port was there before asking, "Would you like a glass?"

"Thank you. I'll help myself."

Before he could rise, Elspeth motioned him to stay seated. "I'll retire to the sitting room and have Beeton serve you."

"Please don't leave. I'd like to continue our discussion."

Elspeth hesitated. Though she wanted to stay and talk with him, she also wanted to prove that someone at Lyndhurst could behave with the sort of social finesse he had every right to expect there. "I could have Beeton bring the port to the sitting room," she suggested.

Chapter Five

Beeton carefully poured one glass of port and handed it to the viscount. The tea tray was set in front of Elspeth and the bottle of port left near Lord Greywell on a silver tray before Beeton left the room. There was silence while Elspeth poured herself a cup of tea, but as she settled back against the cushions she resolved to speak.

"I hope you'll believe I feel the greatest sympathy for your plight, Lord Greywell. As you must realize, no one consulted my wishes in this matter, and it has long been my intention never to marry. That is very hard on my father, I suppose, but then I have never believed I must sacrifice myself for his well-being. Mr. Blockley frequently sermonizes on the duty of daughters to obey their fathers, which may be well enough for women of tender age who have no principles of their own to guide them. I myself have decided opinions, and they frequently do not coincide with Sir Edward's. I am persuaded I must adhere to the set of principles I perceive as being correct for myself."

Greywell looked surprised. "It's a matter of principle with you not to marry?"

"Well, no, not a matter of principle *per se*." Elspeth flushed under his steady gaze. "I'm sure there's not the least thing wrong with most women's being wives. They have almost a calling for the responsibilities and duties expected of them. I know a little of myself, Lord Greywell, and I'm aware that I would make a wholly unsatisfactory wife for any man."

"In what way, Miss Parkstone?" His voice held a trace of amusement.

"I'm not biddable, for one thing. You heard Papa. He considers me stubborn."

"Still, I've met a number of women who weren't particularly biddable, and they've made adequate wives."

"I shouldn't want to be an 'adequate' wife," Elspeth informed him, bristling. "It has long been my goal to excel in whatever I choose to do. Papa may discount my influence on his household, but it is considerable, because I've made a study of running Lyndhurst efficiently."

"That seems only a recommendation for your entering into matrimony."

"Not at all!" she protested. "Lyndhurst is my home. What I've done here would be impossible to accomplish somewhere else. Every establishment has its own practices, and I would antagonize a whole staff with my insistence on my way. I would find it very uncomfortable to live under even the most time-honored traditions; they would feel like unbearable restraints to me."

One of Greywell's brows lowered in thought. "Hmm. I wonder what traditions we have at Ashfield that would seem restrictive to an outsider. We celebrate Christmas, of course, and have a public day in the summer. The Long Gallery is chilly, but we often take tea there instead of in one of the warmer sitting rooms because it's been done for years. I suppose I wouldn't feel entirely averse to changing that arrangement, though there *is* something rather whimsical about sitting among all those portraits of ancestors."

"That's not exactly what I mean." Elspeth took a sip from the teacup and set it down on the table. "But it doesn't signify. That's only one of the reasons I don't intend to marry."

"Tell me another," Greywell urged. He was sitting comfortably in a chair opposite her, one long leg draped over the other, his broad shoulders resting easily against the chairback. "Really, I'm fascinated. For years I'd thought there was no disadvantage for a woman in marrying, unless it was out of her station to disoblige her family."

"How could you think that?" Elspeth was genuinely astonished.

"Why, a woman doesn't even have control over her own money when she marries. It is entirely at her husband's disposal."

"In my experience a husband doesn't generally disabuse the privilege, ma'am. There are any number of wives who haven't the first notion of how to handle money."

"Was your wife one of them?" she demanded.

His posture instantly became more rigid, and his eyelids narrowed over unreadable eyes. "We weren't discussing my wife."

"Forgive me. I didn't intend to be rude." She toyed with the teacup she'd set down, though she had no intention of pouring herself more. "This attitude men have about women's capabilities is wholly absurd, you know. Most women are more than able to manage a household within a reasonable allowance. I see them do it all the time here in the country. Perhaps the situation is different in London, where there is so much to tempt one into indulgence. But one does hear more often of a gentleman gambling away his patrimony than of a woman causing penury through her mismanagement of the household funds."

"Gambling can be a vice with women as well."

"Oh, I dare say, but there are few opportunities in our neighborhood to lose more than a few shillings at cardplay."

"We have digressed from our central topic, Miss Parkstone," he said. "You were telling me why it wasn't advantageous for a woman to marry. You, to be specific. I'd enjoy hearing more of your reasons."

"I have a purpose here in our parish. Any number of people depend on my services." She would not be more specific about Sir Edward's love children. They were none of Lord Greywell's business. Perhaps he didn't even know of them. She glanced at the impassive face opposite her, unable to tell what he was thinking.

"Many women feel there is a purpose in marrying and raising the next generation," he said. "Some feel it is the most worthwhile of purposes."

He had touched a sore spot with Elspeth. Actually, she quite liked children, and, given her inclination toward uplifting her fellow man (and woman), it seemed only logical that she would have very definite opinions on childrearing. Which she did. But she would never have the opportunity to put them into practice, because none of Sir Edward's women was the least inclined to offer her child into Elspeth's keeping, and it would have been almost impossible to raise such a child as she wished, anyhow. Even her advice to these women was as often as not totally ignored, a circumstance which caused Elspeth great frustration, and in some cases made her wish she'd never gotten involved. She was unable to meet Greywell's eyes now, and found herself fingering the silky tassel on the gown's apron.

"I would agree with that," she said softly, "but not every woman can have the opportunity."

His puzzled gaze remained on her down-turned head. "Apparently you've had the opportunity, more than once."

Elspeth looked up. "Did my father tell you that? You mustn't pay any heed to him. He's convinced every man who ever spoke to me is a potential suitor. But that's beside the point." Elspeth was not above wishing him to think well of her; there was something decidedly lowering about being thought so undesirable that no one wanted you. "I suppose I could have married had I wished. As I have said, I didn't wish to marry."

"If you'd married a man from the neighborhood you could have continued your parish work," he reminded her as he withdrew an oval snuffbox from his pocket and flicked it open. "And if you married someone elsewhere, well, there is parish work to be done in almost every community. Marrying would not likely have taken away that purpose from your life."

Elspeth was silent. The clock in the hall chimed ten times. Really, it was late enough that she could, without absolute rudeness, excuse herself and go to bed. As though he sensed her imminent decision, Greywell began speaking in a low, persuasive tone which he hadn't employed before.

"I had no intention of doing anything but stay at Ashfield with Andrew until Uncle Hampden's letter came. Actually, I dismissed his letter as well, until Abigail insisted I give some consideration to it. She seemed so wholly certain you would be willing to care for the poor child, and that your intervention would be beneficial to him. Why I should pay the least attention to her is beyond me. I often think she's quite mad. But there is also something very influential about her when she has hold of an idea. I prefer not to think of it as witchcraft," he said, with a shrug of his shoulders. "There are simply occasions on which she speaks with such authority, when you yourself are floundering, that you cannot help but pay attention. She isn't talking to your head, but to your heart. A very effective weapon, I assure you."

"Yes, I can see how it would be. But—"

Greywell lifted a restraining hand. Only an inch, but he, too, held authority when he wished. "I want the child to live. Whether it is Abigail playing on some superstitious belief within me that I'm not even aware of, or whether it is my recognition that if matters remain as they are, he won't, I'm not even going to try to ascertain. Either way, the end result is the same. I've come to believe that your coming to Ashfield would benefit Andrew. There's no reason you should sacrifice your future for his—you had never met anyone in the family until this afternoon. My uncle seemed to think that you would, as did Abigail, but I found it difficult to imagine, myself."

"It's not that I wouldn't come to help your little boy," Elspeth protested, a feeling of alarm spreading through her that he might misunderstand. "If I thought there was something I could do . . . Even if that's unlikely, I would be willing to come for a few weeks . . . to visit . . . to care for him."

He smiled gently at her. "That's kind of you, my dear, but I don't think your father would approve of such an arrangement. You are not exactly of a class to be a hired nursery maid, or whatever you would be. And I very much wish to leave Ashfield. Please don't think hardly of me, but the memories are too painful and I feel useless where Andrew is concerned. My gloom may be affecting him as much as that of the rest of the household, Miss Parkstone; I cannot overlook that possibility. I am needed at the Congress of Vienna, or so they insist."

His gray eyes regarded her intently, his hands forming fists on his knees. He had leaned slightly forward in his effort to gain her comprehension of what he was saying. Elspeth could feel the beginnings of a nervous quivering in her hands, and she hid them under the apron. He was about to propose marriage; she knew it, and she was afraid, because she wanted to help him. Not enough to marry him, though. That was impossible. Out of the question. There must be some middle ground where she could prove the sincerity of her sympathy and yet not actually marry him.

He continued to to speak. "If I went to Vienna, I would want to leave you at Ashfield with full authority to manage there as you wished. It would be unfair to leave you with such responsibility unless you were my wife, Miss Parkstone. I couldn't possibly go, leaving you with the child, unless we were married.

And I think you would find there were some advantages in marrying me. You would have an establishment of your own, without the inconveniences Sir Edward occasionally must provide. There is parish work to be done there as well as here, I'm sure. We could arrange a settlement which would virtually allow you the use of any money of your own, in addition to a quarterly allowance I would provide. Of course, the settlement would state that only your children would inherit from you; Andrew would be entirely my responsibility so far as his patrimony was concerned."

When her face blanched, Greywell instantly stopped speaking. There, he'd done it again. What had he said now? "My dear Miss Parkstone, whatever is that matter?"

Elspeth waved a shaking hand. "Nothing, nothing. It's just . . . I cannot possibly marry you! Please, don't say anything further. I should like to help. Truly I should. But I've told you I don't wish to marry."

Trying to suppress his impatience, he spoke very slowly. "Yes, so you've said. Nothing you've told me, however, provides an insurmountable obstacle. You would have a greater degree of freedom at Ashfield than you have here. Have I not made that clear? There would be nothing to interfere with your leading precisely the sort of life you wish, with the additional advantage of your being a titled, married woman with a new purpose in your life."

Her hands still fluttered nervously in her lap, and he had what he thought was a flash of insight into her distress. "You're alarmed about what would happen if Andrew died, aren't you?" he asked, relieved to get to the root of this problem. "My dear lady, you cannot possibly think I would blame you should the child not survive! I know you would do whatever was in your power, but these matters are not altogether in our hands, as I'm sure you would be the first to recognize." Her agitation did not seem to have lessened. She observed him with wide, frightened eyes, and fortunately another inspiration came to him. "I see what it is! You're worried that there would be speculation if the child died that you'd wished to provide the Greywell heir yourself, and had not taken proper care of him. Never think it! People already expect the child to succumb. No one would consider such an unworthy, uncharitable possibility."

Elspeth rose to her feet, choking over the words she tried to get out. "No, no! Please! I'm not feeling at all well. I must excuse myself. Believe me, I wish I could help you."

She was gone before he could say anything, and Greywell sat stunned in his chair. Whatever was amiss with the woman? An uncharacteristic scowl settled on his face, and he poured himself another glass of the port, wishing it were brandy, but not willing to ring for anyone. Had she taken him in dislike? It hardly seemed possible, when she kept protesting her desire to help him. He had been considered a very eligible bachelor before he married Caroline. His countenance, his address, his aristocratic position, all were accounted more than acceptable.

Miss Parkstone was obviously somewhat erratic in her behavior, he told himself, to assuage his self-esteem. So it was no doubt all to the good that she wouldn't have him. The thought of spending the rest of his life with her was somewhat unnerving. Greywell didn't doubt her goodness or her virtue. He could even accept on faith her intelligence and her domestic competence. But wasn't she likely to end up as dotty as Abigail Waltham, with all the fits and starts she'd exhibited in one single afternoon and evening? Was she the kind of woman he wanted to raise his child? Surprisingly, he still felt she was his only hope, despite her odd behavior. The idea had taken hold of his mind that she alone would be able to coax Andrew to health. Greywell fervently wished Abigail had never put the thought in his head.

A considerable time passed while he sipped at the port and stared disconsolately into the fire. Once he put on a new log, which was quickly consumed by the flames, the substantial piece of wood disintegrating into ashes in a matter of minutes. How easily something once so solid could disappear! One day Caroline was with him, laughing, thriving; the next day she was dead. And her child. Would he, too, vanish into the obscurity of a grave?

"Where's Elspeth?"

Greywell turned sharply at Sir Edward's voice.

"Didn't she stay up to entertain you?" the baronet asked, clearly disappointed.

"We talked for some time. She retired a while ago, not feeling particularly well."

"Didn't she play the pianoforte for you? Really, it's too bad of her. She's quite good at it."

"I'll accept your word for that." Greywell passed a hand along his brow, feeling rather weary himself. "We discussed the possibility of her marrying me, but the idea seemed to distress her."

"Distress her? But the arrangement would have every advantage."

Greywell could tell Sir Edward wasn't really surprised, despite his protest. "You didn't expect her to agree, did you?"

"I hoped she would." Sir Edward's eyes were as evasive as his words, flitting off toward the hearth.

"Miss Parkstone seemed genuinely concerned with little Andrew's health; she listened to everything I had to say on the subject. The reasons she gave for not wishing to marry were rather inadequate, I thought, and since I was able to alleviate most of her specific worries, I was a little surprised at how adamant she remained."

"I don't know where she got this aversion to marriage," Sir Edward grumbled. "Her mother and I were perfectly happy. That should have set a good example for her. I thought at first she was merely discriminating. After all, who could take Knedlington seriously? And if she'd wanted to annoy me, she could have accepted Blockley. One would have thought he was just the sort of pious gentleman she would be most likely to think herself in love with. But no! She was horrified when it came to his actually offering for her. And I don't think it was snobbery. It didn't seem to have occurred to her that his calling so frequently was with matrimony as his intent." Sir Edward lifted the bottle of port in his pacing about the room, but he didn't ring for a glass. With his eyes averted from Greywell, he muttered, "She's hopelessly naive, you know."

"You surprise me. Living in the same house with you . . ."

" 'Who is so deaf or so blind as is he/ That willfully will neither hear nor see,' " Sir Edward quoted, much to his visitor's astonishment.

"Miss Parkstone is obviously aware of your . . . activities. Her sight and hearing don't appear to be in question."

Sir Edward frowned at him. "Her understanding is superficial. Elspeth disapproves of my 'activities,' as you call them. She doesn't like having a lot of half brothers and sisters wandering about the neighborhood, but she feels it's her duty to see to their welfare. Her annoyance with the whole situation has made her an incredible prude, Greywell. I can't talk to her about it. I'm her father, for God's sake. Maybe you could talk some sense to her."

Greywell was hastily reviewing his various conversations with Elspeth for some clue that her father was wrong, but everything he remembered only served to substantiate the baronet's statement. Her confusion was not maidenly modesty; he had realized that at the time. There was a much more painful expression of her agitation whenever any mention of physical intimacy was made. Even her departure had coincided with his remarking on her possible future children, something to which he hadn't really given a thought. Greywell was still in mourning for his wife; he had no intention of establishing a physical bond with Elspeth—now. But marriage was forever, and especially if Andrew died, Greywell would wish to try for further children. The Foxcott family had not been prolific. If he didn't provide an heir himself, the title would die out.

It was only at this point in his reflections that Greywell realized Sir Edward had finished his remarks with the comment about talking sense to Elspeth himself. "You can't be serious," he said, his voice chilly. "I've just met Miss Parkstone."

Sir Edward was exasperated. "You've asked her to marry you. I can't think what further recommendation you need to be the one to enlighten her."

"She refused me."

"Well, of course she refused you! I'm not saying you should seduce the girl. Just talk with her. Make her understand there's nothing wrong with intimacy between a man and a woman, at least if they're married. She isn't likely to come around if you're too pristine to talk about it."

Greywell, who was deciding again that the whole situation was a farce, stared coldly at his host. "Really, Sir Edward, you haven't the first notion of decorum, have you? Miss Parkstone would be justifiably upset if I raised the issue with her, and I doubt it would do the least good. Such an aversion isn't rational, and can't be explained away rationally. I'm sure with time and patience and affection something might be done to overcome it, but I haven't the time, I doubt I have the necessary patience, and there is, as yet, no question of affection. I think we would do best to forget the whole scheme."

The room was beginning to chill, and Greywell rose from his chair to stand regarding Sir Edward's back. The baronet stood gazing into the dying embers, his shoulders slightly slumped but his booted feet spread apart in an almost defiant stance. He turned slowly to face Greywell.

"As you wish, of course. I can't force you to marry her, or her to marry you. Her mother would have approved of the match, I think. It's not much of a life for Elspeth, living here with me. She's an exceptional woman, you know, just requiring the right man to give her enough room to be herself. Though she didn't inherit her mother's looks completely, she's a handsome woman, and she'd look even better with a little guidance in her wardrobe, and with her toilette. She wouldn't shame you."

"There's no question of that," Greywell said gently. "I regret it didn't work out, Sir Edward. Though I think you might have known it wouldn't," he couldn't help adding.

" 'Hope springs eternal' and all that." The baronet sighed as he crossed the room to the door. "There won't be another occasion when someone with as great attractions as yours offers for her." At Greywell's dismissive gesture he grinned ruefully and said, "I'm not talking about your countenance or your aristocratic station, my dear fellow. I'm talking about your plight. That's what would appeal to her if anything did."

Lord Greywell's plight *did* prey on Elspeth's mind. She dreamed of a child wasting away while black-frocked women went about their household duties, ignoring him. The babe lay in a cradle already swathed in black, in a dark room where no one entered. There was a loud clock with a black face and black hands which ticked away the minutes mercilessly, coming ever closer to what Elspeth knew would be unbearable gongs of doom. She woke to the early-morning light in a sweat.

Was it her duty to marry Lord Greywell and try to save his son? Elspeth felt sure it couldn't possibly be a duty, even a Christian duty, but the question continued to nag at her. It was true she would have gone if it hadn't been necessary to actually marry Greywell. Much as she was accustomed to the neighborhood around Lyndhurst, there were numerous things in her situation which bothered her. Having so many of her father's illegitimate children continually thrust on her notice was unnerving for one of her moral rectitude. And she knew that Sir Edward would go on quite well without her; knew, in fact, that he wished she would leave so he could pursue his pleasures without her disapproving presence. Also, there was Mr. Blockley to consider. Elspeth felt, especially since she'd lost her temper and thrown the queen cake at him, that they could no longer be comfortable together, which made her parish work more difficult. Even at Lyndhurst her life did not hold out much promise of regaining its previous precarious balance.

Elspeth climbed out of the four-poster bed and padded across the carpet in her bare feet. Her room was exactly as she liked it, neither frilly nor overcrowded, the lovely old oak furniture so highly polished it seemed to glow in the pale light. Elspeth drew open the burgundy draperies to find that it had snowed during the night, leaving a sparkling cover over the lawn beyond her window. No wonder everything felt so still, she thought, picking up a hairbrush to draw it absently through her loosened tresses. It was probably later than she'd imagined at first, too, with the deceptive winter light, but her maid had not yet come with her standard cup of hot chocolate, so it couldn't yet be eight o'clock.

There was a light frosting in the bottom corners of the window, a tracery as lovely as the finest lace. Elspeth leaned her forehead against the cold pane, remembering the times she had eagerly pressed her face to the glass as a child, raptly observing the first snow, the first green bud, the first haying, the first fallen leaf. It was a great pity that daily excitement couldn't stay with you when you grew up. Elspeth turned aside from the window as her maid entered with her morning chocolate.

"There's not so much snow Lord Greywell won't be able to leave, is there?" she asked.

"I shouldn't think so, Miss Elspeth. Three inches, maybe. Only a regular dandy'd be bothered by three inches of snow. His lordship don't look like a few inches of snow would bother him, now does he? A fine gentleman he is, miss, from what I've seen of him." The girl set the tray down on a bedside stand. "Shall I help you dress now, or should I come back?"

"Now, please. I'd like to breakfast early." With any luck, Elspeth could be finished before the viscount ever descended to the Breakfast Room. She found Sadie totally unwilling to accept the plain gray day dress she'd already decided on.

"You've company, Miss Elspeth," she protested, drawing forth a blue wool with several falls of lace at the elbows. "An old-fashioned dress," she proclaimed it, "but ever so nice on you."

Once again Elspeth submitted to the girl's ministrations, thinking it couldn't be wrong when Lord Greywell had come all this way to inspect her. He shouldn't leave with the impression she was dowdy, at least. After last night it would have been almost an insult to revert to her more mundane dress, as though she were mocking him for ever thinking he might be willing to marry someone like her. Elspeth tried to put all thoughts of the sickly child from her mind.

Unfortunately, the dressing of her hair took longer than she had anticipated, and she didn't reach the Breakfast Room until almost her usual time. Lord Greywell was already there. Elspeth forced a smile to her lips. "Good morning. I hope you slept well."

"Very well, thank you." He stood until a footman had held her chair for her and then, resuming his seat, observed, "You set a remarkably fine breakfast table, Miss Parkstone. I haven't seen this much variety since my last large house party."

"My father and I both like a little bit of a lot of things. It's odd of us, I suppose, but one gets into the habit of indulging oneself. We usually have only a cold collation for luncheon, though sometimes in winter we have a warming soup." She hesitated before asking, "Will you be staying for luncheon?"

"No, I should be getting back to Ashfield. It makes me nervous leaving Andrew there alone for very long."

Elspeth concentrated on buttering a muffin. "Of course." The horrible dream forced its way into her mind, and she winced, but could not bring herself to say anything.

Watching her, Greywell wondered if she'd had second thoughts. Why, otherwise, had she flinched that way, as though he'd hurt her by insisting on leaving? There was no sense in broaching the matter again if she preferred not to consider it. But if she'd changed her mind? Would it be reprehensible of him to back off now? Compromising, he said, "I was hoping you'd show me the gothic ruin I passed by on my drive in, before I left."

"In the snow?"

He'd forgotten the snow. "If you'd prefer not to . . ."

"Oh, no, I love walking in the snow," she confessed. "If you haven't a pair of boots to withstand this kind of weather, someone could fetch a pair of Papa's."

"My own will do," he said, and for the rest of the meal he asked her questions about the surrounding countryside, Aylesbury, and Lyndhurst itself, carefully keeping each topic perfectly neutral. When she had finished eating, long after he had, she excused herself to get her outdoor wrap.

Elspeth reappeared in a navy-blue cloak lined with ermine, her hands thrust into an ermine muff. The effect of the outfit was somewhat spoiled by the heavy boots she wore, but she appeared unperturbed by the incongruity. When they met in the hall, she pulled the hood up over her head so the ermine lining framed her face. "Ready?" she asked, offering a faint smile.

Greywell nodded and took her arm. There was a flagstone path, freshly swept, that led from the east door of Lyndhurst across the lawn and through a stand of trees toward an ornamental pond. At the stand of trees one could look back over the gray stone building, somewhat forbidding in the dull light of the winter morning, or down the slight slope to the still water of the pond. The path had been swept only as far as the trees, but Elspeth never hesitated as she stepped into the fresh snow, looking back to see the pattern their footprints made in its pristine surface.

"My father's grandfather had the ruin built," she explained as they skirted the pond on a path made invisible by snow. "I can't imagine how the taste for ruins developed—fake ruins, I mean—but ours is quite a good one, for all that. In the summer it's covered with ivy and looks very realistic with the stone bridge just beyond it. In the winter it's a little bleak, and slightly dangerous if you don't watch your footing. The snow tends to hide some of the moldering stones."

Rounding a small orchard of bare-branched fruit trees, they came on the gothic folly abruptly. "It's even more of a surprise in the summer, when the leaves of the trees block out even a glimpse of it as you approach," she said. The stream which fed the pond had a usable stone bridge over it, but the icy incline was not inviting under the current conditions. Water lapped against the sides, sluggishly swirling on toward the invisible pond. "You could see the ruin from the drive over there."

Elspeth pointed to a spot in the distance where the view wasn't obstructed by trees.

Greywell hadn't said much on their walk. He was grateful for her apparent acceptance of his silence. Most women he knew felt it necessary to fill up any empty space with sprightly chatter, but not Miss Parkstone. When she didn't feel like talking, or didn't have anything to say, she walked along beside him, comfortable in her own thoughts. Even Caroline, he realized with some surprise, had seldom let a silence fall between them, even when he was reading the paper.

A few flurries of snow started to fall. Elspeth moved a little aside, so his hand fell from her elbow, and handed him the muff. Then she scooped up a handful of snow in her tan chamois-leather gloves, packed it into a hard ball, and took sight on a rock on the opposite side of the stream. "Would you like to lay a wager on whether I can hit it or not?" she asked, her eyes sparkling with easy camaraderie.

"Well," he replied, dangling the muff from one hand, "if you could hit Mr. Blockley's hat from an upstairs window with a queen cake, I fear I'd lose."

"Did Papa tell you that?" Elspeth was indignant. The color rose to her cheeks, matching her cold-reddened nose. "He said he wouldn't spread it about. Probably everyone in the neighborhood knows by now," she grumbled, tossing the snowball back and forth between her hands. "He thought it a very good joke, but I shouldn't have done it. It was childish of me. Still," she added, an impish smile appearing, "I enjoyed it enormously." And with that she sent her snowball sailing across the stream, where it landed with a satisfactory splat against the rock she'd chosen.

"You have a good arm," he congratulated her, handing back the muff. He scooped snow off the stone side of the bridge, formed it into a ball, and sent it after hers. It hit in precisely the same spot, shattering into fragments that spun off in snowy profusion.

"So do you." Elspeth realized they would soon be returning to the house, where he would no doubt stay only long enough to see his valise packed and warm himself against the cold drive back toward Coventry. Inside her muff she clenched her hands together and forced herself to speak, her eyes kept steadily on the gurgling stream. "I wish you would reconsider my offer to come to Ashfield to care for your son. I had the most awful dream last night. And now winter has set in, which is the most dreadful time for sickly babies. You could say I was a distant relation, perhaps. After all, I was your uncle's wife's godchild. There's some sort of connection in that. People wouldn't be surprised at your having someone come to help out at such a time. If you went off to Vienna, there couldn't even be a whisper of impropriety in my staying there."

A long moment passed while he studied her averted face. A possible solution to their impasse had come to him while they walked, but it would be so difficult to phrase it without offending her, without drawing into the light the dark fears she probably hid even from herself. "I'm afraid that's impossible, Miss Parkstone," he said finally, regretful. "If you come to Ashfield, you really must come as my wife. But let me reassure you on that head. We have only met, and I am a recent widower. The marriage I propose is one of convenience. Granted, it is more convenient for me than for you, but I would hope you could find real benefit in it yourself. I would not expect the ordinary marital . . . obligations from you under the circumstances. The succession is, I trust, provided for. Our arrangement could be one of companionship without the more intimate aspects of married life. If that is the way you would prefer it," he added conscientiously.

Inside the muff Elspeth's hands twisted in an agony of embarrassment, but her face was already so rosy from the cold that her agitation there was only evident in the wild way her eyes skittered from one object to another, never coming to rest on Greywell. "But what if your child were to . . . . I mean, if he didn't survive," she asked in a choked voice. "I'm sure he will, but one must consider all the alternatives."

"I prefer not to consider that eventuality unless absolutely necessary." He sighed and absently gathered another handful of snow, pressing it together as he continued, "I'm the last Foxcott, Miss Parkstone. It's my obligation to produce an heir to the viscountcy if at all possible. I'm sure you can understand my feelings in the matter. The question probably won't arise. If it does . . ." He tossed the snowball at the same target as before, hitting it squarely. Then he turned to her, gently lifting her bowed head with both hands, so she faced him fully. "I would have to expect your compliance, in that case.'' He could feel a shudder run through her, but whether it was from the cold or from nervousness, he couldn't tell. Her eyes remained on his face, so wide they reminded him of a frightened animal. But he would not, could not, compromise on this issue. His offer was, he felt, already more than generous, and probably hopelessly foolhardy.

Elspeth moistened her lips. She wanted to remove his hands, but knew she would be unable to face him if she did, and he deserved to be addressed as forthrightly as he had spoken. Had he decided on this unusual offer because he didn't really like her? Or had this always been his intention? If she could be sure the child would live . . . But that was a terrible thing to even think! How could she make a decision based on whether a child would live or not? The very thought was appalling! Of course he had no intention of consummating their marriage now, when he had so recently lost the wife he loved, a woman who had given her life to produce his son and heir. What he offered her was the sort of marriage she could never have hoped to have, one without the painful demands of physical intimacy . . . unless his son died.

Feeling a little short of breath at what she was about to do, Elspeth, unable to speak, nodded her head. This didn't seem to have the desired effect on his lordship, who merely raised one eyebrow in question. Elspeth tried again, nodding more vigorously.

''You could agree to those terms?'' the viscount suggested, wishing she would express herself verbally.

''Yes,'' she whispered. She would *not* let the child die. Too much depended on his living. ''Thank you,'' she added.

Only Greywell's eyes betrayed the faintest amusement. ''Thank *you* . . . Elspeth. Please call me David. It seems only proper that we be on a Christian-name basis, if we're to be married.''

''When . . .'' Her voice broke on the word; her throat felt totally parched. ''When would we marry . . . David?''

''As soon as I can obtain a special license.'' His hands dropped from either side of her face, and he withdrew a watch from his waistcoat pocket to check the time. ''With luck I could have it by this evening, tomorrow morning at the latest. The day after tomorrow? Would Mr. Blockley be willing to marry us by special license?''

''I . . . think so.''

"Good. I'll speak with him before I leave. Your father's permission I take for granted," he added ruefully.

"He'll want to discuss my dowry." Elspeth turned away from the gothic ruin and headed toward the house, cold, agitated, and determined. "At times he can be very businesslike."

"I'm glad to hear it," Greywell murmured.

Chapter Six

Two days. Elspeth left Greywell with her jubilant father and went directly to her room, where she stood dazed for several minutes. When she'd left the room that morning she'd had no intention of leaving it permanently. At most she had thought she'd go to Ashfield for a short span to care for Greywell's child. Elspeth told herself, as she crossed to the window, that she could go back downstairs and reverse her decision, but she knew she wasn't going to. Outside a thin sunlight made the snow glare, though it did little to melt it.

The white lace dress over a white satin slip would do perfectly well for a wedding dress if the pale-rose corsage was replaced with white satin and the full-blown roses were removed. There wasn't time to have anything new made up, and for such a small gathering as this wedding would be, the expense would be absurd.

There was the housekeeper to confer with, the neighbors to apprise of her change of status, the visit from Mr. Blockley to sit patiently through. Barely enough time to organize a full-scale departure, let alone consider the possible consequences of her acceptance of his lordship's suit. Elspeth would be leaving every person she had ever known—for a friendless vicinity she had never seen. And Greywell would leave her there with his son, going off to do his duty for his country. Leave her there alone with a possibly hostile household staff and an unhealthy baby. Well, that was what she wanted, wasn't it? A chance to do something of her own for a change, to rid herself of the familiar patterns of daily life, which had begun to seem impossibly dull.

Greywell left, and returned the next morning, only to closet himself with Sir Edward and their solicitors for hours on end. The length of these meetings seemed excessive, but her father only said, "There's nothing amiss, Elspeth. Everything must be gone over and written down and signed. It can't be done in an hour, and you'll see it all before it's signed."

Elspeth spent the hours trying to decide which of her childhood treasures to take with her. There was the first ivory fan her mother had given her for her fifteenth birthday, and the jewelry box that played a tune. Her father had brought it back from London many years ago for her mother, and subsequently given to her. There was the jewelry she seldom wore, saved for her in the locked safe in Sir Edward's study, to be carefully packed for the journey. But there were things she must parcel out among the servants and her neighborhood friends, too many decisions to leave time for her to think of what lay ahead. It was like living in a dream (or a nightmare) where she could see herself act, but didn't quite feel as though she was in her own body.

That last evening, after the solicitors left, she sat in the drawing room with her father and Lord Greywell, discussing the most mundane topics: how to transport her trunks, whether her mare should be tied to the carriage or sent over with a stable boy, when Sir Edward would make a visit to Ashfield. Elspeth was surprised to hear he intended to visit her in her new home at all, but she was perfectly willing to plan for his coming at Christmastime. Greywell wouldn't be there, of course, but that really had nothing to say to the matter. And it occurred to Elspeth that her father might not literally intend to come at all, but merely be saying so for Greywell's benefit.

It didn't bother her. Nothing much bothered her just then, since she didn't feel real. Sir Edward urged her to play the pianoforte when conversation lulled. Greywell (she must remember to call him David) turned the music for her. He seemed pleased with her playing, mentioned that his mother had had just such a style as hers, a very sensitive ear for fine music. Elspeth noticed that the little finger of his right hand was slightly deformed.

"I got it caught in a door when I was a child," he explained when he noticed her gaze. "It never healed properly, but it works all right."

There were a million things she didn't know about him, but that didn't matter, either. If there were important things to learn, she would learn them in time. He didn't know a thing about her, either, of course. Elspeth wasn't sure there was anything important for him to learn about her.

She slept soundly that night and had her breakfast on a tray in her room. They were going to the church at nine, and there was just enough time to dress. At the last moment, instead of the pearls she'd intended to wear, she dug frantically through the luggage to find the jewelry box. With a sigh of relief she withdrew the little gold chain with its gold locket and flicked it open to stare at the miniature of her mother. On her wedding day she wanted at least this remembrance of her beloved parent with her. Would Mary Parkstone have approved of what she was doing? Elspeth clasped the chain about her neck with shaking fingers, trying to convince herself her mother would have understood.

Mr. Blockley wore his most solemn countenance in front of the church when Elspeth descended from the carriage. Every fiber of his cadaverous body was rigid with disapproval, but he managed a slight smile for Greywell.

The service was short, and binding. Mr. Blockley managed to emphasize all the grimmer aspects of marriage, his doleful gaze resting inevitably on Elspeth's pale face. But when he had pronounced them man and wife, Greywell touched his lips to her cold forehead and murmured, "We've made our own promises, my dear, and they are as binding as any spoken here."

Elspeth managed a wan smile.

"We can drive straight through or stop the night at Daventry," Greywell told her when they had left Lyndhurst and Sir Edward well behind. "You don't have to decide now. I've sent word to Ashfield to expect us at either time. Are you warm enough?"

Elspeth had changed to a dress of gray Circassian cloth and muffled herself in the blue cloak with its ermine trim. The bricks at her feet were still warm and the carriage rug rested over her knees. "Yes, I'm comfortable, thank you."

The sense of dissociation she had experienced for the last two days had suddenly disappeared when they left the small wedding breakfast at her home and climbed into the carriage. A feeling of panic had seized her as she waved goodbye to her father and the assembled staff. Her life had just changed permanently, and the smiling, well-wishing faces did nothing to reassure her she'd made the right decision. The housekeeper had been quietly weeping into a handkerchief, and Elspeth strongly wished she could do likewise. But her smile remained frozen on her face; her arm ached as she waved through the carriage window until all of them were out of sight. Greywell had rearranged the carriage rug after she sat back, but he didn't speak to her, either guessing she needed a few minutes to think, or having nothing to say.

It felt strange to be alone with him in a carriage jostling over the hard-packed roads. He sat surprisingly still, his gloved hands resting on his thighs. Elspeth wondered what he was thinking while he watched the passing landscape. It was difficult to put herself in his place, when she was having so much trouble with her own thoughts and reactions. Was he satisfied that he'd done the right thing? It could not have been easy for him to decide to marry her, with his wife so newly dead, just in the hopes she would be able to bring about a turn for the better in his son. Well, he must be relieved that he could go off now and leave the situation in her hands.

What Greywell was remembering was another carriage ride, after his first wedding, an affair so different from this one as to make this look a shabby occasion in comparison. Caroline had wanted a full society wedding, with all the trimmings, and he had obliged. Everything had been of the first elegance, with all the ton in attendance. They had been married in the spring, three and a half years ago, when the weather was warm with promise and flowers bloomed in hopeful profusion. They had left the festivities in this very carriage, but they had not sat silent as he and Elspeth did now.

Caroline had cuddled against him, chattering away happily about anything and everything that came to her mind. She hadn't seen Ashfield but she was already planning changes she would make, telling him she would make their home the most sought-after of country residences. "Everyone will want to come and visit us," she had promised. "We will give the most delightful house parties."

"Let's have a little time alone together first," he had laughed, kissing the pert little nose, and then the full, provocative lips. Her mouth had trembled under his, eager and yet hesitant. He had been so careful, guiding her toward the consummation of their marriage. Her inexperience had been wondrous to behold her willingness to learn a charge on his patience and care. She was only eighteen at the time, a woman protected and untried, but she had loved him, had wanted to please him. During that carriage ride they had progressed, slowly, inevitably, toward the bedchamber that night. Greywell was not aware that he uttered a low moan.

"Are you all right?" Elspeth asked.

It was the wrong voice, shattering his memories to leave the present in all its stark reality. "Of course," he said, a little curtly. Though he reminded himself she had no way of knowing what she'd done, he could feel a slight resentment developing in him. This pious woman, in her somber gray gown, could never replace his beloved Caroline, who had been full of joy and light and tenderness. "I wish you would do something for me," he said.

"Whatever I can," she replied, pleasant, though she was a little alarmed by his forbidding expression.

"You may think that because Ashfield is still a house of mourning it's necessary to dress in a subdued manner. I wish you will not. What we all need there is a little color and brightness, for the child's sake. We have been too somber these last months, quite naturally, of course, but it's time we changed that. Shop for a new wardrobe, if necessary. You're aware of the quarterly allowance you'll have at your disposal; if it proves insufficient you have only to speak to me—or write me when I'm in Vienna. I don't want you to have to spend your own money."

"The allowance seemed extraordinarily generous." Elspeth wondered if it was the same as allotted his first wife, and if so, how she had managed to spend the half of it. "Most of my dresses *are* a little somber. Is there a decent modiste in Coventry?"

Caroline had done all her shopping in London. "I'm sure there must be. You can ask Emily Marden. She's a neighbor, and she's always well dressed. You might want to get a recommendation from her for a personal maid, too. Caroline's maid returned to London."

Elspeth was relieved to hear it. Nothing would have pleased

her less than to deal with a woman who had been her predecessor's advocate. She didn't bother to tell Greywell that she felt perfectly capable of choosing her own maid. But by the time she got around to that task, he would probably already be gone, and there was no need to upset him unduly. "I shall certainly speak with Mrs. Marden."

"Good. I've instructed Mrs. Green to prepare the Blue Bedchamber for you. It was my mother's room, but you may find you need to do a little refurbishing when you have the time. That sort of expense will come from the household fund, which will be under your administration entirely while I'm abroad. Mrs. Green will ask your approval of certain expenditures, and I think you'll have no reason to quibble with them. She's been housekeeper at Ashfield for twenty years or so. I've always found her entirely trustworthy."

His voice droned on, explaining arrangements at Ashfield, instructing her in the things she would need to know. But Elspeth had spent a hectic two days, and her exhaustion caught up with her as the carriage swayed gently along the toll road. Greywell discovered, midway through an exposition on estate management, that she had fallen asleep. She still sat almost upright in her corner of the carriage, her head slightly drooping on her chest, her hands folded calmly in her lap. Her new husband was irrationally annoyed. For the life of him, he couldn't remember *anyone* who had fallen asleep when he was talking, and certainly not in the middle of the day.

They had intended to stop for refreshment in Brackley. Elspeth was still sound asleep when they reached the town. Greywell, a note of long-suffering in his voice, directed that a change of horses be made and a packet of bread, cold meats, and cheeses be sent out to them. He could have gotten out and stretched his legs, perhaps even had a glass of ale, but he staunchly refused to move with Elspeth soundly sleeping on the seat beside him. She would have been perfectly safe, of course, but he needed the small sacrifice to fuel his resentment. Elspeth was not Caroline; this wedding day was nothing like his previous one. Greywell was determined to feel sorry for himself.

When Elspeth finally awoke, an hour out of Brackley, she did not apologize for falling asleep, since she wasn't aware she had fallen asleep when he was speaking. "I'm famished" were the first words she spoke.

Greywell had not opened the packet of food, though he was himself quite hungry, and had been for the last hour. With a weary elegance he produced the food wrapped in its mundane brown paper and set it on the seat opposite them. "We passed through Brackley while you were asleep."

Something in his tone made her eye him warily. "You should have wakened me."

"I was sure you needed your rest more than a meal just then. This way we'll lose less time on the road."

The cheese smelled delicious, and Elspeth reached across to help herself, but there was no knife to cut the bread or the cheese. "It's rather like a picnic," she said, breaking off a chunk of each with her fingers. "No one ever remembers to bring the cutlery on a picnic."

Greywell considered this a criticism of his planning, even though she spoke cheerfully. "I'm not in the habit of dining in a carriage. The inn at Brackley has a remarkably fine private parlor, where I have stopped innumerable times on my way to and from London. My intention had been to eat there."

"Oh, I know. Really, I don't mind this at all. It was clever of you to think of bringing something with us."

Greywell considered this condescending and an obvious attempt to cajole him out of his bad mood. "It isn't my preferred method of dining."

Elspeth lost patience with him. "I can see that, Greywell, but you might as well make the best of it. I certainly intend to. There's beef and lamb and something I can't identify. Shall I make you a sort of sandwich?"

"Thank you, I'll help myself." He didn't like it that she'd called him Greywell, after he'd gotten her to call him David. It set quite the wrong tone to their marriage. He was beginning to wish there were no marriage to have a tone to it. Finding himself glaring at her, he switched his attention to the food. Elspeth was a great deal more attractive when she was asleep, he decided, remembering how her face had softened and the long eyelashes had curved up from her cheeks. A stray curl had fallen down under her chin, bouncing gaily with the movement of the carriage. Awake, she looked prim once again, and her words refused to please him, no matter what she said.

Elspeth had begun to realize this and resolved to say nothing further until absolutely necessary. Unfortunately, in the short span of time she'd known him, she'd had no opportunity to observe him in a bad temper. Her father's moods were no mystery to her, and she assumed that in time she would be able to accommodate herself to Greywell's, but it would take time to learn them, and for the present she was determined to do nothing which would further annoy him. Then, too, she was a little annoyed with the fastidious way he was partaking of their picnic. One would think he'd never before been forced to eat anything with his fingers!

Their ride, in profound silence, seemed to last for an agonizingly long time. It was dark by the time they reached the turn-off to Daventry, and he turned to her to inquire politely, "Do you wish to break our journey here?"

"I'd just as soon head on to Ashfield, if that's agreeable with you."

"Perfectly agreeable."

The coachman had stopped the carriage at dusk and climbed down to light the lanterns on either side of the vehicle. Their light was so feeble it did nothing to illumine the surrounding countryside, though it served the purpose of making them visible to other drivers, Elspeth supposed. She had wanted to see what this new area looked like, but had no desire to spend the night at an inn with Greywell, where they would have to pass the time by conversing with one another. In the darkness of the carriage they could each wrap themselves in their private thoughts.

After a while Greywell announced they were passing through Rugby. "I went to school here as a child," he added. "My mother felt Eton was too far away for a boy of my age."

Elspeth murmured her acknowledgment of this fascinating tidbit about his past.

The years at Rugby had been much easier for him than for a lot of his contemporaries, he thought now, merely because he'd been so close to home. His parents had visited him regularly, bringing baskets of fruit and boxes of sweetmeats. Caroline had begged him to tell her tales from his schooldays each time they'd passed through Rugby, though at no other time. Apparently Elspeth wasn't the least interested. Not that he was inclined to regale her with such anecdotes, anyhow.

They were close to Ashfield now. Elspeth could feel it in the way Greywell's posture changed, by the way he gazed through the carriage window, looking for familiar landmarks, no doubt.

A journey's end always engendered a certain impatience in her. She began to pull on her gloves, which she'd removed much earlier to eat and hadn't bothered to replace because she'd held them in her muff. Her hat was crooked and the ribbons untied, her dress crumpled from the long nap when she hadn't been paying attention. She did her best to rearrange herself, knowing it was altogether likely Greywell's staff would be brought together to welcome her.

"We won't be there for another twenty minutes," he said.

"It will take me all of twenty minutes to put myself together," she replied, making a face at him in the darkness.

He had held Caroline's hand that last four miles, asking, "Are you nervous? Everyone is going to love you." Caroline hadn't made faces at him. Greywell had wonderful night vision.

The doors of the house were opened before the carriage came to a standstill. Elspeth had only time to discern that it was a three-story brick structure with stone corner quoins before she was led up the two shallow flights of stairs to the front door. As she had expected, the staff was assembled. She was introduced to the more senior members by her husband, and more briefly to the others by Mrs. Green, who maintained a civil demeanor though her curiosity about the new bride was perfectly obvious to Elspeth. Whether hostility lay beneath the curiosity the new mistress could not tell.

Most of the faces were carefully bland. The one exception was the nursery maid. She was a girl several years younger than Elspeth, and rather prettily plump. Her anxiety shone from large brown eyes and hands she kept firmly clasped over her apron even when she curtsied to Elspeth.

"How does Andrew go on?" Greywell asked her, speaking for almost the first time. No one had congratulated him; he had not expected they would. His own face was drawn. Entering Ashfield with Elspeth was a painful experience for him.

"About as usual, my lord," she answered. "Bates is with him now."

Elspeth was eager to meet the wet nurse. "I should like to see Andrew directly," she told her husband.

"If you would just say a word to the staff first."

Every eye was on her. Why hadn't she thought to prepare something to say to them? First impressions were always of such importance. Elspeth forced herself to be calm, and smile at them. "Thank you for your kind welcome. I'm sure we will all work well together. Lord Greywell has sung your praises to me, and I look forward to getting to know each of you better. I shall need your assistance in familiarizing myself with Ashfield and in carrying on when Lord Greywell departs for Vienna. My first objective is to see the child grow in strength and health, a purpose with which I feel sure you are all in accord. With God's grace we will see him toddling about this very hall, robust and happy, within the next year."

She nodded her dismissal, accepted Greywell's arm, and began to climb the Great Staircase, an elaborate mahogany edifice with carved panels on either side. The newel posts were topped with detailed wooden carvings of baskets of fruit, and the walls were hung with magnificent oil paintings, the quality of which she didn't doubt.

Greywell did not like to compare Elspeth's speech with the one Caroline had given. After all, Caroline had been only eighteen at the time, and somewhat intimidated by the assembled staff. She had stuttered a little, which had merely served to endear her to everyone. Elspeth had surprised him with her fluency; he had noted the light of alarm in her eyes before she turned to address them. But she had years of experience as mistress of a home not all that much smaller than Ashfield, and her ease had not been as captivating as Caroline's winsome charm. The servants had awarded Caroline their undying devotion; he imagined they might grudgingly give Elspeth their respect. He would have liked to squeeze her hand where it rested on his arm, but he couldn't quite bring himself to do it. She didn't need the reassurance Caroline had needed. Elspeth was altogether a different sort of woman: proud, self-contained, pious. There was no need to tell her she had done well; she would know it.

The nursery was on the top floor, and though it wasn't quite as depressing as it had looked in Elspeth's dream, it was hardly a cheery sanctuary, either. Elspeth was surprised at how small the room was, when she had counted three doors coming off the hall before reaching it. Surely there were larger, airier rooms in which the babe could sleep. The wet nurse had a bed opposite the cradle, to be immediately available, day and night. Greywell explained that the nursery maid slept next door.

Bates, the wet nurse, was older than Elspeth would have expected, well into her thirties. She wore a brown fustian dress and soft slippers. When they entered she was trying to induce the baby to suckle a little longer, but he fretted, whimpering and turning his head away from the nipple. Bates gave an exaggerated sigh as she looked up to say, "It's always the way with him."

The child was very small. Elspeth had a hard time accepting that he was more than three months old. There were a few wisps of brown hair on his head, and his eyes were squeezed tight shut while his little fists hammered ineffectually against a blanket that wrapped him tightly. "May I hold him?" she asked, directing the question to Bates, who was sliding her bosom back under the shapeless dress.

"Of course, ma'am."

Greywell realized his oversight in introducing Elspeth. He had been too intent on studying his son for any signs of improvement. "This is my wife, Lady Greywell, Bates. She's eager to help us improve the child's health."

A little sniff of disbelief escaped Bates before she relinquished the child to Elspeth's waiting arms and murmured, "Milady."

Though Elspeth tried to receive the child carefully, the slight jostling made him open his eyes, pucker his little face and wail at her. "Well, that sounds just fine," she said, smiling at him, as she loosened the receiving blanket around his tiny limbs. "You need to exercise those lungs a little more vigorously than you were when we came in, my dear boy."

His continued crying didn't seem to bother her. She walked about the room, talking to him, telling him about their journey and commenting on the room's oppressive atmosphere. "We're going to get you a nice new room, Andrew, where there's more air to breathe. Where the sunlight will stream in and fall on your face and make you feel more lively. And we're going to have a crib made ready, one that's painted white and has pictures of little ladybugs and violets." She stopped in front of Greywell, challenging him with her eyes to deny what she was promising. Instead he tucked a finger in his son's little fist and asked, "Will that help?"

"Who knows?" The child had stopped crying, and Elspeth continued softly, "We're going to try everything. Fresh air. A change of surroundings. Even a change of diet," she added, glancing apologetically at Bates. "Whatever works we'll continue, what doesn't, we'll stop. Just because some form of care is traditional doesn't mean it works for every child, or that it is necessarily good. Take the way we ordinarily wrap them up as tightly as possible. The theory is that it makes them feel secure. And for some children it works wonderfully. But I've known others who felt unbearably restricted by such close binding. For them it was necessary to give more freedom, and to clothe them a little more heavily for when their blankets fell away from them. We'll have to see how it is with Andrew. I'd like you to bring his cradle to my room."

"But when he's here with Bates, she can feed him in the night," Greywell protested, taking note of Bates' indignant frown.

"I shall bring him to her, never fear. As you know," she said, with a wicked grin, "I had plenty of sleep in the carriage today."

Greywell was not inclined to argue with her. For what other purpose had he brought her here, if not to do something about his son? He was loath to antagonize Bates, but surely his new wife's wishes came slightly above the wet nurse's. Besides, he was tired, depressed, and still feeling slightly out of temper. Arguing with Elspeth at such a time didn't appeal to him in the least.

"Very well," he agreed.

Bates couldn't resist putting in a word. "He be needing changing now, milady."

"So I noticed," Elspeth said, good-natured in the face of the older woman's burgeoning antagonism. "Would you do it, Bates? Then I'll take him with me."

"Might be you should take a few extra cloths with you," Bates mumbled as she efficiently changed the now-placid child. "He spits up a lot."

Elspeth gathered a stack of freshly laundered cloths from the pile and accepted the child from the reluctant Bates. "I'll take good care of him," she promised. "Does he still wake in the night for a feeding?"

"Not so often now."

Greywell considered the mechanics of getting a footman up to the nursery to carry the cradle, and decided it would be simplest if he carried it himself. He wasn't pleased with the arrangement; he wasn't in the habit of lugging furniture around his own house. But for the sake of a quick escape from Bates' piercing eyes, and to accommodate his new wife, he lifted the heavy wood cradle, sure he'd throw his back out, and led the way down the stairs to the Blue Bedchamber. It was in another wing entirely from his own, and the one that had been Caroline's, but it was close to the stairs to the nursery floor.

A fire had been lit on the hearth, and there were several branches of glowing candles. Elspeth directed Greywell to put the cradle near the canopied bed with its heavy blue velvet hangings and gold tassels. A maid had already unpacked her smallest case and laid a nightdress out on the bed. Elspeth didn't like Greywell's seeing it, since it was a rather frivolous garment, one the staff at Lyndhurst had given her as a wedding gift (though surely only Mrs. Hinton had chosen it!). A touching gesture, to be sure, but hardly practical under the circumstances, with its rows and rows of lovely lace, a great deal of which couldn't have shielded a sixpence from view. Elspeth took a quick look about the room, the babe still in her arms, sound asleep.

"It's a fine room," she said. "A little ornate for my taste, perhaps, but that's mostly the furniture. I've never cared overmuch for all these lion-legged chairs and benches and occasional tables. But I suppose it's the original furniture, recovered from time to time, and I would dislike breaking your family's tradition by removing it."

Greywell was sure she wouldn't mind in the least and told her coolly, "You may do whatever you please with it. However, if you decide to replace it, I would ask that you have this furniture relegated to some other room, or stored away in the attics. Some future generation may be more enamored of it than you are."

"I dare say."

He had grown up with this furniture. His own chamber was full of similar pieces; the whole house was full of it. Dear God, what had he done bringing her here?

A strained silence had fallen between them, alone in her new room, and she broke it not by speaking to him but by starting to hum a gentle lullaby as she settled the baby in his cradle and tucked the blankets around him. When Elspeth turned to him again, his face was carefully schooled into polite civility.

"If there's anything you need, you have only to ring for it," he said. "I'll have one of the maids come to help you undress."

"That won't be necessary. I can manage for myself."

"They'll expect it of you."

Elspeth frowned at him. "I don't really care what they'll expect, Greywell. When I have a maid of my own I'll be perfectly happy to let her do for me. In the meantime, I'll do for myself."

Stubborn. Her father had been correct in his judgment. Greywell acknowledged her decision with a slight lifting of his black-clad shoulders. "As you wish. May I at least arrange for a maid to bring you coffee or tea in the morning?"

"Hot chocolate, at eight."

"Excellent." His voice held a false note of heartiness. "I'll bid you goodnight then, my dear. Sleep well."

"Thank you." Elspeth had already turned back to the cradle before she said, rather absently, "Sleep well."

Chapter Seven

The experience of having a baby sleep by her bed was a new one for Elspeth. Andrew made all sorts of strange sounds, and half a dozen times during the night her heart speeded up with fear that he was choking or suffocating. Once when she picked him up to comfort him, he spit up all over her nightdress, and she was glad she'd put the lovely lacy confection in the wardrobe and worn one of her old flannel ones. He never seemed to come fully awake, until six in the morning when he howled for food.

Groggily Elspeth stumbled out of bed and wrapped herself in a dressing gown. He sounded so urgent she didn't bother to do anything with her hair, allowing it to remain in the braid down her back as she scooped him up and hurried to the nursery with him. Bates, who had probably gotten her first good night's sleep in three months, was a little more cheerful this morning. She put the babe to her breast, crooning to him, even as she tugged a bell cord near her chair.

"Lucy brings me my breakfast soon's I'm up," she explained. "You have to keep up your strength when you're feeding a child."

"Precisely. I wonder if you would mind going over with me what your daily meals consist of. That way I will be better able to judge if you're having sufficient nourishment."

Bates rolled her eyes but complied. "For breakfast a little cold meat or game pie. Then at eleven or thereabouts a biscuit with half a pint of stout. I have my dinner at one: meat, bread, and potatoes, with occasionally a piece of sago, rice or tapioca pudding, and some green vegetables. Or maybe fresh fish. With a pint of porter. Then about eight in the evening half a pint of stout with another biscuit, and for supper, at ten or half-past, a pint of porter with a slice of toast or bread and cheese."

"And never any fried meats? They have an adverse effect on some children."

"Well, now, sometimes it's a bit of fried fish. It never seemed to bother the little fellow."

"Hmm. And the vegetables? Cabbage, cucumbers, pickles, and several others can make difficulties for some babies. Have you had any of them?"

"I'm partial to cabbage," the woman admitted. "No one never said it was a problem."

"Yes, but for the child's sake let's cut it out of your diet for a while and see if that helps." Elspeth was walking slowly about the room, taking in its appointments and the various containers lying about on the dressing table and chest of drawers. Her eyes widened at one bottle, and she reached for it with an exclamation that sounded suspiciously like "Eureka!" Bates had been watching her but looked not the least disturbed at Elspeth's discovery.

"Do you give him this regularly?" she asked.

"The castor oil? Why, of course, milady. Everyone knows it's what every child needs."

Elspeth shuddered. "Never, never give him another dose, Bates. It is not what every child needs. In fact, it is the cause of more disturbance to a child's health than any one other concoction I can think of."

"But I've given it to all my babies!"

"Then you are fortunate indeed that they've survived, especially those with weak constitutions." Elspeth carried the bottle to the window, pulled the stopper from it, and proceeded to pour the contents out, unconcerned with whether they would smear on any windows below them. "Dear God, it's incredible how many people believe in its efficacy, when it is entirely injurious to a constitution such as Andrew's! A healthier child could manage; obviously many of them do. Didn't you ask the doctor about it?"

Bates regarded her sullenly. "Not this one, but the very first time I was a wet nurse, the doctor *insisted* I use it, and so I've done ever since."

"Some doctors are as ignorant as their patients," Elspeth grumbled, tossing the empty bottle in a waste receptacle. "I'm not blaming you, Bates, but you must believe me, it's entirely the wrong thing to give Andrew. Ask the doctor, if you doubt my word. I'm sure Greywell would only employ a doctor who knows what he is doing. And I will not be convinced that a doctor who knew Andrew's condition would prescribe castor oil!"

"Well, I didn't know," the poor woman muttered, staring at the little bundle in her arms. "I wouldn't be doing anything to hurt the little angel."

Elspeth laid a hand on her shoulder. "I understand that, Bates. Together we're going to get him healthy, if it's at all possible. I'll speak with the kitchen help about your meals. You do know that stout and porter are the only beverages of that nature you should drink, don't you? They're both strengthening, but others might affect the child adversely."

"That's all I drink, Lady Greywell. Honest."

"And you don't give him anything to make him sleep at night, do you?"

"Never!" Bates was indignant. "I heard of a woman once used to give a baby syrup of poppies! That's criminal! I'd never do such a thing!"

"No, no, of course you wouldn't," Elspeth said soothingly. Unless someone had told you it was all right to do so, she thought, not angry with Bates but with the strength of folklore medicine among the country people. Much of it was genuinely beneficial, too, which made it all the more difficult to eradicate the dangerous practices. Elspeth had spent a great deal of time around children in her parish work and in seeing that her father's illegitimate offspring were well cared for. Several years ago she'd wanted to have a little booklet printed which would give advice on child care, information she'd gathered from the local doctor and midwife, but her father had pointed out that most of the women in the district weren't literate enough to read it. That had inspired her to institute classes in reading for them, but she'd never gotten back to her original project. Perhaps here she'd have the time . . . and the authority that was so necessary. Her father had also told her, in no uncertain terms, that people would think she, an unmarried, childless woman, was mad to write such a booklet.

Andrew had begun to fuss. Bates took him from her breast and changed him before looking to Elspeth for guidance. "Did you plan to take him back to your room now?" she asked.

Elspeth wasn't sure what she'd planned. "Will he be awake for a while?"

"About an hour. Then he'll take another nap."

"I'll take him with me," Elspeth decided, accepting him from Bates' arms. His eyes were wide open, staring at her. They were a deep gray, like his father's. Elspeth wondered, as she walked down the stairs, what his mother had looked like. She wasn't going to ask Greywell; she'd ask Mrs. Green if there was a portrait. It was not difficult to imagine that Caroline had been beautiful.

The hall was deserted, with only a faint morning light reaching it. She walked down to the window to look out over a snow-covered landscape. It must have snowed more in the night, she thought, holding the baby up to see out the window. "One day all this will be yours," she told him, gesturing to the lawns and trees. "And the sooner you get strong and healthy, the sooner we'll go out and explore it together. Not that I intend you should stay cooped up in the house as you have been. We'll bundle you up in your warmest clothes and take a short walk this afternoon. Long enough to get some fresh air, but not long enough to chill you. If the light's too bright for you, we'll put on a bonnet with a brim to shield your eyes."

The silence in the corridor was broken by the nursery maid's footsteps as she carried a loaded tray up to Bates. The girl didn't notice Elspeth by the window and hurried on up the stairs humming happily to herself. Did she always do that? Was Greywell mistaken that his staff were downhearted and morbid about the child's chances of survival? Elspeth assured herself it no longer mattered, save that she do her best to see them all bright and cheerful, especially in Andrew's presence. Which might prove a little difficult, if she antagonized them. And it was difficult not to antagonize people when you were forcing them to change their ways.

"But we'll manage, won't we?" she asked the silent baby as she wandered back to her room. Taking a blanket from his cradle, she spread it on her own bed, covered it with several cloths, and laid him down on his stomach. His eyes continued to follow her, and he had to lift his head a little to do it. "Good," she said. "We're going to give you lots of things to look at so you exercise those muscles. And we're going to get you kicking your legs and pulling with your arms. Our doctor in Aylesbury said that was very important. It's all well and good to feel all cozy and secure in a tight blanket, Andrew, but you need a little exercise to work up an appetite."

The next hour she spent encouraging him to take an interest in her movements and the objects she brought to him. He was fascinated by the lacquered lid of her powder box, which she carefully wiped clean of any traces of powder before allowing him to grasp it in his little fist. She laughed at him, and talked to him and cuddled him until he started to doze off from sheer exhaustion. Then she put him in the cradle, kissed his pale forehead, and said, "Sleep well, little love, and wake ready to drink more milk than you've ever had before. You're going to need to keep up your strength with *me* around."

He was already fast asleep by the time a maid came in bearing a tray with hot chocolate at eight. Elspeth was severely tempted to go back to sleep when she'd drunk it but forced herself to dress and join her husband in the Breakfast Parlor after she'd left Bates sitting with the child in her room. Though she had chosen the most cheerful of the dresses that were already unpacked, it was not one of her more becoming outfits. The mustard color brought out a sallowness in her skin and the fullness of its skirt made her look frumpy, but it was that or a dark green, a dark blue, or another gray. Elspeth didn't have much choice.

Greywell had risen when she entered the room, his eyes quick to take in the unsuitable costume. "It's the only thing I had that wasn't depressing," she told him as she took the chair a footman held. "When the rest of my clothes are unpacked there are a few other things I'll be able to wear."

"You don't look as though you slept well. Are you feeling all right?"

"I'm a little tired," she admitted. "In time I'm sure I'll accustom myself to Andrew's little squeaks and groans, but they were a bit unnerving."

"He doesn't have to sleep in your room." Greywell gave her an "I told you so" look, though he hadn't told her anything of the kind.

"I *want* him to sleep in my room. I want to spend the majority of his waking hours with him, just now, at the start. He needs to get familiar with me, to hear my voice even when he's sleeping so I won't be a stranger to him."

Greywell studied her while she buttered a slice of toast. Her eyes looked larger because of the light circles under them. "I don't want you to exhaust yourself, my dear," he remarked kindly, before dismissing the servants for a more private talk.

"I shan't." Her expression became earnest. "He's a darling boy, Greywell, and I feel so good having a purpose. I've already discovered something that might have been keeping him poorly. No, I don't intend to tell you what it was. You might misunderstand. Just be assured I shall do my best to see he gets the proper care, and I've learned a great deal about babies over the last few years."

"Hmm. Don't you think it would be wise if you talked with Dr. Wellow before you made any drastic changes, Elspeth? He's been watching the child's progress since he was born."

"Well, of course I shall talk to him! The sooner the better. I don't think there's anything in the regimen I'm proposing which will alarm him in the least." Elspeth frowned momentarily, setting down her piece of toast. "Though he might perhaps have some reservations about my intention to get Andrew a little fresh air. Doctors are notorious for believing all sorts of vile things are afloat in the air. But this isn't London, or even an industrial area. Good country air is a lot better for a child than something like that stuffy room he's been spending all day in. Isn't there a larger room which could be used for the nursery?"

"We'd originally intended to keep him in the room that connects with Bates, but when he appeared so sickly . . ."

"Yes, I see. It's not something that has to be changed immediately, because I intend to keep him with me for a while." Elspeth took a bite of the ham, pondering her next request. "May I have a crib built for him, like the one I described last night? He's too old for a cradle, even if he's not too big. Babies need some room to move about in, Greywell. They need to exercise their arms and legs, to roll over and shift about."

"My own crib is in the room that was to have been the nursery. It's not painted white, and it doesn't have ladybugs and violets painted on it." Greywell grimaced, whether at her idea of a proper crib or at his own she couldn't tell. "In fact, it's an antique, rather rococo, with a lot of gold leaf on it."

"I'll look at it," she promised, skeptical. "It might do if we hung a few cloth toys within his reach that he could bat about. Really, he must have more to look at than a dark room! Even in the poorest households I've visited the babies have had something to play with and look at."

"There are any number of things in the other nursery. I think Bates has left them there because he didn't show any interest in them." He took a sip of cooling coffee. "Caroline made quite a few things for him that were put away."

"But he should have them!" Elspeth insisted. "They will be treasures to him when he's older, knowing his mother made them for him. Or perhaps you would rather they be kept unused so they will still be new when he's old enough to appreciate them."

"She made them for his use." Greywell dismissed the subject with a wave of his hand. "Do as you please, Elspeth. I'm willing to trust your judgment with Andrew, as long as the doctor finds your 'remedies' acceptable. I thought you would like Mrs. Green to show you over the house this morning, but I wouldn't be surprised if we had some visitors. Word always seems to spread so quickly in the country, and there will be those who wish to call on you. You might have one of the maids press a different gown, one that would be more suitable to company. Your trunks were put in the room next to yours until there was time for you to supervise their unpacking."

"Will your neighbors find it objectionable that you've remarried so soon?" Elspeth regarded him curiously, apparently not disturbed by the possibility.

"Some of them may. I wouldn't let that worry you. They won't come if particularly offended, and if they do come, they'll be polite."

"Do you intend to tell them you'll be leaving for Vienna soon?"

"Yes. Would you rather I didn't?"

"Not at all. I hope you will." Elspeth popped the last bit of toast into her mouth and chewed it thoughtfully. "I think it wouldn't be a bad idea to stress my role with Andrew, either. For the time being I plan to spend a lot of time with him, and it would be a nuisance to have an excessive number of bride visits with which to contend."

Greywell's brows came down in a settled frown. "Surely you know how important it is that you be accepted in the community, Elspeth. For your sake as well as my own, and eventually for Andrew's. I hope you don't intend to put up people's backs by not receiving them. That would be quite the wrong way to go about things."

"I promise you I have no intention of offending anyone, or of reducing your consequence." Her level stare across the elaborate breakfast table was haughty. "You may be sure I know precisely how to comport myself, Greywell."

"It's not that I doubt you do, my dear," he said, trying for a more placid tone, and not quite achieving it. "You conceive of Andrew as your first duty, and I admire your devotion to it. Nonetheless, you should remember there are any number of people here who can care for him, while there is only you who can greet our guests as my . . . wife and the new mistress of Ashfield. So you must not confuse your priorities."

Elspeth gave a dainty sniff. "I wouldn't dream of it, my dear sir. If you will excuse me, I'll have Mrs. Green show me around my new . . . domain."

Her husband groaned inwardly as she made an elaborate curtsy to him and glided regally, chin up, from the room.

As with any really large house, there wasn't time, on the first inspection, to do much more than gather an impression of most of the rooms. Certain rooms seemed to be favorites with Mrs. Green, possibly because of their truly excessive furnishings and decorations. Her expertise ran to knowing the names and relationships of all the Foxcott family immortalized in portraits in the paneled Long Gallery, where there was, she explained in answer to Elspeth's question, no portrait of the late Lady Greywell, it having been planned for the following summer.

"There is a miniature, though. I'll show it to you," the housekeeper offered. "What a beautiful woman she was, with the most glorious golden hair and glowing green eyes. And her complexion! Well, I've never seen the like of its creamy texture. So very sad."

Elspeth turned aside as the housekeeper dabbed at her eyes, studying the portraits hung the entire length of the enormously long room. When Mrs. Green had regained control of her emotions, she led Elspeth through another succession of rooms. The North Drawing Room was hung with magnificent tapestries, and the South Drawing Room with a succession of murals and mirrors. Elspeth found the latter overwhelming and hoped it wasn't the room used most frequently for company. The Great Chamber, the Double Cube Room, the Saloon, the Chapel, the State Bedroom, the Long Library, the Miniature Room. It was all too much to absorb at once, but Elspeth maintained a demeanor of interest and approval. Really there was a sameness to the rooms after a while: all highly decorated with the most ornate furniture and trappings, enough gilt about to please even Midas. Elspeth eyed one room, called the Queen's Closet, which she intended to have for her private retiring room. Her own bedchamber wasn't divided to make a good sitting as well as sleeping room, and the closet was only two doors down from it. Fortunately, there was very little furniture in it to be gotten rid of.

Several aspects of her tour were of special interest to the new mistress. Mrs. Green had hesitated before taking her into her predecessor's chamber, where everything had been left much as it had been when poor Caroline died. Her silver-backed hairbrushes were still laid out on the dressing table, and little knickknacks were scattered about the room. It was the only room that had been recently redecorated, and it was still too ornate for Elspeth's taste. Because she didn't wish to appear too curious, they didn't stay long, though Elspeth intended to return when Greywell was safely on his way to Vienna. Greywell's own chamber was merely indicated to her with a wave of Mrs. Green's hand, but Elspeth knocked on the door and his valet allowed her a cursory glance over the mammoth chamber. That room, too, she would explore further at her leisure. Elspeth was not, she assured herself, unduly nosy; it was a matter of acquainting herself with the whole of her new residence, and with the external setting of a rather enigmatic husband.

In the Miniature Room Mrs. Green lovingly took down the promised miniature of Caroline, which was indeed as beautiful as she had promised. Elspeth murmured the expected appreciation and sorrow. Actually, she felt both, but they disturbed her more than she had expected they would. No wonder Greywell was so overwrought by the loss of this enchanting woman. What a pity Andrew would never know her as his mother in anything but a miniature. She carefully replaced the frame on the wall, only to have her eye caught by a display of snuffboxes immediately beneath it.

"And what's this?" she asked, indicating the collection.

"His lordship collects snuffboxes, milady," Mrs. Green said, sounding somehow surprised that Elspeth wouldn't know. "It's a great occupation with him. There must be fifty in this room alone, and you'll find them scattered throughout the other rooms when you have a chance to investigate them more thoroughly. In addition he has several dozen in his study and in his bedchamber, I'd guess, his more recent acquisitions."

"He collects snuffboxes?" Elspeth asked, incredulous. "Whatever for?"

"Why, because he likes them, I suppose. Some of them are very pretty."

And some of them, thought Elspeth, glaring at two with naked nymphs, are totally objectionable. Did Greywell intend to leave them lying about the house when his son was growing up? What sort of education was that for an impressionable young mind? She preceded Mrs. Green from the room without voicing her puritanical thoughts.

"We won't go to his lordship's study," Mrs. Green decided, bypassing a closed door. "He'll be there now with his estate agent, arranging matters for when he's abroad. Ah, here's Selsey now. Do we have visitors?" she asked, smiling coyly at the butler.

"Indeed. Mrs. Waltham has just arrived. At the front door," he added, making Elspeth wonder if this was something unusual. "I was just about to inform his lordship and her ladyship."

Elspeth glanced down at the mustard-colored dress she wore. "Tell Lord Greywell I'll join him in ten minutes. Where have you put Mrs. Waltham?"

"In the North Drawing Room, milady."

With a nod she hurried off to the Blue Bedchamber, where a maid had already ironed and hung out several of her dresses. She found the girl talking with Bates, who sat hemming a handkerchief beside the sleeping baby's cradle. Wonderful, she thought, now I can get dressed in front of both of them. Elspeth was beginning to wonder if her idea of keeping Andrew in her room was such a good one after all.

The maid assumed her assistance would be needed in Elspeth's changing, and her mistress did not disillusion her. Without the girl's help it would have taken her a great deal longer to present herself in the drawing room, but the baby woke just as she was leaving the room and she had to force herself not to go back and pick him up. She was sure the smug look Bates wore was meant for her.

The North Drawing Room was the one with the beautiful tapestries and a minimum of ornate furniture. The fireplace surround, it was true, was anything but plain, with its stucco embellishments of twisted columns, chubby cherubs, and a profusion of floral designs, but there was a spaciousness to the room which absorbed these details into something very elegant. When Elspeth entered the room she found Greywell seated opposite an absurdly dressed woman in her fifties with sharp brown eyes and a sagging face. The name Waltham had rung some bell with her when Selsey announced her, but it was only now that she remembered Greywell had said this woman knew of her.

Elspeth came forward with a welcoming smile, but the old woman frowned at her, saying curtly, "That's not Elizabeth."

"Elspeth," Greywell corrected.

"Elspeth, Elizabeth, it doesn't matter," Abigail insisted. "This is not the woman I know. For God's sake, Greywell, you've gone and married the wrong woman!"

Her two companions stared at her until Greywell hastily recollected himself and said gallantly, "This is certainly the woman I intended to marry, Abigail. She's the woman Uncle Hampden wrote me about. If there was some confusion, I fear it must have been on your part."

"I am *never* confused. We were discussing Elizabeth Parker quite clearly. I've known the woman all her life, and this is not she!"

"Very true," Elspeth admitted, accepting the chair Greywell held for her. "You must be Mrs. Waltham. I've very pleased to meet you. Greywell has told me you're a close neighbor of ours."

The woman snorted her indignation. "And where do *you* come from?"

"Near Aylesbury. My father's home is called Lyndhurst."

"Never heard of it. Who's your father?"

"Sir Edward Parkstone."

"Never heard of him either."

Elspeth looked to Greywell for a little encouragement, but he remained withdrawn, a brooding look on his face. To Mrs. Waltham she said, "Perhaps one day you'll meet him. I'm expecting him to visit at Christmastime."

"That's neither here nor there," Abigail muttered. "If you were the right Elizabeth, I'd already know your home and your father."

"Yes, well, I'm sure it's a great disappointment to you. I've come to see if I can't induce a little more strength in Lord Greywell's son, you know. That's the important thing, isn't it?"

Abigail regarded her with the sharp brown eyes. "What makes you think you can do that?"

"I have a certain amount of experience with the children in my neighborhood. It has been rather a project of mine to see that they have enlightened care."

"Enlightened," Abigail scoffed. "The old methods are always the best methods."

"I'm afraid I can't completely agree with you there." Elspeth looked to Greywell once again for some support, but he did no more than give her a perfunctory smile. What the devil had gotten into him? Elspeth hoped he didn't intend to act this enigmatically whenever a guest arrived to meet her. "Some of the old wives' tales," she told Abigail, "are injurious to infants. The bad has been passed along with the good."

"And you think you can tell the difference?" Abigail demanded.

Elspeth refused to be intimidated by her companion's outrageous behavior. "I hope so. I've been instructed by an excellent doctor and midwife, back at Lyndhurst. Of course, everything depends on God's will," she added virtuously.

"*Now* you remind me of Elizabeth," Abigail chortled. "That was the one thing I was going to warn you about, Greywell, but I decided better of it. Elizabeth is a very devout woman."

Greywell smiled sweetly on the two ladies. "That is a coincidence. Imagine there being two such virtuous women in England, and my being recommended to both of them. I can't think how that came to happen when I'm such an unworthy fellow myself."

The light mockery in his voice made Elspeth bristle. "I don't know that I would consider anyone who collected snuffboxes by the dozen 'unworthy,' but it does denote a certain frivolity which I was surprised to learn of in you, Greywell. There are several of them which I consider unacceptable left lying about. Andrew is, of course, too young to be affected as yet, but there is the morality of the maids and footmen to be considered."

At first Greywell thought she was teasing him, but, as that did not appear to be a part of her nature, he reluctantly came to the conclusion she was perfectly serious. Abigail's bright eyes had swung from Elspeth to Greywell, eager for his reply, sheer delight emanating from her at the possibility of being witness to their first (she presumed) married quarrel. After all, they'd only been married a day.

"I'm sure the servants' morality can withstand the sight of a few artistic snuffboxes," he replied, seemingly indifferent. Greywell had no intention of arguing with his new wife in front of *anyone*.

"Just the same," Elspeth replied, "when you are gone I shall put away the indecent ones until you return, and then I hope you will keep those somewhere where no innocent eye could fall on them."

He would have liked to nip this sort of prudery in the bud, but Abigail was waiting for just such a scene, and he refused to give it to her. Fortunately, Selsey appeared to announce another visitor just as a footman brought in the tea tray. In the ensuing commotion the subject was dropped. But not forgotten—by either of them.

The vicar, Mr. Clevedon, was followed by several other neighbors, including Emily Marden, the young matron Greywell had suggested might guide Elspeth in acquiring a suitable wardrobe. She was accompanied by her husband, and was enormously *enceinte*, which didn't give Elspeth a proper opportunity to decide whether or not she agreed with Mrs. Marden's style of dress. The procession continued throughout the morning, concluding with Sir Markham Treyford, his wife, Julia, and their twenty-six-year-old son, Francis. Elspeth was amused by the highly unlikely combination of a florid country squire, a tight-faced, gaunt woman, and a willowy, dreamy young man, but when she attempted to convey her good humor to Greywell with an arch look, he pretended not to see it. For that piece of effrontery, she flirted a little with the son. Not that Elspeth would have called it a flirtation, but Greywell, watching her earnest attention to the young man, certainly did. Lord, was there no end to his new wife's ability to put him out of countenance?

When their visitors had at last departed, and before another onslaught for the afternoon could begin, Elspeth bundled herself in the blue cape and hurried up to her chamber. Andrew was awake, but once again tightly wrapped in a blanket in his cradle, with Bates rocking cozily in a chair beside him.

"I'm going to take him outside for just five minutes," Elspeth explained, bundling him in yet another blanket. "He needs an opportunity to fill his lungs with some rich country air."

"But it's freezing out of doors," Bates protested.

"No, it's warmed since this morning. He'll be perfectly comfortable, I promise you. I'd like to see a little color in his cheeks."

Bates muttered something about frozen lungs, congestion, and runny noses, but not so loud that her comments need be considered as an address to her new mistress. She sat with her hands folded firmly in her lap, as though to prove she had nothing to do with the dangerous expedition Lady Greywell proposed. Elspeth never stopped talking to the child, which was another thing Bates objected to. The new mistress had some very strange notions, if one of them was that a child of less than four months could understand a solitary word she spoke. The poor lamb, in Bates' opinion, was not going to enjoy the cold air one bit, either, as her ladyship assured him he would. The purpose of having a nice warm fire in each of the rooms at this time of year was that it was *cold* if one didn't.

Outside the air was crisp and snow crunched under Elspeth's boots. Almost as much for her sake as for the child's, she welcomed the opportunity to be away from Greywell and his house and his household staff. Talk about tradition! Everything in the place was rife with it, and here he'd told her that wouldn't be the least problem. All their patterns were established, their rituals and superstitions firmly in place. Bates, Mrs. Green, Selsey, all of them. Elspeth knew they didn't want someone else taking Caroline's place, and she didn't blame them, but she missed the kind of affectionate respect in which she'd been held at Lyndhurst. There the servants had mostly known her since she was a child; they knew she would be demanding but fair, that they could come to her with their problems, that she was concerned with their illnesses. Here she doubted anyone would ever give her a chance to be more than a stranger.

Elspeth heard a carriage on the drive, denoting yet more visitors. Her five minutes were up; she must take the baby directly back to the nursery and freshen herself up for more company. Somehow things weren't working out exactly as she'd expected. She braced her shoulders and marched back into the house to meet yet another of Greywell's curious neighbors.

Chapter Eight

"Andrew does seem improved since you came," Greywell admitted one evening when he was sitting with Elspeth in the Saloon. They had spent an hour there together each evening since their arrival six days before. Aside from their meals together, and the times when people called, it was the only time they had spent together. Neither of them regretted the shortness of this exposure.

"Yes, I think he is. He's eating better and not spitting up as much. His color is much healthier and he's been more active, according to Bates. She'd like to resent me, but she's devoted to the child and she can see the improvement, too." Elspeth tried to suppress a yawn. Her days had been full and exhausting—taking care of the child, acquainting herself with Ashfield, greeting visitors, going over routines with the housekeeper and several other members of the staff. Tonight she really should spend more time with Greywell, since he was leaving for Vienna in the morning, but her nights were always disrupted by Andrew's cries and murmurs; she was bone-weary. "Was there anything you especially wanted me to know before you leave?"

"I think we've gone over everything at one time or another." Greywell was aware that most of their conversation had consisted of his passing along information (which Elspeth considered strictures) and her long-suffering acceptance of his instructions. Surely there was no more martyred expression than the one she wore when he merely pointed out some way in which she could better adjust to the routine of this household. There was the instance of the dairy maids, a totally unnecessary interference. It had been the practice at Ashfield for literally centuries for the dairy maids to milk the cows, but Elspeth had insisted they had quite enough to do with emptying and cleaning the milkpails and, of course, supplying the milk, cream, and butter to the household. She had insisted the cowkeeper could quite as easily take over this share of the burden, since he was, after all, in charge of the cows and had to be there anyhow. Elspeth had said, "What in the name of heaven is the use of his standing there and watching those poor girls work their fingers to the bone? At Lyndhurst we did it differently, and there was a fair division of labor." Greywell hadn't wished to hear how they did things at Lyndhurst. All she was managing to do was cause disruption among his staff.

Elspeth was a little surprised now to find he'd exhausted himself on subjects regarding the sanctity of Ashfield procedures. She'd begun to think there was no end to the things he intended to make sure she adhered to. "Well, in that case," she said, stifling another yawn, "I think I'll go to bed now. Of course I'll join you for breakfast in the morning and see you off."

It would have been easiest just to let her go, but Greywell was suddenly determined to make one last effort to instill a little caution and respect in her for his home and his inheritance. "Before you do," he said, lifting one elegant hand in a gesture of restraint, "I want to thank you for your efforts on behalf of Andrew. If you will just concentrate on his development, everything else will flow along smoothly as it always has. There's no need for you to concern yourself with making changes at Ashfield. I'm sure Andrew will absorb a great deal of your time. To add any further burden to that fatiguing one would be excessive. You will need some time to your own devices, and I hope you will take it. Let Mrs. Green handle household matters and enjoy yourself as you can."

"Oh, I shall enjoy myself. Don't fret about *me*." Elspeth's tone held just a hint of mockery. "If I find myself with time on my hands, after I've read the latest book or ridden my mare, I shall see what I can do for the vicar. And of course I will wish to go shopping for a new wardrobe. Mrs. Marden said there are two quite acceptable shops in Coventry. How long do you expect to be gone?"

"It's impossible to say. Rest assured it won't be any longer than necessary. If an emergency should arise, send a private messenger. I very much doubt negotiations will be completed by Christmas, so I hope your father will visit as he promised." Greywell watched as she covered her third yawn. "Off to bed with you, my dear. You're always up early with Andrew. We'll say our goodbyes in the morning."

Because he had eaten particularly well the previous evening, Andrew slept until seven-thirty in the morning. This would have been ideal, except that Elspeth knew Greywell intended to leave fairly early and she had expected to join him in the Breakfast Parlor a little after seven. She leaped out of bed and tossed on a dressing gown just as a light knock came at the door. Thinking this would be Bates, worried at the baby's lateness, she called, "Come in," as she stooped to pick up the child. Her braid of hair had fallen forward over one shoulder and loose wisps of hair curled about her ears and forehead.

"It's all right, Bates," she said as she cuddled the child against her shoulder. "He's only just now woken." And she turned to find Greywell standing immobile in the doorway, staring at her. "Oh. I didn't know it was you. I'm afraid I've overslept."

"So I see. I didn't mean to disturb you. May I hold him?"

Elspeth handed the wide-eyed Andrew to his father. The baby, who had been fussing, immediately stilled in Greywell's arms, blinking curiously up at the face so far above him. Greywell's expression was hard for Elspeth to decipher: it was tender and yet sad, hopeful and yet touched with despair. How awful to feel such conflicting emotions when you looked on your child, she thought, feeling a wave of reluctant affection for Greywell. Really, he only wanted to do what was right for his son.

"I'll take good care of him," she promised. "By the time you return, he'll be strong and healthy."

He believed her. Somehow he had no trouble believing Elspeth would accomplish just about anything to which she set her hand. Greywell told himself he should be grateful to her for his being able to leave everything in her capable hands. And he *was* grateful, as far as Andrew went. As for the rest of it . . . Well, there was no more he could say now. She would do as she wished when he was gone, of that he was as certain as he was of his own name. The startling and traitorous thought that she looked adorable with her sleepy eyes and the clinging tendrils of hair he pushed firmly from his mind.

"You'll want to take Andrew up to Bates," he said. "They're bringing my carriage around, so I'll say farewell to you both now. I'll write to you, and I hope you'll send me word of Andrew's progress. And of your own, of course," he added, belatedly.

"I shall. Don't worry if you haven't time to write often. I understand how busy you'll be." Elspeth accepted the baby back from his arms and smiled up at him. "I hope your mission will be wonderfully successful, Greywell. Godspeed."

"Take care of yourself." He bent to kiss her forehead. "I'll be back as soon as possible."

When he turned and walked out the door, Elspeth felt the slightest bit of regret, for which she could not account. After all, she knew him only slightly better than anyone else at Ashfield. Well, she decided with a sigh, it's all for the best he'll be away. When he's here, we're at odds, and by the time he returns I'll be so entrenched there will be nothing for it but for him to get accustomed to me. She had every intention, too, of getting accustomed to him, when the time came. Accustomed to his various moods, that is.

As Andrew's health progressed, Elspeth took more interest in the world outside Ashfield. She was a little disappointed to find that the parish was a prosperous one, where the vicar required little assistance in the way of making clothing for the poor or ministering to the sick. The only project she could think of to put in motion was one to teach some of the illiterate how to read and write, and she had a difficult time drumming up enthusiasm for it among the people she'd met.

Emily Marden, for instance, thought it unnecessary. "Why would they want to learn to read, my dear Lady Greywell?" she asked as she and Elspeth headed into Coventry one day on a shopping expedition. "If they had wanted to learn, they would have learned as children. We have a perfectly wonderful dame school here, you know. Your husband's grandfather helped to establish it eons ago, and each of the Greywells since then has taken a personal interest in it. Very few of the children leave school without knowing how to read and write."

"But there must be adults who don't know," Elspeth insisted. "Surely any number of them come from other parts of the country, where they didn't have the opportunity as children."

"You don't know much about the area yet," Emily said with a tinkling laugh. "There never was such a place for people staying put. Of course, there are a few people who've come from outside, but if they're smart enough to settle in the village, they probably already know how to read!"

"Well, perhaps I'll just ask around."

Emily patted her hand. "Yes, do. There may be people I don't know of, though the question once came up at Crawley and it turned out every one of the servants knew at least the basics. That would be most unusual in some parts of the country, wouldn't it?"

"It certainly wasn't the case at Lyndhurst." Before I undertook my little project, Elspeth could have added, but didn't.

To Greywell she wrote:

Andrew is thriving these days. His new crib is ready (you will recall I thought the old one too dark and gloomy), so we have set it up in the original nursery next to Bates' room. I've had new curtains made, light, airy ones, but have saved the old mauve hangings in the attic as you requested I do with the furniture. Andrew seems to like the crib and bats at the little cloth animals which dangle from a band across the top. You aren't to worry that he can get them in his mouth! We've given him safer things to chew on. Bates is delighted with his progress, as I am.

Emily Marden and I went shopping in Coventry the other day and I've ordered five new dresses. One of them is jaconet muslin over a peach-colored sarsnet which she insisted upon, though the weather is far too chilly for it now. She has the most incredible taste in headdresses! You will be surprised to hear she talked me into a leghorn hat with a large brim and a crown ornamented with four rouleaux of peach-colored satin twined with white cord. It makes me feel exceedingly frivolous!

The question of the dairymaids has been settled. The cowkeeper will milk half the cows.

I am interested in undertaking a project of teaching illiter-

ate adults in the neighborhood how to read and write. Mrs. Marden says there aren't any. I find that difficult to believe! I shall look into it further.

By all accounts things progress slowly in Vienna. I hope you are not discouraged.

Your obedient servant, Elspeth

When Greywell received this missive, he was tempted to write her that he would prefer she not call herself his "obedient servant" if she had no intention of following any of his instructions, but he forebore. With so many of the British delegation to the Congress seemingly more intent on attending parties than to the matter in hand, he found himself overworked as one of the few who were determined to find a long-range solution to the division of Europe.

So he wrote back:

Your report on Andrew's progress is encouraging. I should like to see him right now in his new crib batting at the cloth animals. Thank you again for your care of him.

The Regent should have come himself instead of sending Castlereagh. He would have appreciated the balls and petits soupers, *the operas and the promenades a great deal more than Castlereagh does. Besides, most of the Allied sovereigns are here, and it is something of a slight that he should disdain appearing. Nonetheless, I have hopes that progress will be made sometime soon; my fear is that it will be the wrong sort of progress. I press for something which will be less disastrous and not bring so much misery.*

I was pleased to hear you had gone shopping with Mrs. Marden. She has exquisite taste from all I've witnessed. She is probably also right that there are few illiterate adults around the village.

Is your father still planning to come for Christmas? Some will come home for the holiday but there is too much work for me to get away. I hope you will understand.

Yours, etc. Greywell

Much to Elspeth's surprise, her father did come for Christmas. He arrived the week before, laden with all the paraphernalia for hunting. The staff in the stables were delighted by his interest, and by the two fine hunters he brought with him. Emily Marden's husband, John, willingly provided an introduction for him to the local meet, and agreed to accompany him to Leicester once for a meeting with the Quorn under the famous Assheton-Smith. On the day they were gone, only two days before Christmas, Emily Marden came to Ashfield for a visit.

"I don't begrudge him his hunting," she began, nervously folding her hands over the the huge mound of her stomach, "but the baby is due any day now, and I should so dislike his being away when my pains begin."

It was Emily's first child, and Elspeth wondered if Caroline's death in childbirth was weighing on her mind. "You can send for me the moment you feel the slightest discomfort," she assured her guest, "should it come at a time Mr. Marden is from home. Or even if you'd just like the company. I've sat with several women, you know. Are you frightened of the pain?"

"A little. My mother said it's all worth it in the end, and that you start to forget it after a while." She gazed fondly down at where Andrew lay gurgling and kicking his legs on a blanket spread on the floor. "I suppose most of all I'm simply impatient. I want it over with and a baby of my own to show for it."

"It's a great pity there's so much pain associated with having a baby," Elspeth mused. "And the men get off with so little of it."

Emily laughed. "So far as I can tell, they don't get any of it at all."

"Not at the birth, certainly. I meant at the conception."

Her companion regarded her curiously. "Why should they feel any pain at the conception? They don't even know it's happened, and it's not their bodies it happens to."

Confused, Elspeth tried to explain. "Well, I meant when men and women were . . . intimate. That pain."

"Pain?" Emily's brow wrinkled in a frown, and then cleared. "Oh, you mean the first time for a woman. But that's such a brief thing, hardly even noticeable. And it doesn't cause the man any pain, surely. I rather think they like proving how *masculine* they are." And she blushed with the temerity of speaking so frankly.

Elspeth wished she would speak a little *more* frankly. What was it Mrs. Marden was actually saying? That there was no pain in that ludicrous configuration human mating consisted of? Impossible! She herself had heard the groans and cries of pain. It had nagged at her, of course, that if there was really so much pain, why did people indulge in it so freely? Her father, for instance, had never shown any other evidence of wantonly causing himself pain. If anything, he was a consummate hedonist. On the other hand, he would thoroughly enjoy proving his masculinity, even at the cost of a little (or a lot?) of pain.

"Do you . . ." Elspeth began, and thought better of it. "My mother died when I was only fifteen," she tried again.

"I'm so sorry," Emily murmured, wondering at the abrupt change of subject.

"Yes, well, she didn't . . . I wasn't . . . Greywell agreed . . ." There was no way she could put it without sounding hopelessly naive. She, a married woman. What would Mrs. Marden think of her? Already she was regarding Elspeth with a slightly puzzled lift of her brows. Elspeth decided it was easier to give up on the subject. With a forced cheerfulness she said, "It's not every woman who can have a child to raise the day she's married, is it? Andrew is such a dear."

Emily wondered if Lady Greywell's mind had wandered a little during this conversation, since she hadn't been able to keep track of its direction, and she was usually very good at that. With her husband she needed to be. "Yes, you're very fortunate. And I do admire the way you've taken hold here. Andrew's health has so vastly improved, and you are so very fond of him. Poor Caroline! But she would be pleased to know her son has someone like you to care for him."

"I'm not at all like her, am I?"

"Like Caroline? Good gracious, no!" Afraid this might sound rude, Emily hastened to say, "She was a very small, ethereal-looking woman. She had the most beautiful long blond hair with wide green eyes and the merriest dimples. Everything was a lark for her. I don't think she took anything seriously, which was what made her so much fun to be with. I swear she could wrap any man around her little finger. Greywell was besotted." Emily clapped a hand over her mouth and lowered her eyes. "I'm sorry! My tongue runs away with me sometimes."

"There's nothing to be sorry about," Elspeth assured her, but feeling the tiniest bit disturbed. "We have an understanding, my husband and I. He needed someone to care for his son and manage things for him here, and I . . . well, I wanted to get away from Lyndhurst. It was the best offer I was likely to receive."

"I cannot believe that!" Emily declared, loyal already to this strange woman. "Not that Greywell isn't a splendid match, but there must have been all sorts of men who took an interest in a woman of your merits."

"Men aren't particularly interested in merits."

Emily considered this for a moment, and sighed. "You may be right. Most of them are interested in the beauties that everyone else acknowledges. My cousin is going to London in the spring for her first season. Lord, she'd rank as a diamond of the first water, if my aunt could afford to outfit her properly. She's very like Caroline in looks, actually, but with a meager wardrobe I'll bet she won't have half the attention Caroline got. Not that she hasn't any other merits! She's quite a charming girl."

"Would she be willing to accept Caroline's clothes?" Elspeth asked abruptly. "They're just sitting in the closets in her room, of no use to absolutely anyone. I don't think Greywell would mind, you know. I doubt if he's given any thought to disposing of them, but they really should be used before they're entirely out of fashion. Yes, that's exactly what should be done with them, they should be given to your cousin so she will have a proper introduction to London."

"Oh, I don't think you should—"

"Nonsense. Greywell has left me in charge of Ashfield. It would only be hurtful to him to come back and face all her clothes again. I shan't do anything with her little knickknacks, of course, except perhaps box them away for her son one day, or for Greywell himself if he's sentimental. Certainly there will be things of hers he'll wish to keep. That would be understandable, but not her clothes, my dear ma'am. Her clothes should find some good use."

Emily would not deny her cousin the opportunity to have the elaborate and extensive wardrobe of which she knew Caroline to have been possessed. With some misgivings, she agreed.

In her next letter to Greywell, Elspeth wrote, in part:

I have sent Caroline's clothes to Emily Marden's cousin, who makes her come-out in London in the spring, and whose family is not able to afford a proper wardrobe. I was sure you wouldn't mind, as this way they will have some benefits, which I'm sure Caroline would have wished. The rest of her belongings I have had boxed and put in the attics for you to go through when you are of a disposition to do so.

This letter Greywell tore into shreds after his first reading, thus denying himself the chance to reread the passages which concerned Andrew's continued growth and improvement. He did not deign to comment on the matter of his dead wife's clothing in a subsequent letter; in fact, he considered never writing to Elspeth again.

Sir Edward did not depart from Ashfield when the Christmas season passed. The prolonging of his visit gave Elspeth some concern, since she didn't want to suddenly find herself with a batch of illegitimate children in her new neighborhood. That would have been absolutely too much to bear!

"Wonderful fox-hunting here," he told her daily. And he did indeed go out almost every day with the hunt. Elspeth was aware that no women rode with the local group, which was encouraging in its way. But there were the evenings.

After dinner he would announce, "Well, I'm for Coventry," and, though Coventry was indeed close enough for him to easily reach for an evening's entertainment, Elspeth had noticed, from an upstairs window, that he did not ride his horse in the direction of the town, but toward the village in exactly the opposite direction.

There was the excitement of Emily Marden's confinement of a daughter to distract her. And the almost daily visits of the queer Abigail Waltham. For a while, after Greywell's departure, the old woman had stayed away from her, as though miffed she hadn't turned out to be the right woman. But recently she had begun coming for these strange visits, where she appeared in the house without arriving at the front door, and tracked Elspeth down wherever she might be in Ashfield, whether in the nursery or her own chamber or the Queen's Closet or one of the drawing rooms.

Abigail was perhaps the most bizarre person Elspeth had ever met. And it wasn't just the odd way she dressed; in fact, that seemed to have improved somewhat lately. What was so absurd was that the moment she entered a room she would be talking, just as though they were in the middle of a conversation. Yet all the while Elspeth sensed something sly about her, something withheld from these discussions that apparently went on in her head, with or without Elspeth's compliance.

"Yes, I know just what you mean," she was saying one day as she entered. "There are entirely too many people who take foxes for granted. Whereas we all know sometimes a concerted effort must be made to keep enough of them alive for there to be sufficient sport each winter. I for one will put up with the destruction they cause, for the sake of a little sport, but there are those who would exterminate them like rats."

The old woman had found her in the nursery this time, hanging another of the little cloth animals she'd just finished making. Andrew was cooing and wriggling his little body about excitedly. Elspeth never knew exactly what to say to Mrs. Waltham at times like these, so she murmured something unintelligible, tagging on a "Good day, ma'am."

"It's going to snow again," Abigail replied. "If there's not a hard freeze it won't keep them from the hunt, fortunately. My husband rode with them until two days before he died."

"Some gentlemen are certainly avid about their hunting."

"I wouldn't have it any other way. Wonderful sport, hunting. Much less violent than this pugilistic stuff, and a great deal more enterprising than the cockfights."

"Mrs. Waltham, would you like to hold the baby?" she asked, hoping to distract her visitor's attention from such gruesome subjects.

"Hold him?" Abigail peered nearsightedly at the chortling Andrew. "Why, yes, I'd like that very much. It's been years since I've held a baby." She was very careful as she took him in her arms, and she smiled down at him, but a tear crept down her cheek. "We never had children, Burt and I. Not for want of trying. Sometimes I thought it was how much fun we had trying made it so we didn't have them. But that was a lot of puritanical nonsense. There's no harm in enjoying yourself. I don't believe we were put here to walk around in sackcloth and ashes. That makes no sense at all. There are problems enough without making them for yourself."

"You don't think there are certain . . . sacrifices expected of us?"

"Bah! People who go around making sacrifices are martyrs,

and not of the least use to anyone else. It's not what you give up but what you give that's important. And it's not the people who go around proclaiming their piety who are the ones we should admire, but the ones who quietly live their lives in accordance with their principles. Charity begins at home." She eyed Elspeth fiercely. "There are some who'd try to push their charity on folks who don't want it or need it. That's the worst kind."

Elspeth could feel the flush rise to her cheeks. She was sure someone had told Mrs. Waltham about her plans to teach reading to the illiterate adults in the neighborhood. "Some projects are designed to help the needy help themselves."

"When the 'needy' want help, they'll ask for it. If you try to push things down their throats, they'll just resent you."

This was a thing Elspeth had never mastered, the ability to know when something was being asked for and when she was thrusting it on someone. She had certainly encountered the phenomenon of being resented for her efforts often enough. "It's just that one doesn't want there to be suffering," she said lamely.

Abigail wiggled a finger at her sagely. "A body's dignity is just as important as his belly being full. Don't forget that."

"No, of course not," Elspeth replied, though she really hadn't given it much thought.

The baby was quiet in Abigail's arms, staring at her wizened face. She studied him for a long while before proclaiming, "He's going to look like Greywell. That's all to the good, you know. If he looked like Caroline, he would only be a reminder of her loss. And this way he might even be taken for your own child, since your coloring isn't so different from Greywell's, and you have that sharp chin, too."

"I don't want him to be taken for my child," Elspeth protested. "He should grow up knowing who his mother was. That's his birthright."

"Yes, yes. Of course he should know who his mother was." Abigail impatiently handed Andrew back to Elspeth. "But you won't have to be always explaining to *other* people that he isn't your child because they'll assume he is."

There seemed no point in arguing with her. Elspeth settled the baby back in his crib before turning to her guest. "Would you like a cup of tea?"

"Greywell has a splendid brandy."

It was only one o'clock, but Elspeth refrained from mentioning the early hour. Mrs. Waltham was an eccentric, and one treated her as such. If she wanted brandy at one o'clock in the afternoon, Elspeth would not deny her. Visions of this neighbor sitting home all day drinking endless glasses of brandy rose in Elspeth's mind, but she sternly forced herself to make no well-intentioned remark on the dangers of imbibing. They seated themselves in the North Drawing Room, Elspeth with her fragile cup of tea, Abigail with her hefty dollop of brandy, and contemplated each other.

"Your father's quite the sporting fellow, isn't he?" Abigail asked, that strange sly look in her eyes again.

"He's especially fond of hunting."

"Aye, and more than the fox."

The tea slopped onto Elspeth's saucer. "What . . . what do you mean by that?"

"A vigorous man he is, for his age. He told me you used to raise quite a fuss about his pursuit of the ladies . . . back in Buckinghamshire."

"When did he tell you that?"

"The other day," Abigail said, most unsatisfactorily. "You have to expect a man of his energy to still be interested in the ladies."

"Not when he leaves a string of children behind him."

"Well, he's a bit careless, I dare say, but some men are just like that. They lose their will to keep to the straight path when they lose their wives. He was never a rake when your mama was alive."

Elspeth set down her teacup; her hands were shaking too badly to hold it steady. "Did he tell you that, too?"

"Certainly. We have no secrets between us."

The conversation had taken so disorienting a turn that Elspeth felt too confused to question, and too alarmed to comment on it. When had Sir Edward and Mrs. Waltham become so intimate? Even the word "intimate" made her shiver.

Abigail took a large sip of the dwindling brandy. "There are women who have the same sort of vigor as Sir Edward," she said, meditative now, her eyes closed. "Women who've known the pleasures of the body."

Oh, my God, Elspeth thought.

"Some women think of that sort of thing as their duty, and

others think of it as their pleasure. It's a great pity when a woman can't appreciate her own body, or a man's. She misses the delights she was meant to have. It's as much a sin to deny yourself that pleasure as to commit any other sin of omission. I'm very impatient with women who make a burden of what should be a joy."

"How can it be a joy when it's so painful?" Elspeth blurted.

"Painful? Nonsense!" She narrowed her eyes at her companion. "An itch is only painful if you don't have the relief of scratching it. Hmm, it *is* an exquisite sort of agony, like eating some spicy dish that burns your mouth but tastes so delicious you wouldn't forgo the delight of having it. Or the satisfaction afterward. And the closeness it brings with a man! There's nothing to compare with that. All your life you could go along trying to persuade yourself you can manage inside your own head, with the use of your own body, but why should you when you can have the comfort of sharing your joys and sorrows with someone else? It's more than just a physical act—if you want it to be more."

"But it's so . . . undignified."

Abigail gave a croak of laughter. "No, my dear, it's beautiful. Two human beings as God created them, taking a little warmth and comfort from one another, leaving each other with a few minutes of joy to ease them over the rougher times, the lonely times. What's so frightening about a naked body? Even my old body isn't so 'undignified' as you may think. There are those who can still appreciate it," she added a little huffily.

Elspeth wrote to Greywell: *I have the most horrid suspicion my father is "spending time" with Mrs. Waltham.* To which he wrote back: *At least Abigail's too old to bear children.*

Chapter Nine

Eventually Sir Edward left, but not until the middle of February. At parting he enjoined his daughter to have a care for Mrs. Waltham. "She's a dear woman," he said as he climbed into his traveling carriage. "Odd, of course, but I for one like her that way. It's the eccentric ones who add a little spice to life. Nothing is as engrossing as unpredictability. You remember that, Elspeth. A predictable woman is deadly boring, unless you happen to be devoted to her, of course. Your mama had a streak of unpredictability about her, you know. Now I don't see that in you so much. Except the queen cake. Yes, that was definitely unpredictable."

He laughed and patted her cheek. "You may have hidden fires in you, my girl. Give them a chance to burn. You're forever taking a snuffer to everything. Not that you haven't done a splendid job here at Ashfield. I'm proud of you; Greywell will be proud of you."

His praise pleased Elspeth, and she tried to remember it (and not the other things he'd said) as she went about her duties as chatelaine of Ashfield. Andrew continued to thrive. He was beginning to crawl about whenever placed on the floor, and the staff made renewed efforts to keep everything immaculately clean. Things were, in fact, going along so well that Elspeth took more time for herself those days. She restrained a natural tendency to interfere in parish charitable works, and instead donned her new slate-blue riding habit with the gold braiding she and Emily Marden had chosen for her in the fall. Having spent so much time indoors, she now felt a certain relief in riding her mare about Ashfield and the surrounding countryside as the weather worked its gradual way toward spring.

It was on one of these daily rides that she met Francis Treyford again. He had come with his parents that first day she was at Ashfield, but she hadn't seen him since, though she'd met Sir Markham and Lady Treyford any number of times in the interim. Elspeth recognized the willowy figure slightly before he was quite close enough to discern his features. The windblown blond locks scattered wildly above perfectly arched, thin eyebrows, wide blue eyes, and a long, thin nose. He had narrow bowed lips and the creamy complexion of a woman. Since he wore no hat, he was unable to doff it as he pulled in his horse, but he made a sweeping gesture all the same.

"Lady Greywell! How charming to meet you!" He offered the dreamy smile she remembered. "I've been away or I would have called on you. How are things at Ashfield?"

"Splendid. Andrew grows healthier each day, and the household seems to run smoothly without much effort."

"I suppose Greywell is still in Vienna."

"Yes, the deliberations go on interminably. His letters indicate a certain frustration, but he's made no mention of returning here." This was Elspeth's standard reply. For no particular reason she added, "I don't mind, except that Andrew has probably already forgotten what he looks like. Poor Andrew never sees another male at Ashfield."

"A sorry plight for the little fellow," Francis said. "I tell you what, I shall visit him. Can't leave him surrounded by females all day. How old is he now?"

"More than seven months. He's begun to crawl."

Francis looked surprised. "Has he now? I didn't think they started to move so young. But then, I haven't any experience of children, you see."

"Well, he doesn't get too far before he collapses, but he's a wiry boy, and I wouldn't be surprised if he could get anywhere he wants within the month." Elspeth pushed back a strand of hair that had come loose from her bonnet. "Would you like to ride back with me now and see him?"

Francis, whose offer to visit the child was made as spuriously as most things he did, was slightly disconcerted. "Well, I was . . . That is, I had intended to ride into Coventry." Then he shrugged and smiled at her. "I can do that anytime. Certainly I will come back to Ashfield with you, as long as you promise me some tea and a bite to eat. I haven't had a thing since breakfast."

There was no way for Elspeth to know he'd only eaten this meal at ten, his usual hour, and she hastened to assure him of a plentiful tea. "Where have you been?" she asked as they directed their horses back to the stables.

"London, mostly. Though I did spend a week with a friend in Hertfordshire. He's a poet, too."

Elspeth regarded him with interest. "You're a poet?"

"Perhaps I shouldn't presume to call myself one," he said modestly, "but, yes, I do scribble a bit."

"How wonderful! May I see something you've written one day?"

Francis was not the least inhibited about showing his work. "I have something I've been working on in my pocket, as it happens. At tea I'll read it to you."

He was not a success with Andrew. Not knowing precisely how to treat the child, his behavior fell somewhere between what it would have been in greeting a dog and conversing with the village idiot. Elspeth hastened him off to the drawing room, where he pulled out a few sheets of crumpled paper as she gave instructions for tea. When she returned her attention to him, she found him deeply engrossed in rereading his own poem, the dreamy light in his eyes again. He was quite a nice-looking man, she decided. Softer somehow than Greywell, with his light coloring and his smooth skin. And she especially liked this habit of his of going off into reveries. They made him seem more spiritually attuned than the majority of the people she met.

And his poem was ambitious in that direction, with its intent to discuss the human soul, its deepest workings and its loftiest relations. Francis told her that before he began reading, which was a wise decision on his part, since she was soon lost in the metaphysical ramblings of blank verse. But he did have the facility of cloaking his thoughts in images of the countryside, the passage of the seasons, and the simple beauty of everyday things. He read it, too, with an amateur player's musical resonance, and when he stopped and looked up at her, his face was suffused with unaffected pleasure.

"That was very moving," Elspeth said, hoping it was the right thing to say. "I have to admit I didn't understand all of it. One is used to listening more for a story in a poem, and yours, at least to my mind, is more subtle than that."

"Ah, subtle. How clever of you to understand that, Lady Greywell." He bestowed a beatific smile on her, as he folded the sheets and replaced them in his pocket. "Though the groundwork is philosophical, I hope the purity of the natural images will induce people to consider it for its language as well. This is but a fragment of a far larger work, you understand. That's why you didn't perfectly comprehend it. You would have to read the whole to fully grasp the importance of this particular segment. Occasionally I dabble in lighter verse, of course. I'm particularly fond of the sonnet. Perhaps you'd care to hear one of those another day?"

"Oh, yes. That would be most enjoyable," Elspeth assured him. She felt sure she'd be capable of understanding a sonnet.

Two footmen brought in the tea tray and a tray laden with cakes, bread and butter, and biscuits, as well as fruit from the succession houses and some slices of cold meat and cheese. Elspeth had been quite specific in asking for a variety of foods for her visitor, fearing she had kept him from a more lavish meal at some inn in Coventry.

"Please help yourself to whatever you want," she said as she poured him a cup of tea. She was a bit disappointed when he took only one slice of meat and a piece of bread and butter.

"Thank you." He ate daintily, his long, elegant fingers hovering nonchalantly over the fine China plate. "I don't hold with any one school of poetry, you know. As far as I'm concerned, there are merits and disadvantages to all of them. I pick and choose," he said, helping himself to a slice of cheese and a peach. "And I study those poets I most admire."

"Who are they?"

"Shakespeare, Milton, Dryden." Francis gave an explanation of his reasons for choosing each of them as a model of accomplishment while he took two biscuits and a slice of cake. He had not finished talking before he finished the food on his plate. Elspeth was astonished at how much he managed to eat while seeming only to discuss so rarefied a subject as poetry and poets.

Before he had completed his discussion he had once more filled and emptied his plate of another biscuit and another slice of cake.

At last he drained his cup of tea and rose. "I mustn't stay a moment longer. You know, Lady Greywell, you are undoubtedly the most attentive companion I have yet come across. Don't let me bore you with my theories on poetry! There are a dozen subjects on which I can converse creditably, I promise you. Horses and hounds, opera and the theater, even women's fashions. Next time I shan't be such a single-minded fellow, if you will give me leave to visit you again."

"But of course. Anytime."

In a gesture of extreme gallantry, he carried her hand to his lips. "Greywell is a lucky devil to have found you," he murmured. "I shall write a poem—a sonnet of course—on the subject."

Elspeth laughed. "I doubt you could find fourteen lines to write on the matter, Mr. Treyford, but you are welcome to try."

His visit had cheered Elspeth, and she sat down almost immediately to write a letter to Greywell in which she lightly made fun of Treyford's enormous appetite for cook's Savoy cake and for his own philosophical poetry. She even jested about Treyford's awkward behavior with Andrew, but added to be just:

> *Still, he is an engaging young man and probably a friend of yours, so you mustn't think I shall avoid him in future. He says he's going to write a sonnet about how lucky you were to have found me! If it is quite ludicrous enough to appeal to you, I'll send it along. Did I mention that I've put a number of your snuffboxes in your study in a closed case? Only the "Lady Godiva" type, the gold enameled one with the diamond thumbpiece, and the Sacrifice to Venus, as well as the Marcault and the repoussé gold plaque one, though I've stuck a few others to the back of the open case where they're not so obvious, like the Triumphs of Alexander one. I understand the last is after a painting of Charles Le Brun, but the staff aren't likely to know that, are they? The gold-mounted tortoiseshell with the gouache miniature I didn't think safe enough even in your study, so I've put it in one of the drawers in your chamber under a stack of cravats. It seems to me Venus is a very convenient excuse for drawing naked ladies!*

The tone of her letter rather pleased Greywell, despite her continued insistence on sounding like a prude. She had, after all, *mentioned* "naked ladies," when she really hadn't had to. And her good-humored mocking of Francis Treyford had made him laugh when he read it. Francis was six years younger than Greywell, but they had spent time together as boys, being close neighbors. Greywell had long held a similar view of his friend to that which Elspeth expressed, a gentle, affectionate, yet rueful acceptance of Francis' languid preoccupation. It did not for a moment occur to him that Francis posed any sort of threat to the tranquillity of his household. So he wrote back:

I'm glad you'll have Francis to divert you from your daily routine, since you've mentioned Emily Marden is preoccupied with her child. Your letter reminded me that, tall and thin as he is, he's always had the most incredible appetite. He isn't that interested in physical activity, so I must suppose his brain burns up an inordinate amount of excess nourishment with his constant devising of obscure verse. He's a harmless puppy, though, and good company when he wishes to be.

This letter reached Elspeth some time after the news that Napoleon had escaped from Elba, early in March, and after she had begun to wonder if Francis was, after all, a "harmless puppy." And now that there seemed a chance that Greywell would return to Ashfield, with the Congress so rudely interrupted, she felt entirely confused about what her wishes were on the subject. For Andrew's sake, of course, she wished that his father would come home. But as for herself . . .

After his initial visit, Francis had become a regular caller. As often as not he appeared when there was a chance of a meal, but this did not long remain his primary purpose in coming. He was, Elspeth presumed, fed at his own home, though he soon assured her he was not able to eat a bite unless he was in her company. Elspeth did not believe him for a minute, considering this a part of his poetic fancy, which she knew was inhabited by the most amazing hyperbole.

And yet . . . it was flattering, his obvious attachment to her. And it was difficult not to return his regard in some very tiny way. He was a fine-looking fellow, with his whimsical eyes and his shaggy blond locks. His mind, too, was so elevated, so intent on the finer things of life, the spiritual benefits of philosophical poetry. Who could resist such an appeal? Not Elspeth. Not entirely.

"Listen to this," he would say, lounging on the sofa in the North Drawing Room with a leather-bound edition of Shakespeare's sonnets in his hands.

"Some glory in their birth, some in their skill,
Some in their wealth, some in their body's force;
Some in their garments, though new-fangled ill;
Some in their hawks and hounds, some in their horse;
And every humor hath his adjunct pleasure,
Wherein it finds a joy above the rest;
But these particulars are not my measure,
All these I better in one general best.
Thy love is better than high birth to me,
Richer than wealth, prouder than garments' cost,
Of more delight than hawks and horses be;
And, having thee, of all men's pride I boast.
Wretched in this alone, that thou mayst take
All this away, and me most wretched make."

Then he would cry, in the wretched, appealing agony of his deep-timbred voice, "But I don't have you! This is my challenge, my burden to bear. Ah, Elspeth, you will make my poetry purer from the very struggle you cause."

"What nonsense!" she would lightly retort. "You've dreamed me out of whole cloth, Francis. Made me up to be your guiding light. How ridiculous you are." But she did not think him at all ridiculous, really. There is something few can resist in being made the object of such passionate infatuation. And Elspeth, with her disapproving husband, found a certain comfort in Francis' devotion. It was so aesthetic.

"Will he come home now?" Francis asked every day. "Why don't you hear from him?"

"He's not in the habit of writing very often. I imagine I'll hear soon enough."

Too soon, was what she feared. Sometimes she thought he might actually be on his way home, thinking it would take him little longer to journey there than for a letter to reach her. Perhaps assuming she would be expecting him, since the Congress had had to be abandoned and a new attempt made to conquer the little Frenchman. Elspeth was torn between wanting him to see Andrew and Andrew to see him and wanting him far away so her interludes with Francis could continue uninterrupted. She took to hanging around the Great Hall about the time the post was brought from the receiving office, so she would know as soon as possible what to expect. When the awaited letter finally arrived she snatched it unceremoniously from the silver salver on which Selsey had deposited it and hurried off to the Queen's Closet to peruse it in peace.

I've come with Wellington to Brussels, he wrote.

Elspeth barely read the rest of the letter, she was so relieved. She refused to consider what this signified in herself. All she acknowledged was that Andrew would have to wait a little longer to see his father . . . and she would have more time with Francis.

Francis proclaimed himself to be ecstatic. Right in the North Drawing Room he sat down at a desk to pen an Ode to Fortune, while Elspeth sat on the sofa a few feet away from him, patiently crocheting a lace collar, a slight smile curving her lips. Odes were not precisely Francis' forte, he explained when he sat down to read it to her, but he had felt so inspired he was convinced she would excuse him.

Was ever fate so sweet a mistress
As now she is to me?
Wrapped in the glorious light of love
What better place to be?

The soul is touched with celestial harmony
The heart with a golden glow,
An enraptured man hath not the words,
One fair lady could bestow.

Fortune touched me with her wand
Delaying the day most feared
Will now the lady defy such a sign
As the angels themselves have cheered?

Spare me now the gloom of the clouded day
Of the torrents of rain and despair.
Thou alone hast the power in a single hand
To make the day sunny and fair.

"It needs work," he conceded at her slight frown. "Anything you dash off is bound to be improved with a little future consideration, but the thought is there."

Since it was one of the few of his poems she'd understood, Elspeth did not disagree with him on that point. It was the thought itself which disturbed her. Not so much his continued declaration of his own love for her (which she regarded as sheer exaggeration), but there had been something in there about her love for him. Surely she didn't love him. She was fond of him, to be sure, but that hardly constituted love. Elspeth would have thought herself remiss if she allowed Francis (as she now called him) to think she loved him.

"I'm a married woman," she reminded him now. "You really shouldn't be writing poems about loving me or . . . or my loving you. You know I'm fond of you, Francis, but that's not at all the same sort of thing as loving you."

"Then who *do* you love?" he demanded, the dreamy light gone from his eyes. "Not Greywell. You hardly know him, for God's sake!"

"Well, I don't love anyone, I suppose. I don't know you very well either, do I?"

"Better than you know Greywell," he insisted. "You and I have a great deal more in common than you and he."

Elspeth was feeling a little alarmed. "That really doesn't matter, you know. I'm *married* to Greywell. That isn't something that can be changed. And I wouldn't want it to be changed," she added rather hastily.

Francis smiled angelically. "No, of course not. There is something so much more satisfying about a love that isn't of the body, Elspeth. It's of a rarer, more purified nature, isn't it? One feels the torment of the soul cleansing one's spirit."

Obviously he didn't understand at all, but Elspeth hardly felt up to arguing with him about the subject of bodies and souls. "I really should go up to Andrew now," she said, rising. "He'll just be waking from his nap."

When he had reluctantly left, with a sweet smile of complicity, Elspeth wandered to the nursery in something of a daze. Was she falling in love with him? It was true she looked forward to his visits with something a great deal stronger than an anticipated visit from Emily Marden would have inspired, but that didn't mean she loved him. That meant she was a little lonely, and his company was more amusing than Emily Marden's. Not that she didn't like Emily Marden! Elspeth was exceedingly fond of her, and really should go to visit her again very soon. She would have done it before now, if she hadn't been afraid of missing one of Francis' unannounced visits.

That very evening she sat down and wrote to Greywell, at the new Brussels direction.

It's a great shame there will be more fighting now, and that you have had to go to Brussels. You would love to see how Andrew is getting about these days and how much he has grown. I quite understand the necessity of your going, though, and hope matters will proceed as we would all wish. Tomorrow I shall visit Emily Marden to see how she gets along with the baby. One day soon I will even take Andrew along with me on these jaunts, as it would give him some new experiences. Spring is a little late in coming, but I get outside with him as often as possible.

She tried, without success, to think of something she could say about Francis (Mr. Treyford in a letter to Greywell, of course) that would not sound compromising. She could hardly say he came almost daily to read his poetry to her, or that his poetry was *about* her. It didn't even sound good, when she thought about it, to mention that he called so often.

There was something about this letter that bothered Greywell, but he was too busy at the time he received it to consider what it was. The chaos which followed the news of Napoleon's escape was a matter he had taken in hand, since there were many who seemed not to know how to handle the surprising event. His influence at the Congress had not been what he had hoped, and he felt his abilities might now be better employed in sorting out the hopeless muddle . . . before he went home. There were reasons to go home—Andrew, Ashfield, even Elspeth—but he couldn't force himself to do it. Certain that his talents were still needed, perhaps needed more than ever now, he stayed on in Brussels, sending home only a brief note to Elspeth saying: *Your father has written what a fine job you're doing there. Forgive my delayed return, but it is necessary. Do give my love to Andrew and amuse yourself with Emily Marden. Spring will doubtless make everything more cheerful and allow more activity, but not, I hope, of an interfering kind on your part.* (He had remembered the snuffboxes at this point, and the dairymaids.) *I shall be home as soon as feasible.*

His cavalier attitude irritated Elspeth. Certainly there was every reason for him to stay in Brussels if he wished, but he needn't have mentioned her interfering, and he needn't have sent his love only to Andrew. At the time, she could have done with some expression of affection from him, even if he didn't really mean it.

How sadly I've degenerated, she thought as she set the letter aside on her escritoire in the Queen's Closet. I would never have considered wanting his affection when I married him, only his respect for what I could accomplish. Now I want him to offer me something he couldn't possibly feel, just because Francis is so wretchedly prompt in offering me his agonizing declarations of devotion.

By the time Elspeth received this letter at the beginning of May, Francis' poetry had subtly changed. His struggles with his soul on the subject of his love for another man's wife, already a major part of his new verse, had recently taken a new turn. He had taken to impassioned descriptions of Elspeth herself, in which his euphemisms got more and more absurd, as they got more and more intimate. Her "twin orbs," she realized after a second reading, did not refer to her eyes at all but to her breasts. At first she had wondered why he called them delicious, rather than enchanting. On realizing her mistake, she had blushed furiously and said, "You mustn't write such a thing."

"There is no way on earth I could prevent myself," he declared, fervent. "It would be a disgrace to my talent to shun the very natural beauty of your body, my dear Elspeth."

Knowing she should put a stop to this dangerous game, she yet could not quite manage to deny him the right to visit her, and read her his increasingly erotic poetry. The reason she was unable to do so was that it moved her, in a very unascetic way. For instance, she got quite an unusual physical reaction from his reading about Cupid's cave and Cupid's torch. It made her feel quite warm all over, and rather breathless. A delicious shiver ran through her, and when he was finished reading, she couldn't look at him, but walked over to the vase of flowers on the table in the corner and rearranged them with nervous fingers.

"Would you like to go for a ride?" she asked. "Andrew will sleep for some time now, and I could use a breath of fresh air."

Elspeth had learned that he preferred sitting indoors reading his poetry, but he gallantly accepted the invitation. He was a natural horseman, with an easy elegance in the saddle that pleased her. His languidness didn't vanish, but he appeared more masculine when he was on a horse. And she wanted him to appear more masculine just now, when her body tingled with unaccustomed sensations.

Their horses seemed to feel the tantalizing breath of spring in the air, frisking down the path away from the stables. Buds on the trees were finally beginning to open, and the grass was a fresh, vibrant green. Elspeth had noticed how many birds there were around Ashfield, and she asked Francis now if he could identify any of their cries.

"A few of them—the rook and the magpie. You really can't miss either of them, though, can you?" His gaze went to the trees along their path where some hidden bird was spilling out his glorious song. "I tell you what—let's dismount and see if we can see him."

He helped her from her sidesaddle, allowing his hands to linger at her sides when she was safely on the ground. His eyes, kept steadily on her face, were soulful and pleading. Elspeth felt a definite tug of desire, a most decided wish to have those fascinating lips on hers. She did not give him permission; nor did she turn her head aside when he lowered his head to hers. The pressure of his soft flesh on hers was a unique experience. She had never before been kissed that way. There was something altogether thrilling about the way his mouth meshed with hers, about the way his lips moved over hers, gently rubbing, pressing, drawing on something deep inside her. Elspeth shivered with the sheer excitement of it.

"You're scaring the birds away," a voice said from nearby.

Startled, Elspeth hastily pushed Francis from her and looked about with large, panic-stricken eyes. There was nothing to be seen. The voice had sounded suspiciously like Abigail Waltham's, but there was no one around them. They were in a stand of trees, with the horses grazing on new tufts of grass, but there was no other living creature within her view. In fact, the birds had taken flight; she had heard the rustling of their movement as Francis kissed her, but paid no attention to it. Now their song was gone and she and Francis stood frozen, waiting for Mrs. Waltham to manifest herself.

She took her time in doing it. When one is fifty-two years old, one doesn't climb down from a tree with any great degree of speed. It wasn't a large tree from which she descended, and it had branches growing fairly close to the ground, but Elspeth watched her come into view with astonishment. Francis let out a peal of delighted laughter.

"You frightened off a whitethroat," Abigail said when she had her feet firmly on the springy earth. Her shawl was snagged and the rest of her clothes terribly disheveled, but she cocked her head to one side, very much as a bird might, and studied the pair before her. "Did you come to see the birds?"

"Oh, yes," Elspeth said quickly. "Francis . . . that is, Mr. Treyford wasn't sure what kind it was but I liked the gushing, jerky little song it made. We used to have a blackcap at Lyndhurst, but its song was different."

"They don't sound at all alike," Abigail sniffed. "I'm afraid you don't know much about birds, my dear Lady Greywell."

Was it Elspeth's imagination, or did she stress the "Lady Greywell"? "I'm afraid I don't," she admitted, hanging her head.

"How did you get up in that tree?" Francis asked, still smiling.

"How do you suppose I got up in it?" Abigail demanded. "I climbed it, of course. I climb it every spring to get a close look at the birds, and when people don't come along to frighten them off, I can spend hours observing them at close range. Now I'll have to wait till another day to see them."

"I'm terribly sorry," Elspeth murmured.

Abigail eyed her thoughtfully. "You should be."

"Yes, well, we didn't know you were there."

"Obviously," Abigail snorted and turned her back on them to trudge toward her house, leaving them to stare guiltily at one another.

Francis didn't look as guilty as he should have, Elspeth thought as she muttered something about getting back to Ashfield.

"There's no hurry, now she's gone," he said.

"I want to go back now."

Francis shrugged. "She's not a gossip, Elspeth."

"It doesn't matter." But it did matter, a great deal. Elspeth could not have borne the idea of Mrs. Waltham telling anyone what she'd seen. Fortunately, she was sure Francis was right: Abigail wouldn't mention it to a soul, not even Greywell. She allowed Francis to help her into her saddle, holding herself stiff and awkward until he had mounted his own horse. They rode back to the stables without speaking.

Chapter Ten

Elspeth spent a great deal of time that day thinking about Francis. And even more time thinking about herself. She had always assumed she was above temptation, simply because she'd never before been tempted, she realized now. It was surprising, and upsetting, to learn that she was as beset with human frailty as anyone else she could think of. Elspeth knew she shouldn't allow Francis to visit her any longer. Actually, she reluctantly admitted, she should have forbidden his visits some time ago, when he first declared his love for her, or at least when his poetry became so provocative.

Realizing her mistake did not necessarily mean she was capable of adjusting it in future. Something in her attempted to justify her conduct. Elspeth wasn't particularly pleased with that whiny voice that assured her she deserved a little pleasure from life. It said: see how hard you've worked to take care of Andrew and to run Ashfield to the best of your ability. It said: Greywell doesn't care for you, and he'll never care for you, because he's still in love with his dead wife. It said: what you do is your business and if it doesn't hurt anyone else, no one has the right to complain about it. Worst of all, it said: everyone knows your purity is too great to be ruined by a little dalliance.

Elspeth knew she should fight this voice determined to undermine her high standards. On the other hand, she was beginning to understand that she was infatuated. There had been any number of young women near Lyndhurst who had suffered from the same affliction, and Elspeth had been able to recognize it in them without the least difficulty.

In herself, she could call it whatever she chose, but it amounted to the same thing. The only problem was that she hadn't realized then what she did now—it was a very strong emotion. Especially after Francis had kissed her, she wanted to experience that kiss again, and she wanted him to hold her. In her mind she didn't really go further than that, thinking of him holding her, pressing her against his chest . . .

When she tucked Andrew in for the night, she was abstracted, and afterward she couldn't remember whether she had gone through her usual ritual of telling him his father loved him, and that she loved him. But when she went back to look in, he was fast asleep, holding one of the toys his mother had made. Elspeth sighed and wandered off to her room, too distracted to find a book to read, and certainly in no mood to write a letter to Greywell.

At one moment she would believe she had the strength not to see Francis again. At another she knew she wouldn't. At times she even blamed Greywell for what was happening: if he hadn't been away so long, she wouldn't have had the opportunity to form this attachment to Francis. Sometimes she merely blamed fate, though that seemed an unfair thing to do, when Francis was writing odes to fate for the good fortune of their having the time to be together. Really, it was a terrible muddle, and she went to bed with a pounding headache.

Nothing was changed in the morning. Elspeth awaited Francis' arrival with a certain trepidation that had not formerly bothered her. The tightness in her chest was almost outweighed by the fluttery feeling in her stomach, but not quite. All morning he didn't come . . . and then all afternoon he didn't come. Elspeth tried to occupy herself with Andrew, but she found herself constantly moving to the window that overlooked the drive.

Andrew was cranky. Bates told her he was teething and not to expect any immediate improvement in his behavior. For the first time, however, Elspeth could feel the impatience rising in her, and, rather than snap at the poor child, she left him to the care of the nursery staff. Unable to settle down to a book or to any handwork, Elspeth roamed about the house, finding herself critical of the way the fireplaces had been cleaned or the furniture dusted. She almost mentioned these things to the housekeeper but decided she was being particularly picky today and that tomorrow she would doubtless find nothing amiss with any of the rooms.

It was too late by the time she thought of it to call on Emily Marden, so she went to the pianoforte and played for the hour remaining before dinner. Almost every night for the last few months she'd sat at that table in lonely splendor, but tonight she particularly felt it—the loneliness and the splendor. Greywell wasn't even in her thoughts. It was Francis she thought about. Where was he? Why hadn't he come to see her today? Had he been upset by Abigail Waltham's spying on them? He certainly hadn't seemed so at the time. Perhaps he had mentioned something he had to do today, and she'd simply forgotten in her confusion.

Mostly Elspeth asked herself one question: What am I going to do? She was unable to answer the question, but it did occur to her that she wouldn't have to answer it if Francis never showed up again. As though to spite her, after not presenting himself all day, Francis arrived just as she was leaving the dining room to go to the drawing room.

He wore a driving coat with several shoulder capes, and he looked very dashing as he handed his hat, coat, and gloves to Selsey. "Ah, Lady Greywell," he said, for Selsey's benefit, "I hoped I wouldn't interrupt your dinner. I spent the day with a friend north of Coventry and thought I would call on you on my return."

"Have you not eaten, then?" she asked.

"Oh, yes. My friend keeps abominably early hours."

"Come and sit with me in the drawing room. Selsey, please bring in some brandy for Mr. Treyford."

When Francis had disposed his willowy form on the sofa beside her, and Selsey had left the tray discreetly close to his elbow and retired, Elspeth said, "I had thought you weren't coming to visit today."

"Didn't I tell you I was going to visit George?"

"I don't think so. It doesn't matter."

"But of course it matters! You must have wondered where I was!" His face distorted with concern, and he very naturally grasped one of her hands to press it with abject apology. That did not seem sufficient, however, and he leaned over to brush his lips against hers.

Elspeth had meant to tell him not to do that again. Instead, she found herself clinging to him, in a misguided effort to keep her overwrought emotions at bay. He kissed her forehead and her eyes and her trembling chin, all the while saying, "My adorable Elspeth, my lovely, sweet lady," in a kind of chant that mesmerized her. She knew that her hands had gone around his waist, that her lips were responding to his when they came again to play on her mouth.

She had neither the desire nor the will to withdraw from his embrace. Even when his hands slid down along her sides and came to rest tentatively beside her breasts, she made no demur. How could she put a halt to an experience that was bringing the most delicious sensations to her body? All the while he continued to kiss her with an urgency she was beginning to share.

But when his hand moved to cover her breast over the sarsnet gown, she blinked her eyes open in alarm. A shock of longing had run through her. Elspeth gently pushed Francis' hand away from her breast and sat up. "Please, Francis. You mustn't. *I* mustn't." She swallowed before adding, "It's my fault. I shouldn't have let you kiss me. Did you bring a poem with you? Would you read to me?"

His tormented-soul look replaced a brief frown. "No, it's entirely my fault, Elspeth. I know you're a married woman. How I've struggled to resist your charms! My God, it's almost beyond my strength. I've written about it. Here, let me read you this." From his pocket he withdrew a crumpled sheet and proceeded to read it with an abundance of agony in his voice. In the strongest possible terms he expressed the torture being with her daily caused him, and his inability to stay away from her. The poem's conclusion, that he would plumb the depths of his soul for the strength to bear his burden, seemed slightly out of context after what they had just been indulging in.

What bothered Elspeth was something else altogether. She wet her lips and asked, "You didn't read that to your friend George, did you?"

"Well, yes," he admitted, "but I didn't tell him whom it referred to. You needn't worry about that. Besides, he doesn't know you or Greywell. George is rather a hermit."

"I wish you won't read your poetry about me to anyone

else," she said. "In fact, it would be better if you didn't write about me at all, Francis. You might leave something lying around that anyone could read."

He was fervent in his denial. "Never! My poetry about you is locked in a chest each night, and during the day I carry it with me. Even my valet couldn't catch a glimpse of it."

"Still . . ."

"Don't deny me the only chance I have to reconcile my deepest desires with my obvious duty," he begged.

It didn't seem to Elspeth that his poetry did anything of the sort, but she made a nervous gesture with her hand indicating she wouldn't insist. "But I do think you should go now, Francis. I'm a little overwrought and can't seem to think clearly."

He smiled sweetly as he rose. "Of course, my love. Don't fret yourself with what happened. I'll be stronger next time. Just working on the poetry will help me restore my thoughts of you to a higher plain. Trust me."

Elspeth not only didn't trust him, she didn't trust herself. When he had left she went directly to bed, though it was still early. Only after she had pulled the blankets over her did she remember she hadn't gone to say goodnight to Andrew. Bone-weary with the emotional turmoil of the day, she nevertheless rose again and put on a dressing gown before trudging up to the nursery. Andrew was already fast asleep, and Bates regarded her with what Elspeth could only assume was infinite disapproval. She said a wary goodnight to the wet nurse and returned to her chamber, determined to do better the next day with regard to her charge.

For several weeks both Francis and Elspeth behaved in an almost seemly fashion. Of course, Francis agonized in his poetry over what a struggle it was, and Elspeth spent many sleepless hours at night congratulating herself on the restraint with which they both acted. But she was aware, as Francis must have been, that there was an undercurrent of severe physical tension between them. To offset this, Elspeth spent extra time with Andrew, she visited Emily Marden more often, she worked at renovations in her bedchamber and the Queen's Closet. Occasionally, when she was sure no one was around, she snuck a peek at some of Greywell's more enticing snuffboxes. Unfortunately, there were mostly naked women on them, and she would have been more interested in seeing some naked men.

Abigail Waltham appeared at Ashfield less often, though she did sometimes come to visit. "Your father wrote that he's thinking of coming to stay with you again," she said one day in June.

Elspeth had heard nothing of the plan, and wasn't at all sure she liked it. With her father in the house, she couldn't very well see Francis as often. It would have aroused his suspicions, though she assured herself there was nothing of which he need be suspicious. She and Francis were behaving themselves remarkably well. It did occur to her that Mrs. Waltham might have written to him to suggest such a step. "Had you been corresponding with him regularly?" she asked, not meeting Abigail's eyes.

"Of course. Ever since he left here," Abigail was put out that Elspeth would think her connection with Sir Edward was so unimportant as to have terminated the moment he was out of sight. "Doesn't he write you?"

"Not very often," Elspeth admitted. "I haven't heard from him in over a month."

"Does Greywell write you?"

"Of course. I heard from him this morning."

"What did he have to say?"

"Only that a battle was brewing. Apparently Bonaparte has gathered a considerable army about him. Greywell says there's a reckless gaiety in Brussels; everyone knows how important this battle will be, and that it won't be an easy one for Wellington and our allies to win."

"So he intends to stay there until he sees the outcome?"

"I presume so. Certainly he made no mention of coming home."

Abigail regarded her closely. "Do you care?"

"It would be nice for Andrew to see his father."

"For yourself, I mean. Do *you* want to see him?"

Elspeth felt herself stiffen. "He's my husband. I would be pleased to have him home."

Her companion snorted. "He's worth two of that Treyford fellow, my dear girl, though I doubt you realize it. The sooner he returns, the better."

Elspeth did not disagree with her, nor did she mention that Greywell had written that Wellington had accepted Greywell's offer to act as an aide to the general. That was a piece of information she did not intend to tell anyone, mostly because she didn't know how she felt about it. There would be plenty of time to consider it in private, and no reason to alarm anyone in the household.

For it *was* alarming news. Greywell had been a soldier much earlier in the Peninsular War, but he had sold out after an injury temporarily disabled him. It was while he had been in London recuperating that he had met his first wife, and there had been no thought of his returning to battle after that. To Elspeth his desire to immerse himself in the deadly duel now indicated that he hadn't considered his son, but was still in a kind of desperate mourning for Caroline.

When Abigail left, unsatisfied with Elspeth's response but unable to get her to say more, Elspeth went straight to the Queen's Closet to pen a letter to her husband. Perhaps it was a tinge of her own guilt that made the letter sound rather sharp to him when he read it.

My dear Greywell, I am not at all pleased to hear you have agreed to act as one of Wellington's aides. Have you forgotten your responsibilities to your son? The poor child has already lost his mother; how is he to manage if he should lose his father as well? Of course I would raise him to the best of my ability, but your recklessness appals me. Pray reconsider taking such a drastic step. You say there is an immensely important battle in the offing and that Wellington needs all the help he can get. Is it your pride which dictates this step, or some other part of your character? In either case, I consider it highly ill advised.

Greywell received the letter as he was dressing to attend the Duchess of Richmond's ball on the 15th of June, when rumor had it that battle would ensue before the night was out. He had, for several months, refused to attend the entertainments which might have distracted him from his grief and from his work, but he had learned in time that more business took place at these social gatherings than in all the negotiation chambers he had yet entered.

So it was nothing new for him to attend a ball, though the thought still rankled with him. He had not found it necessary to mention them in his letters home, fearing Elspeth would hardly understand the necessity. What he didn't need was some ascerbic comment from her on his social life. And now this! How did she dare to advise him of where his duty lay? She knew nothing whatever of the matter. And perhaps, somewhere in him, he knew she had a grain of truth on her side. If he was killed, poor Andrew would be an orphan—but at least he would be there to carry on the Greywell title.

As he stood patiently waiting for his valet to achieve perfection in his cravat for the distinguished occasion ahead of him, Greywell mentally composed an answer to his wife's letter, something that would give her a proper setdown, but he hadn't time to actually put pen to paper before he had to leave.

The news of the Battle of Waterloo reached Elspeth when she was sitting in the garden with Andrew. Francis was the one to bring it to her, and he knew little beyond the fact that there was a tremendous death toll for the English, though they had eventually proved victorious, with their allies.

Elspeth hadn't told him of Greywell's involvement. "Oh, my God," she said, scooping up the child to hold him protectively in her arms. "When did you hear? Was Greywell in the battle? Is he all right?"

Francis frowned at her. "Why would he have been in the battle? He's one of the diplomats."

The child was regarding her with large eyes, uncomprehending of all her words, but aware from her tenseness that something was amiss. She ran a hand gently through his soft hair, trying to calm herself before she spoke. "He wrote me that he'd become one of Wellington's aides," she admitted, not lifting her eyes to Francis. "I wrote back trying to dissuade him. But I haven't heard from him since. Have you seen a list of casualties?"

"No. I was told about it, and several names were mentioned. Not Greywell's. Which doesn't really mean anything. For God's sake, Elspeth, why didn't you tell me?"

There was a hum of bees in the hollyhocks nearby and the smell of newmown grass. Elspeth had a terrible premonition she would always remember this day, with Francis standing there looking down at her as though he'd somehow been betrayed by her not confiding in him. "I didn't tell anyone. The news would have caused too much anxiety, without there being the chance of anyone doing a thing to change matters." She stood up with Andrew still in her arms. "I'm going to take the child in now. Find out what you can for me, will you, Francis?"

"Certainly." He hesitated for a moment before asking, "May I come this evening? You'll want someone to keep you company."

"Thank you, yes. That's very kind of you."

"Do you still want me not to tell anyone?"

"It would serve no purpose to mention it now. The battle is apparently over. Either Greywell is safe, or he isn't. I'll just have to wait for word."

She gathered her full skirts with one hand and settled the baby against her shoulder. Francis stood watching as she walked toward the house. A variety of emotions passed over his face, but she didn't see any of them. Even at the side door she didn't look back, and he slowly retraced his footsteps to the stables.

Francis was aware of the tenuous nature of the relationship between Elspeth and himself. He liked the ideal of an impossible love between them, but he was also very strongly physically attracted to her. So he wisely chose to arrive that evening after she had put Andrew to bed and was free for the remainder of the evening. Guessing correctly that this latest news would render her even more susceptible to his advances, he nevertheless moved very slowly. It was not that he guessed Elspeth was a virgin. The thought had never occurred to him. She was, after all, married to Greywell, and Francis, not one for paying overmuch attention to the proprieties, would not have considered the possibility of there being no consummation because of the recent death of Greywell's first wife.

It was a warm summer evening, with a light breeze blowing through the North Drawing Room from one of the doors to the terrace which had been left open. Elspeth had taken a seat on a chair, rather than the sofa, which had been her practice for the last few weeks. This prevented the proximity with Francis which had led to that one reckless evening, and she continued to feel it was a necessary condition of their meeting. On this occasion Francis didn't take a seat at all, after the brandy had been brought, but wandered over to the French doors and stood looking out into the fading evening light.

"Would you like to sit on the terrace and watch the sunset?" he asked. "It's a little stuffy inside."

There seemed no reason not to join him on the terrace. True, there was only the stone bench for them to share, but it was still light outside. The rich aroma of summer flowers lingered with the heat of the day, and Elspeth stood for a moment at the railing looking over a neatly tended bed of antirrhinum, sweet peas, calceolaria, and linaria. Farther along there were larkspur and petunias, nasturtium and foxglove, their colors only dimly visible in the fading light. She hadn't cut any flowers for the drawing room that day, being too preoccupied with other matters.

"I often come here in the evening," she said, looking out now over the rolling lawn to a stand of trees on the north. "It makes me feel more a part of Ashfield. At Lyndhurst I roamed about more, taking strolls in the evening to use up some of my excess energy, but Selsey looked totally distraught the one time he found me returning from a short walk. Perhaps he thought I might have fallen and hurt myself, or been abducted by some brigand. I don't know, but I stopped doing it so I wouldn't worry him."

Francis smiled at her. "I'm sure he'd consider you perfectly safe with me. Why don't we walk as far as the trees?"

Dew hadn't really settled on the grass yet, and Elspeth's light rose-colored slippers were perfectly adequate for crossing the lawn. Francis took her hand, in an ostensible effort to prevent her from falling, should there be anything so dangerous as a hole in the ground. As they strolled along, he quoted poetry, not his own, on the beauty of the night. There was something soothing about black velvet skies and ivory moonlight. Elspeth allowed herself to relax under the influence of his melodious voice and the magic of the night. Actually, there was only a bit of a moon, and it cast very little light after the last of the sun's rays had disappeared from the sky.

When they reached the trees, Francis gazed down at her for a long moment. "I remember a path through the trees to a clearing."

"Yes," she agreed, "there's a path, but it will be a little dark to see."

"We'll manage."

Elspeth knew then that she should refuse. The intensity of his eyes was a sure sign of some other intent than a mere stroll through the gray-barked beech trees. The ground underfoot was covered with the silky husks from the budding leaves, a soft cushion on which to lie down if one chose. But Elspeth didn't refuse to follow him. With her hand still in his, he led the way through the small forest to the dimly lit clearing. Almost no light penetrated the thick foliage, but her eyes rapidly adjusted to the darkness.

Without a word, Francis removed his coat and spread it on the soft beech husks, motioning for her to join him. Elspeth gingerly lowered herself to a sitting position, spreading the skirts of her dress down over her ankles. Francis was momentarily touched by this modesty and seated himself slightly apart from her.

"This is a very upsetting time for you," he suggested tentatively. "You must be worried about Greywell. I'm sorry I couldn't find out any more for you. Perhaps tomorrow will bring some news." He reached out to stroke her hair in a comforting gesture, as she might have done with Andrew. But his hands lingered at the nape of her neck, caressing the silken skin there. "You've had a great deal of responsibility over the last few months, Elspeth. You deserve a chance to relax and forget all your worries."

Elspeth stared at her hands clasped tightly in her lap. Her mouth felt dry and her throat had begun to ache with suppressed emotion. She wasn't sure whether she wanted to cry, but his sympathy was almost unbearable somehow. Just for the moment she wanted to lay all her cares in his lap, to escape from the constant confusion of her thoughts. Why should she have to worry about whether what she wanted was right or wrong? Hadn't she earned a few minutes of release? She turned her face to him expectantly.

He did not immediately kiss her. Instead he put his arms around her and hugged her to him, rocking her gently, like a child. "My poor, sweet love. What a lot you've had to bear. I wish I could be the one to make it all right for you." He kissed the top of her head while he stroked her back with long, gliding movements of his fingers. At first she could feel his fingertips only through her thin dress, but soon they were above the material on the bare skin of her back. She shivered.

"Are you cold?" he asked, concerned.

"No. Not at all."

"It's a warm night," he murmured, at last bringing his lips down to meet hers. He could feel her lips tremble under his, but it was with an eagerness that instantly aroused him. Still, he cautioned himself to proceed slowly. She could be startled as easily as a wild animal by any abrupt demands.

It was then he conceived of lovemaking as poetry. He hadn't actually looked at it quite that way before, and he considered Elspeth the inspiration for this new vision of what he'd always thought of as a basic physical necessity. Not that in the ordinary course of things Francis was particularly highly sexed. If he could find a willing woman once every few months, that was quite sufficient for him. But Elspeth was different; he had known it all along. She was a woman among women, an inspirer of poetical fancy, a guideline to the resources of the soul. He was so incredibly moved that he actually composed verses to her body as he began to explore it with his sensitive hands. Nor did he keep these verses to himself. Francis, in the throes of both love and poetry (as well as lust), shared with her each new metaphor (or euphemism) that came into his befuddled brain.

Elspeth was equally intoxicated. As his hands strayed to her waist and then slowly upward, she could feel her body tensing with a wild mixture of painful delight. Her mind accepted his murmur of orbs of snow and ivory hills without really attending. His touch on her breasts even through the light gown sent an incredible feeling of excitement through her.

Was this what it was, then, that had made her father's Fanny cry out as she had? Why, it wasn't pain at all, but an urgency so great she could scarcely contain the crazy desire to moan. But the memory of her father with Fanny brought with it a warning bell in her head. What she was doing wasn't right, and though at the time that didn't particularly seem to matter, Elspeth fought for some sanity. She was lying on his blue superfine coat, and she forced herself to concentrate on the button that dug into her back.

Firmly she pushed him from her, eyes wide and misty. "Francis, I'm sorry. I can't. I shouldn't." Elspeth drew herself, shakily, to a sitting position.

Francis silently ground his teeth and struggled to his knees. "No, yes, well, I suppose you're right. Here, let me help you up." He stood over her for a moment before offering his hand. Francis had seen the desire in her eyes, and he wasn't quite ready to believe he'd been defeated. But when he had her on her feet and attempted to kiss her again, she turned her face away.

"Please, Francis, no." She straightened out her skirts with a meticulous care that annoyed Francis, but hardly managed to calm her. When they arrived back at the house, she bid him goodnight.

Chapter Eleven

A messenger arrived at Ashfield the next afternoon. Elspeth had not yet decided what to do about Francis; that is, whether or not she would see him again. She very definitely wanted to, but she knew what would eventually happen if she did. So she was sitting in the Summer Parlor at the back of the house, trying to justify her desire, when Selsey appeared at the door to announce in a rather quavering voice that the messenger had been instructed to deliver his message directly to her. Elspeth paled but allowed no other sign of her alarm to show.

"Please show him in here."

"He's come all the way from Brussels, milady."

"I suspected as much. We'll give him refreshment as soon as I've spoken to him, Selsey." When the old man turned to leave, she added softly, "I'll let you know as soon as possible, Selsey."

"Thank you, milady."

The messenger was hardly more than a boy. He entered the room with a nervous look behind him, as though he feared being trapped in the elegant, unfamiliar surroundings. Elspeth swallowed hard before rising to face him with a smile meant to put him at his ease. "I'm Lady Greywell. You have a message for me."

"Yes, milady." He reached into a worn leather pouch slung

over his shoulder. What he withdrew was a single sheet of paper, with a plain blob of sealing wax.

If the message had been from Greywell himself, he would have used his seal to close it. Elspeth received the sheet of paper with trembling fingers. The handwriting was not familiar to her. She was too agitated to search out a letter opener, but carefully broke the seal so as not to tear the paper and lose any portion of the message it contained. Her eyes blurred momentarily before coming to focus on the short message:

Lord Greywell has been injured at Waterloo, but not seriously. His right arm is incapacitated and he has asked me to write saying we will return to Ashfield as soon as possible. He sends his regards to you and his son.

It was signed by Greywell's valet.

Elspeth felt the tears stinging at her eyes, but she smiled at the messenger. "Thank you. We're all very grateful for your speed. Selsey will show you to the kitchen, where you can get a good meal." She dug in her reticule for a suitable gratuity for the lad. "If you can take the time to rest here, the staff will show you to a room."

Selsey was waiting near the door and entered almost immediately when she rang. "Please take this young man to the kitchen. He's brought us the news that Lord Greywell was injured at the battle of Waterloo, but not seriously. Greywell and his valet will be returning to Ashfield as soon as possible, so we should set things in motion for his return. Perhaps you would send Mrs. Green to me."

"Very good, milady," Selsey said, his shoulders once again squared. "That's good news indeed."

Left alone, Elspeth found her hands still shaking slightly, and she dropped onto a straight-backed chair with a sigh of relief. Andrew still had a father—and she still had a husband. There had been a moment, when she saw the unfamiliar handwriting, that she had been sure he was dead. Why would someone else be writing at such a time? Somehow she couldn't bear the thought of his being dead, not only because of Andrew, but because of herself. It wasn't that she had any affection for him, really; it was that her guilt would have been horrendous if he had died while she was carrying on a flirtation or worse, with Francis

Treyford. The message had finally shocked her into the enormity of her actions. She, who had always led the most blameless of lives, had allowed temptation to distract her from her obvious duty, from the most elementary of obligations. When she married Greywell she had made a promise, and to not honor that promise was a grievous fault indeed. Elspeth was sunk in a morass of self-abasement when Mrs. Green entered the room.

Together they arranged what needed to be done before Greywell returned. Elspeth tried to disregard the housekeeper's close scrutiny during this interview. If Mrs. Green was interested in how this news affected Greywell's wife, Elspeth had no intention of behaving in any way which would give her the slightest information. When Mrs. Green expressed her thankfulness at his lordship's safety, Elspeth smiled and said, "We are all greatly relieved. Andrew will benefit from having his father around again. The poor child probably won't even remember him."

"That won't take long to remedy." Mrs. Green excused herself, but before she left the room she added, "A boy needs a real man to look up to, I always thought."

Was that some comment on Francis? Elspeth wondered. But she didn't let the remark distract her. Instead she went up to Andrew, explaining to him that his father would soon be home. Though the child didn't understand, it made Elspeth feel better just to say it, over and over. The knowledge was something she wished to impress on her mind.

Francis came during the afternoon. The day was muggy, and Elspeth had Andrew sleeping on a blanket in the shrubbery where he got at least a whisper of breeze. His own room was too warm on days like this, even with the windows open. Elspeth had heard someone ride up to the stables, and she felt sure it was Francis, but there was no way she could avoid him now. This was the time to speak seriously with him, to make him understand she had accepted her responsibilities and would no longer dally with him, if that's what they'd been doing.

As he came around one of the bushes, he was mopping at his forehead with a handkerchief. He looked uncomfortably warm, and Elspeth felt a moment's softening of her resolve. Always before he had looked so cool and unruffled, so far above the discomforts of ordinary mortals. He smiled at her as he stuffed the handkerchief back in his pocket and dropped down to sit at her feet, scarcely noticing the child at all.

"Heat always bothers me," he said. "Especially this moist heat. You look adorable in that hat."

The creation he referred to was a leghorn hat with a large brim, turned up behind in a soft roll in the French style. Elspeth remembered writing about it to Greywell, and she staunchly refused the compliment. "It keeps the sun out of my eyes." Self-consciously she retied the ribbon under her chin a little tighter.

"You still look adorable, with your curls peeping out that way," he insisted.

"Francis, we had a message from Greywell this morning. He's been wounded, but he's all right and he's coming to Ashfield very soon. I suppose as soon as he can travel. I don't think you should call on me anymore."

Francis looked stunned. "Not call on you! I couldn't live if I didn't call on you!"

"Nonsense. We've been behaving very improperly. If you are not aware of it, I certainly am. I know it's my fault. There is some weakness in me that I shall have to make a strong effort to weed out. And in order to do that I simply cannot see you any longer."

"But I love you! Doesn't that count for anything?" His long, elegant hands came up to claim hers. "I thought you felt the same way about me."

"Well, I . . . I don't know how I feel, Francis. I'm very confused right now. But that really doesn't matter, you know. I'm married to Greywell, for better or worse. He has every right to expect me to act according to my marriage vows." Elspeth tried gently to withdraw her hands from his, but he held on tightly.

"Dear Elspeth, you're my inspiration. I've never written such poetry as I have since I met you."

"But it isn't the kind of poetry you meant to write," she insisted, her face flushed. "You've completely ignored your major work while we've . . . dallied. You had meant to write much more serious poetry, something that would make men reexamine their souls and lead better lives. While we've been leading quite . . . exceptionable lives ourselves."

His brow puckered. "Never think that. The poetry of love is justified in its very nature, as is the way we've responded to each other. You don't understand! Love is not something you can control. It's out of our human ability to dictate to our hearts. And their choice is sacred, Elspeth. Perhaps we *have* acted a little improperly, given your situation, but that is not to say we have much error on our side. One would have to show the discipline of a monk not to gravitate to one another's company, to wish to share the fruits of our affection."

"It's one thing not to be able to control your heart, and quite another not to control your body," Elspeth said sadly. "Please, Francis, don't make this any harder for me than it is. You know I'm fond of you, but it isn't *right* for us to do what we've been doing. And we certainly can't continue to do it when Greywell returns. I owe him that much."

At last Francis let go of her hands, but only so he could draw his fingers distractedly through his shaggy locks. He wore a pained expression. "I can't just forget you, Elspeth. I can't shut my heart to you. What about my poetry? The pain you're causing me can only have its outlet in my poetry. That's where I express all my emotions. You have to understand that."

Elspeth sighed. "I do understand it, Francis. Of course you will continue to write your poetry, but you must be very cautious about where you keep it, for my sake. And Greywell is a friend of yours. Don't forget that."

"I can never forgive him for marrying you."

"If he hadn't married me, we'd never have met," Elspeth said reasonably. "But then, perhaps it would have been best if we hadn't met."

"Don't say that! It was our destiny, our fate to meet." Francis went into one of his dreamy trances, coming out of it after a minute or two to say, "And perhaps it was our fate to suffer for our love. Maybe this was the grand design, the struggle I had to go through to purge my soul of its lesser interests. Yes, I do see that that would be a worthy ambition for a poet." He smiled at her, a sad, nostalgic smile. "Very well, Elspeth. We won't see each other anymore. But I shan't forget the light you've brought into my life, the clarity you've given my vision. Knowing you has given me the strength to accept this burden. Without my love for you, I wouldn't be able to bear it, you know. I would have dwindled away like some maiden in a decline."

His grandiose speech left Elspeth rather embarrassed, but she had no wish to contradict him. "You'll have your poetry. That will be something to sustain you." What would she have to sustain her? She looked at the sleeping baby, and realized his happiness was as important to her as her own. "And I have Andrew to care for. That's why I came here. He's the one who will give my life purpose."

Francis stood up and dusted the seat of his riding breeches. There was perspiration on his forehead, but he didn't bother to wipe it away with his handerkerchief. Probably he thought it appropriate as an indication of his distress. He took one of Elspeth's hands in his and carried it to his lips, where he kissed it fervently. "Goodbye, my dear. I shall miss you, your sweet lips, your glorious body, your generous heart, your admirable mind. Remember that I will always love you. No, no, don't deny me the right to tell you that one last time. Someday you will be famous, as the mysterious lady to whom my poetry was dedicated. To the Only Love of My Life. Others will know how I suffered, but they will never know the object of my love." He gazed deeply into her eyes before abruptly turning aside and striding in the direction of the stables.

Elspeth shed a few tears but dried her eyes when the baby stirred. "Come along, my love," she said as she picked him up. "We have a million things to do before your Papa returns."

Greywell had fallen asleep during the journey from Daventry to Dunchurch. His arm ached abominably, and sleep was the only release he had from the pain the jolting carriage caused. A warm breeze came through the open carriage window to waft across his brow and tease his dark locks into disorder. Outside of Dunchurch, when he woke, he surveyed the passing landscape with a certain eagerness. This was truly familiar territory.

Opposite him his valet, Clemson, sat upright, with a grim compression to his lips. He had not approved of Greywell's traveling with the injured arm. If he'd had his way, they'd still have been in Brussels, with the viscount safely tucked in bed recuperating. But Greywell had insisted he was well enough to travel, and that there was confusion enough in Brussels without adding his mite to it. "There are hundreds of severely wounded men here," he had pointed out, "and we would just be in the way of heroic efforts to see to all of them. If we could be of any use, I'd stay. As it is, we're better out of it."

Both of them now studied the passing fields, the heavily

leafed stands of trees, the few large houses set far back from the road. Clemson was thinking of the comforts of Ashfield, and how he'd be relieved to be there once again after the horror of the streets of Brussels, filled with wounded and dying men. Before he had found Greywell, he had attended to those he could, but once the viscount was found, he refused to leave his side. Despite the almost cheery note Greywell had dictated to him to be sent to Lady Greywell, Clemson was not, at first, all that sanguine about Greywell's condition. There was not only the arm, which had received an enemy ball, but a bad cut on the left leg and a burn on his shoulder. But they were all healing properly now, thanks mostly to his care. And Greywell, if he wouldn't listen to Clemson's advice, never stinted his valet in the thanks due him.

Despite the pain in his arm, Greywell wasn't thinking of the comforts of Ashfield. He wasn't, even, thinking particularly of his son at that moment. His thoughts were entirely concentrated on Elspeth. Their week together at Ashfield had not been particularly pleasant, and the letters they'd exchanged since then had given him little idea of what sort of reception to expect from her. Certainly she had accomplished his most cherished aim of restoring Andrew to health. For that alone he would always be grateful to her. He unconsciously grimaced. That might turn out to be the only thing for which he could be grateful to her.

According to her letters, she had not particularly interfered in parish business, or even in the functioning of Ashfield—but they were her letters. She might not, in her excess of enthusiasm for controlling other people's lives, even notice if she was stepping on people's toes. That streak of self-righteousness in her was something he didn't think she even recognized. Her smug certainty that she knew what was best for everyone else could be a grueling attribute with which to live on a day-to-day basis.

Now he could see the beeches off to the left of the road, in the distance. They had always been the first indication that Ashfield was really near, though it would be another fifteen minutes before the carriage actually reached the gates and lumbered down the drive to the house. More for the servants' sake than for his wife's, he made some effort to rearrange his cravat, but Clemson leaned forward, scolding him, and took over the task. The valet also brushed his hair and his coat, taking the necessary implements from the case he perpetually traveled with. Greywell felt like a small child, being ministered to in the carriage. If his arm were of more use, he would never have permitted it.

The household at Ashfield had been alerted the previous day as to what time they would arrive, and Greywell felt sure everyone would be assembled. Not that he liked the idea. He was tired and his arm ached. All he really wanted was a bath and his bed. So it was a great relief to him when the carriage came to a standstill to find that only Selsey came forward with two footman to take charge of their luggage.

"It's a pleasure to have you home, milord," Selsey said, beaming.

"It's a pleasure to be here," Greywell responded. "You're looking well, Selsey. No problem with your knees?"

"Lady Greywell gave me some salve to rub on them and they hardly give me trouble anymore."

Trust Elspeth, he thought. "Where is Lady Greywell?"

"She said she'd wait for you in the North Drawing Room with your son."

Selsey led the way, since he didn't want his lordship to have to open the door with his injured arm. There was an unusual amount of activity in the hall, all trying to catch a glimpse of him as they found some excuse for being there. Greywell smiled at those he recognized and nodded to those he didn't. Had she replaced many people? And then he was in the North Drawing Room.

Elspeth was seated on the pianoforte bench with Andrew at her side, *standing* on his chubby legs, and holding precariously to the tips of her fingers. Her gaze came to rest on Greywell, and she smiled. "Welcome home. This is a new start for Andrew. He's only just learning to pull himself up." She returned her eyes to the child. "Andrew, love, look who's here. This is your papa."

No matter what she was, Greywell told himself, he would always value her for this moment. The joy he felt when he saw the boy turn his head toward him, and smile, and try to take a step forward, could not be denied. Without Elspeth the child might not have survived. "Thank you," he said simply as he came to stoop in front of the child, who had landed on his bottom on the floor. "Well, Andrew, we have a lot of getting acquainted to do." He looked at Elspeth inquiringly over the boy's head. "Will he let me hold him?"

"Oh, I think so. He's not particularly shy. Sit down on the sofa and I'll put him on your lap."

Greywell wanted to tell her he was capable of picking the boy up with his left arm but thought better of it. He did as he was told, and Elspeth seated herself beside him, the child in her arms. "Just look at those shiny buttons," she said to Andrew. "I'll bet you'd like to sit in your papa's lap and play with those shiny buttons." Andrew obligingly reached for them, and Elspeth shifted him easily onto Greywell's legs. "He should be dry, but that's one of the hazards of children, Greywell. I dare say you'll be wanting to change soon in any case. Shall I leave you two alone?"

"Please stay," he said, smiling at her as he smoothed the boy's unruly hair. "You've wrought miracles with him, you know."

Elspeth laughed. "No, he's simply grown, as children do. I'm glad you'll be here when he starts walking. How's your arm?"

"Not too bad."

"I thought you'd be tired. I hope you don't mind my not having the whole staff assembled for you."

"No, I'm grateful." Greywell ran his hand over Andrew's arms and legs as though to check that everything was as strong and healthy as it looked. Then he raised his eyes to Elspeth again. "You look different. I don't remember any curls, and certainly no dresses as delightful as that one."

"Emily Marden urged the new hairstyle on me, and helped me choose a new wardrobe." When Andrew wriggled on Greywell's lap and extended his arms to her, she made an excusing gesture with her hands. "He's used to me. Besides," she said as she accepted the child, "you'll want a bath and your bed after the journey. And it's time for Andrew's nap."

Greywell rose as she did. "I'll want to speak with you later, to find out how everything went while I was away, but, yes, right now I need to rest." He laid his left hand gently on Andrew's sleepy head where it rested against Elspeth's shoulder, and then raised it to touch her cheek. "You look lovely. I can't tell you how much I appreciate what you've done for Andrew."

Elspeth flushed. "There's no need to thank me. I'm very fond of him."

"Yes, I can see that." He followed her out into the hall and up the stairs until she left him to climb to the nursery. She seemed somehow different to him, subtly altered from the way he'd left her last autumn. Not just in her appearance, which was vastly changed for the better, but in her—what?—humility? No, perhaps not that. Greywell decided it was too soon for him to make any judgments. He entered his bedchamber and willingly submitted to Clemson's ministrations.

It was late afternoon by the time Greywell came searching for her. He found her in the Summer Parlor, alone, revising a menu for the next day. During his absence she had kept the dinner fare to simple meals, but now he was back she intended to be more extravagant again, imagining he would expect it. When she looked up to find him standing in the doorway observing her, she asked, "Do you prefer roast lamb to capon?"

"To boiled capon, yes, but I'm very fond of roast capon. You needn't trouble yourself over what to feed me, Elspeth. And Mrs. Green knows my preferences as well as I do."

"I suppose she does," Elspeth admitted, trying not to find the remark unnecessarily condescending. She hadn't, after all, spent enough time with Greywell to have the least idea what his food preferences were. Relying on Mrs. Green's knowledge wasn't the same; Elspeth wanted to feel fully knowledgeable herself.

Greywell stood for a moment just inside the door of the room. His arm was in a sling, so one sleeve of his jacket merely hung from his shoulder, but he looked dashing rather than sloppy. Elspeth had forgotten how striking his eyes were, how broad his shoulders, and how very tall he was. Francis was a great deal shorter, and his face so smooth as to appear boyish. There was nothing boyish about Greywell. Everything about him was excessively manly, she thought, from the thick, unruly hair so like his son's to the care lines on his sun-browned face. And the way he stood, so decidedly sure of himself, so determinedly in the here and now. Quite the opposite of Francis' dreamy face and willowy body.

"You should sit down," she said, concerned for his wound.

"I'll sit down when I need to."

Though his tone was neutral, she knew he was irritated with her remark. "I was only thinking of your health."

"I feel quite well," he said stiffly, and then relented, always remembering Andrew. "I stopped by to speak to Mrs. Green. She said you've taken everything well in hand."

To Elspeth it sounded as though he'd been checking up on her. Of course, she would expect him to do that, but he didn't have to put it so bluntly. "I think I've managed not to destroy her household routine too badly."

He looked startled for a moment, then sighed and took a chair opposite her. "I think we're talking at cross purposes, Elspeth. I went to see her because I always go to see her when I get home after an absence. She thinks of herself as another mother to me, and would be vastly put out if I neglected her. What she said about you was of her own volition, not at my inquiry. I admit I had expected her by this time to have a grudging admiration for your efficiency; I didn't expect her generous praise and obvious affection."

"We've gotten along very well."

"So it sounds," he agreed, rueful. "Apparently you didn't tell them I had decided to join Wellington's staff."

She had been looking at the paper in her hands but now lifted her eyes to his. "I couldn't see what purpose it would serve. They would only have worried about you."

"I'm glad you didn't. If I'd thought of suggesting it to you, I would have. Your last letter did make me have second thoughts, Elspeth, but it was too late. I'm sorry for the additional worry I caused you."

She gave only a toss of her head. "You did what you thought you should. I wouldn't have felt right if I hadn't remonstrated with you on Andrew's behalf."

Greywell decided to let the matter drop. His annoyance at the time he'd received the letter was long past, and she had had the right to say what she had—on behalf of Andrew. "So, my dear, what else has been going forward here? What have you been up to, other than running the household and taking care of Andrew?"

The question meant nothing out of the ordinary. He really was curious to hear what she thought of the area and the household, and wondered how she'd spent her time. He wasn't at all prepared for the dusky flush that invaded her cheeks, or the way her eyes refused to meet his. What the devil *had* she been up to?

"Nothing much," she managed to say. Had Mrs. Green made

some mention of her frequent visits from Francis Treyford? Was that what he wanted to know? Because she couldn't bring herself to look at him, she hurried on, "I've seen a bit of Emily Marden and Abigail Waltham. And I've done a bit of renovating in my room and in the Queen's Closet, which I've taken over for my sitting room. I hope you won't mind."

"Not at all. It sounds a good choice to me."

"I had everything I didn't need put in the attics, as you ordered."

It was Greywell's turn to flush, though in him the color was not really discernible under his tan. "I was a bit overbearing when I brought you here. Forgive me."

"There's nothing to forgive. You were quite right in wanting to keep the furnishings. I really wouldn't have thrown them away, you know."

"Of course not. The furnishings at Ashfield *are* a little ornate. Perhaps in time we could tone them down a bit. I really have no particular love for that heavy style. It was in fashion when the house was originally put together."

"They don't bother me so much any more. I suppose I've grown accustomed to them. But a few of the rooms could use a little lightening." Elspeth felt she had successfully distracted him from his original question.

Not so. "And was that enough to keep you occupied? In a neighborhood where you knew so few people I worried that you'd be lonely."

Elspeth couldn't really believe he'd worried any such thing. What she thought was that he was fishing for some reference to Francis, and she decided it would be prudent to be the one to offer up his name. "Well, Francis Treyford came to visit me regularly. He read me his poetry."

"Awful stuff, isn't it?" Greywell asked, with an amused light in his eyes. "Francis has been at it for years, and I don't think anyone on earth even understands it."

If she felt she should come to Francis' defense, she thought better of it almost immediately. Instead she said, "Some of the short pieces he read me were intelligible," with a flippancy that grated on her nerves. Really, it was too bad of her to be maligning Francis to cover her guilt. "But tell me about your travels, about the Congress and the battle. You've had a lot more happening in your life than I have in mine." Which was doubtless true, wasn't it?

"The Congress was frustrating and the battle was hell," he offered succinctly. "Someday I'll tell you about both of them, but not yet, I'm afraid. They're both a little too close for me to make a good tale of them."

Elspeth was disappointed. What *were* they going to talk about if not what he'd been doing the last six months? And it occurred to her that he would, if he had any consideration for her at all, attempt at least some sort of recounting of his activities. If he was to bar her from reflections on the important matters in his life, there would be little else than household episodes to discuss between them. Francis had been a good deal more open in his conversation. "As you wish, of course, but I had hoped for your thoughts on your experience, not a rousing adventure tale, Greywell."

"If you'll agree to call me David, I'll tell you a little about the months in Vienna," he offered.

There was a quizzical light in his eyes, and Elspeth lifted one shoulder in an embarrassed shrug. "Of course . . . David."

He spoke of Castlereagh and Metternich, of the settlement of the Polish-Saxon question, of the insistence on re-erecting old barriers in Italy, and the overlooking of Napoleon himself. Even when Napoleon had escaped and begun to regroup his army, Greywell insisted, the sovereigns of Europe refused to accept the new situation. "There always has to be some compromise between self-interest and the interests of the civilized world as a whole," he said, "and it was difficult to get each of the groups to agree on where the compromise was best made. In the end I felt completely ineffectual in changing the course of events. I have no desire to join whatever negotiations will now take place." He indicated the sling with a rueful glance. "Fortunately, I won't have to explain my absence."

"You intend to stay here, then, and manage the estate?"

"Except for jaunts to London, yes. You and Andrew can accompany me or not as you wish, but I would like you to see a little of London, Elspeth."

"Why?"

"Because I think you would enjoy it." He smiled at her, once again noting the new gown and the hairstyle. "There's a great deal to do there—the theater, the shops, the entertainments. I don't think you'd be corrupted, my dear."

Again a rosy color invaded her cheeks but she said only, "I'll think about it. Shall I take you up to Andrew now? He'll have woken from his nap."

Puzzled by her discomfort, Greywell agreed.

Chapter Twelve

No one at Ashfield said anything to Greywell about Francis Treyford. This was not in an effort, necessarily, to shield him from the knowledge of Elspeth's activities. They didn't, after all, know precisely how matters had worked themselves out between the two, and no one was going to gossip about the new mistress without sufficient foundation. The staff at Ashfield actually had, as Greywell learned from Mrs. Green, developed a great deal of affection for his new wife. Not that they had expected to. At first they had been exceedingly reluctant to welcome her into their rather close-knit society. They had been fond of Caroline, proud of her beauty and spirit, and accepting of her negligence toward the staff. One did not expect a young girl to understand all the obligations of privilege. And Caroline hadn't understood them, but they had assumed that given a few years and some children of her own, she would settle down and take her proper place as mistress of the manor, so to speak.

The second Lady Greywell, on the other hand, had a perfect understanding of her responsibilities—with regard to the management of the household. It was true that she'd put a few noses out of joint at the very beginning, but the improvements she made were so reasonable and fair that her servants quickly came to trust her judgment. And her concern for their well-being was as obvious as her devotion to the child, who wasn't even her own.

So their acceptance of her had grown almost imperceptibly from one of forebearance to one of active appreciation to an ever-strengthening affection.

For all they knew, her relationship with Francis Treyford was perfectly harmless. Certainly they hoped so, and even among themselves they did not discuss the subject, for fear someone would bring up something the others didn't want to hear.

So Greywell had no hint of anything amiss, except those surprising blushes of his wife's. And one other thing. She carried herself differently. He was at a loss, at first, to put a finger on the change. It was not the clothes, and it was not the hairstyle, though both things added immeasurably to her appearance. When he was in the same room with her, he would study her, the way she sat in a chair, or walked across the room, the way she stooped to pick up the child or concentrated on some handwork.

Probably, he decided, it was having the child. Though she hadn't borne Andrew herself, she had adopted motherhood with a real enthusiasm. Her concern for the boy could not have been greater if she'd been his mother, despite her insistence that he must always know Caroline had carried and given birth to him.

Or maybe, he thought again, it was simply having a household of her own over which to reign. She did it magnificently, he had to admit. There was very little going on at Ashfield of which she was not aware, or in which she had no say. When he came, she willingly relinquished the parts of the estate management which were his prerogative, though she continued to show an interest in them, plying him for details of anything new which arose, anything he found it necessary to change, any little matter in which she might have erred, wanting to know, she said, for the future.

What did she expect in the future? That he would go away for an extended period of time again? It was certainly not his intention. He was content to think of spending the majority of his time on the estate, enjoying his son after missing all those months while he grew. Then too, his preoccupation with Caroline for those first years of their marriage had sometimes kept him from taking the time to investigate what could be done at Ashfield to make it a more profitable venture, to improve the lot of the laborers and cottagers. Elspeth might, inadvertently, have fostered this attitude in him; Greywell was not inclined to give her so much credit. He had always intended to do something, and now he would have the leisure to carry out his schemes.

There was certainly more than enough time. Much as he adored his son, and spent a goodly number of hours with him, he could scarcely consider that a major occupation. Sometimes he wondered how he and Caroline had managed to fritter away so many days in idleness. Thoughts of Caroline came less frequently now. His obsession had passed, his grief had abated. And yet there was one thing about her memory, now neatly tucked away in the recesses of his mind, that continued to gnaw at him. For the first week after his return he could not put his finger on it, but it always arose when he was watching Elspeth.

An amorphous physical desire had eventually returned to him. He hadn't acted on it—as yet. But he thought perhaps it was this that was bothering him, and that Elspeth was beginning to inspire something like lust. Perhaps this made him feel disloyal to Caroline's memory, he thought one day as he watched Elspeth from the study window. She was gathering flowers in a basket, her leghorn bonnet knocked to a slightly disreputable angle when she tucked a curl up under it. The desire to spend more time in her company was constantly growing in him.

On a whim, he set down the ledger he had taken from a shelf and left the study. By going out a side door he was able to catch up with her before she noticed him, and he stood for a minute listening to her hum as she worked. Was she happy, then? It wasn't a question that had occurred to him previously.

"You look charming, my dear," he said, softly so as not to startle her.

Elspeth swung around with a peculiar look on her face. Greywell was at a loss to identify it. Annoyance? Alarm? It was gone before he could quite say. "Oh . . . David. Thank you." She smiled, but absently, tucking the flowers she'd just cut in with the others. "I wish I were better at arranging flowers. And I don't actually like cutting them down this way. Everyone should just come down to the garden to see them, so they could die a natural death."

He had the impression she was aimlessly chattering, something he didn't remember about her from their original meetings at Lyndhurst. Saying something for the sole purpose of covering her confusion. But what was there to be confused about? he wondered. "I thought we might take a ride together when you're finished."

"Is your arm well enough for that?"

"I think so." The sling was gone now. "I didn't have anything too ambitious in mind, just a ride over to the village."

"Yes, well, that would be lovely. I'll have to change. Say, in about half an hour?"

Her enthusiasm seemed forced to him, but he nodded and left her, returning briefly to the study before going to his own room to don riding apparel. Caroline would have tossed her arms around his neck and kissed him, because she never thought he did enough with her. Most of their expeditions had been at her instigation, when he would laugh and touch her nose and say, "Very well, my little love. I can finish the books later."

It was when he saw Elspeth standing beside her mare that something finally clicked in his head. Yes, the way she held herself was decidedly different—different the way Caroline had held herself after their wedding night. Before, she had been flirtatious and aware of her body in only a superficial way, knowing she was pretty, that her figure was admired by men. After, she had held herself with a special kind of feminine consciousness. She had radiated a confidence in her womanhood that had been lacking when she was an uninitiated girl. He remembered feeling astonishingly touched by the change.

A similar change in Elspeth did not make him feel touched at all, but slightly ill. Had she somehow been initiated when he was away? It seemed unlikely, given her frame of mind on the subject of physical intimacy, and the promise he had made to allow her to remain chaste should Andrew regain his health. Greywell assured himself he was imagining things. For all he knew, there might be any number of things which would make a woman aware of her own body in that striking way. Perhaps even having a child to care for, feeling like a mother.

Getting into the saddle was a little awkward, but once he was astride there was no problem. The arm didn't ache much any more unless he was forced to exert it. Elspeth watched him with a proper amount of wifely concern, smiling when he indicated there was nothing to worry about.

"Your Clemson has done wonders," she said as they directed their horses toward the village. "I had thought you'd want to call in Dr. Wellow, but there seems to be no need."

"None at all. The surgeon in Brussels told Clemson how to handle it, and I think he would have been extremely put out with me if I'd called in other advice."

"No doubt. He's very protective of you."

Greywell turned to stare at her. "Why do you say that?"

"Oh, not for any particular reason, I suppose. It's just that . . . The day after you returned, I remembered about the snuffboxes I'd put in your drawer, and I thought perhaps I should move them. Not because of Clemson! It just seemed rather silly of me to have put them there in the first place, you know." She shrugged. "So I was going to put them back where I'd gotten them. And I tapped on your bedchamber door, just as a courtesy, since I knew you were down with your estate manager. But Clemson was there, seeing to your clothes, and he was very suspicious of my wanting to come in. He acted as though I might be spying on you, peering in your drawers and such. He said he'd get me whatever it was I wanted."

"And did he?"

"Well, you must know the snuffboxes weren't there any more, so he couldn't very well find them, could he?" Elspeth sounded miffed.

"No, I suppose not. He'd found them there the first night and asked what I wanted him to do with them. I told him to put them in the study. They aren't so likely to bother you there."

"I made a great fuss about nothing. You should, of course, put them wherever you wish, Gr— David. Some of them are quite handsome. Mrs. Waltham told me a little of the history behind a few of them. She's knowledgeable on the most astonishing subjects, isn't she?"

"Yes. She not only knows their history, but a great deal about their craftsmanship. God only knows where she picked up *that* information. Their history she knows from me, of course. Did she ask what had become of the ones you'd put away?"

"Naturally, but I didn't tell her I'd had anything to do with it. I couldn't bring myself to do that."

"There was no need. Abigail asks a lot of impertinent questions which are none of her business. She doesn't even consider whether she's being rude. It's more a matter of curiosity with her, an almost insatiable curiosity. And of course she's known me since I was a child and feels she has a right to involve herself in my life and that of anyone associated with me."

"She said my father was planning to visit again, that he had written to her, but I haven't heard from him recently. You don't suppose she's a little mixed up about that, do you?"

"It's hard to tell with Abigail. Do you still think they were . . ." He left the sentence unfinished out of consideration for her delicacy.

"Going to bed together?" she asked, unperturbed. "Oh, yes, she as good as told me they were. Not that I should be so surprised, allowing for my father's reputation. But I wouldn't have thought Mrs. Waltham was quite his type of woman. He told me he liked her unpredictability. Imagine!"

Greywell was imagining all sorts of things, but very few of them had to do with Abigail. When had this astonishing change come in Elspeth? Not only did she speak of such physical intimacy with a lack of embarrassment, but she showed none of the moral repugnance he would have expected from her. He wished he had some clue to what was going on.

His wish was answered sooner than he could have expected. They were entering the village now, trotting down the single street with no particular destination, when Francis Treyford emerged from a shop to the left of them. Greywell wasn't looking at Elspeth at the time; he was trying to decide whether it would be a good idea to buy her a gift, and if so, which of the shops would be the most likely to have something of interest. None of them was very well stocked, and certainly not with anything of a very exciting nature. He should have bought her something in Vienna, or even in Brussels before the fighting had started, but he hadn't thought of it.

So it was Francis on whom his abstracted gaze fell, and his lips automatically formed a smile of greeting. Before he could say anything, however, Francis' odd expression had registered with him. The younger man's willowy body had stiffened and his face paled, taking on a forlorn and suffering cast. What was more significant, no doubt, was that his eyes were riveted on Elspeth, not on Greywell. It was only when all of this had impressed itself on his lordship that he, too, turned to look at Elspeth.

His wife had had plenty of time to control her countenance into one of friendly interest, and was even now greeting Francis with the offhandedness of old acquaintances. She inquired after his health, his poetry, and his parents.

Unfortunately, Francis was not able, or willing, to respond in kind. He continued to stare at her, a variety of emotions passing quickly over his face. Then he switched his gaze to the viscount for a moment before saying stiffly, "How do you do, Greywell? I'm glad to see you're recovered from your injury."

Greywell didn't think he seemed the least bit glad. In fact, he had the distinct impression Francis would gladly have seen him disappear from the earth that very instant. So Francis had developed one of his hopeless passions for Elspeth, had he? And what of Elspeth herself?

Her face had frozen into the expression she'd adopted, but her eyes were lively with distress. It was impossible for Greywell to say whether this was because she was aware of Francis' devotion and found it embarrassing, or whether she returned it and was alarmed at Greywell's discovering her secret. "You should come by to see us one morning," he said to Francis, out of sheer devilry.

"No!" that young man ejaculated without thinking. And then he added, "I'm about to be off to visit a friend. Won't be around for a while. Perhaps when I return . . ." His voice trailed off.

"Yes, when you return," Greywell rejoined, pleasant. "Do come to see us when you return."

Francis nodded gravely to him, and threw a furtive glance at Elspeth's averted face before marching off to where a small boy waited patiently with his horse.

"Francis seems a bit jumpy today," Greywell said to his wife. "No doubt a short trip will help relax him."

Elspeth regarded him suspiciously, murmuring something that might have been taken as assent.

"Let's dismount and go into Burdock's," he suggested, dropping the subject for the present. "I'd like to get a toy for Andrew."

The child's birthday was approaching, but of course that was also the day of Caroline's death, and Elspeth felt a deep sympathy for Greywell's pain. She didn't mention the birthday, thinking it would be something he wouldn't wish to discuss. For the last few days she'd been trying to decide how to handle the situation without inflicting unnecessarily grim memories on him, but there didn't really seem any solution. Perhaps what he intended was to give the child a present now, and let the birthday pass without comment.

Mr. Burdock's store was small, and rather cozy, compared with the shops in Coventry. Elspeth patronized it when she could, though that wasn't as often as she wished. There were a variety of goods, from ladies' scarves to gentlemen's gloves, with a sprinkling of hardware and toys. None of them were of a quality to match the more exclusive businesses in Coventry, but Elspeth hardly felt little Andrew would notice the difference. She led Greywell to the shelf where a few items were displayed, dismissing the dolls and soldiers as not of interest to Andrew, and the marionettes as too complicated. There were lambs with white wool fleeces spangled with gold, and cardboard models of mail coaches and curricles, jigsaw puzzles and yoyos. Elspeth frowned at the assortment.

"I think perhaps a toy he could pull. He'll be able to manage it very soon, you know, and in the meantime he could push it about sitting down if necessary," she said.

But Greywell's eye had been caught by something entirely different. It wasn't on the shelf of toys, but resting on the floor, half pushed behind a table covered with mixing bowls. The rocking horse was made of wood and brightly painted in white, brown, and red. Elspeth had never noticed it before and wondered that Mr. Burdock had such an expensive item in his small shop, since few people in the neighborhood could afford that kind of luxury.

"It's a little large," she said dubiously. "He might fall off it and hurt himself."

Greywell touched her chin with a finger, smiling in amusement. "Now who's being protective? Little boys take lots of spills, Elspeth, and it doesn't usually do them the least harm. We can put something soft on the floor, pillows, perhaps, and he'll be perfectly safe."

Her eyes met his for a moment. There was something disturbing about his gaze, and the way he had touched her chin. Something familiar and affectionate, almost as though they were an ordinary couple, attached to each other. Elspeth looked away. "I suppose you're right. He'd love to have the rocking horse. But it must be very expensive, David."

He laughed. "I can't see that that's any problem. Have you taken to worrying about money, my dear?"

"No, of course not. It's just that such a large present might best be given for a . . . special occasion."

"Such as his birthday?" Greywell regarded her thoughtfully, drawing a hand along the smooth surface of the rocking horse. "Perhaps you're right. We'll buy a pull toy for him today and save the rocking horse for his birthday. All right?"

"All right." She smiled hesitantly at him. His eyes did not seem to have left her face the whole time. What was he trying to read there? She turned away to choose the nicest of the toys with their strings and little wooden balls, their round red wheels and crudely carved figures. "This one, I think."

He hardly glanced at it. "Fine," he said, brushing her hand as he took it from her.

After dinner each evening it was her habit to go to the nursery to play with Andrew for a few minutes before putting him to bed. Since Greywell's return, he had accompanied her, as he did that night. Instead of returning to the drawing room, however, he suggested they walk in the shrubbery afterward. "It's a lovely night and I have something I wish to speak with you about," he said.

Elspeth felt a momentary panic, but managed to agree in what sounded like a normal voice. "I'll have to get a shawl from my room."

"I'll come with you. I'd like to see the changes you've made, if you don't mind."

She made an awkward, flapping gesture with her hands, but he ignored it, since she didn't actually refuse. They walked down the stairs in silence, and traversed the corridor side by side. At her door he reached forward to turn the knob, entering directly after her. There was no one in the room. Her maid had left a nightdress on the bed and tidied up since she had dressed for dinner.

Greywell was surprised at the change in the room. The heavy draperies were gone and in their place were light cotton ones. The same fabric had been used on one of the walls, and for the spread that covered her bed. It was a simple gold-and-white stripe which enlivened the room considerably, especially when one took into account the new furniture. Elspeth had not stinted on expense in the material or the furniture; both were of excellent quality. But the total effect of the room was of an elegant simplicity to be found nowhere else at Ashfield.

"I bought a heavier material for the draperies for winter," she explained, "though it's the same pattern. I like light, soft colors in a bedchamber. They make you feel good about each day when you wake up."

"It's delightful. I had no idea one could so easily transform a room. Or perhaps it wasn't all that easy?"

"There's no problem, if you know what you want, and if you have the money to purchase it." Feeling a little more relaxed now, she asked if he'd like to see the Queen's Closet.

"Tomorrow," he said. "Don't forget your shawl."

Elspeth shuddered as she draped it around her shoulders and followed him from the room.

There was still some fading light in the sky, with splashes of purple and orange on the horizon. Greywell linked his arm with hers as they strolled down the gravel path. "We're going to have to talk about Francis, Elspeth. No one with the slightest sensibility could have missed his reaction to you this afternoon. It was a great deal more difficult to judge your own response. I hadn't thought you were so skilled at dissimulation."

"I've learned a great deal while you were away," she mumbled, her eyes on the toes of her white half boots.

"Yes," he agreed, and was silent for a while. One of the dogs came to join them, rushing at Greywell with an abundance of enthusiasm, which was met with an absent pat on his head. The dog moved over to Elspeth, but she didn't really notice and he continued to pad along at her side.

A circular stone bench surrounded a small fountain in the middle of the garden beyond the shrubbery, and he led her to it, waiting for her to seat herself before he settled beside her. He was trying to decide exactly how to put the matter when she blurted out a confession.

Elspeth had felt the tension mount as they walked, until it reached a point where she could not keep silent any longer. "I haven't behaved properly while you've been away, David. I didn't really think about how it would appear to you. I'm so sorry, but . . . Francis came to visit me, and he read me his poetry, and he . . . well, he seemed to understand me. He didn't disapprove of anything I did or said or believed. We're . . . spiritually attuned, you might say."

"I see." Greywell carefully brushed some dog hairs off his pantaloons and scowled at the dog, which was pawing at his boots. "What you're telling me is that you think you love him, is that right, Elspeth?"

Never in her wildest dreams had she imagined having this conversation with him. She should have, of course, but it had never really occurred to her that she would have to account for her behavior. Her romance with Francis had been as ethereal in concept as Greywell was solid beside her. It seemed, right now, not so ethereal as tawdry, and she was at a loss to justify any part of it, even to herself. Especially when she realized how close she and Francis had come to making it a physical as well as a spiritual bonding.

"I . . . I suppose I love him," she said.

Greywell sighed. Elspeth read unsuspected depths into that sigh. For the first time she thought what it would be like to be in his position: his first wife had died giving birth to his child, and his second wife had just announced that she loved another man. She sat unmoving, miserable, wanting very much to cry.

"Did you . . . consummate your 'spiritual' relationship?"

"Oh, no!" she cried, unable to admit how close she had come. "No, I promise you we didn't. I swear it!"

Carefully masking the relief he felt, he said, "And what do you propose we do about your affection for Francis? Had you given any thought to that?"

His tone was not sarcastic, but pleasantly neutral, as though she might truly have some solution to an insoluable problem. "Why, nothing, of course! I had told him, before you returned, that we couldn't see each other any more. It has ended, all that."

Greywell was wise enough not to ask what "all that" consisted of. He presumed it had been Elspeth's prudery which had prevented any lovemaking between them, and not some other cause. It was easy enough to imagine her, as she had been when he met her, developing a sanctified kind of love for the poet Francis, which she would never have contemplated acting on in a physical way. And he could even picture Francis doting on that kind of admiration, since it was so much in keeping with the aesthetic imagery in his poems. An unfulfilled love would probably be just what he expected of his life. It wasn't the first time he had conceived an unrequited love; Greywell could remember Francis' infatuation with a Russian princess a few years ago. The woman had never even known he was alive.

The silence that had developed between them was making

Elspeth nervous. She felt there was a great deal more she should say, or explain, but she couldn't quite think how to do it. There were Greywell's feelings to consider, and she herself felt too confused to voice half the unformed thoughts that swam through her head. If he wanted to send her away, how could she bear to be parted from Andrew? And where could he send her? Sir Edward certainly wouldn't want her back at Lyndhurst. She had become very fond of Ashfield. Leaving it would be impossible.

She cleared her throat in the heavy quiet. "If you'll forgive me this once I promise I'll behave as you would wish me to. I don't think anyone knew of my . . . attachment to Francis. He did come to visit more than was perfectly acceptable, perhaps, but no one commented upon it." She remembered Mrs. Green's obscure hint, but decided that didn't qualify. "I think I've run Ashfield reasonably well, and I've tried not to interfere in the neighborhood. The neighbors have come to accept me, and . . . oh, David, I'm so very fond of Andrew. Please don't send me away!"

His brows shot up in surprise. "Send you away? For God's sake, Elspeth, it never crossed my mind to send you away." It had, very briefly, occurred to him that their marriage might be annulled, since it hadn't been consummated, so she could marry Francis. But that would be intolerable. No one would accept either of them in polite society in such a situation, and he didn't think either of them would be willing to accept that kind of disgrace. And there was Andrew. Most of all there was Andrew, who would not for a moment understand if his substitute mother were to disappear. No, there was nothing for it but to continue their marriage as they had originally intended.

"I would like to see you happy," he said after a moment, touching a finger to her cheek, "but I don't think sending you away would accomplish that. Andrew depends on you, as do other members of the household. I see no reason why we can't go on very much as we intended when we originally married, save for your disappointment over Francis. You will find, in time, that such a . . . wound heals, if you let it. That's all I ask of you, Elspeth, that you let it mend. That you don't dwell on it, in either guilt or nostalgia. That you let it go, so far as you're able."

"Oh, I will! I will," she promised, fervent in her gratitude.

"Fine." He rose from the circular bench, ending the discussion. "Shall we go back in?"

The subject was never raised again. Elspeth was astonished at his seeming unconcern with the whole matter. She was appreciative, of course, that there was no evidence of his being annoyed with her, no sign of any moral repugnance or aversion. Greywell was surprisingly kind to her, treating her as if nothing out of the way had ever happened. He was, in fact, much more solicitous than he had been before he went away to Vienna. Each morning he greeted her with a smile and a pleasant query as to how she'd spent the night. His smiles, she noticed, were quite charming. They seemed to radiate from hidden depths within him of which she knew nothing. And they had no hint of the dreamy quality of Francis' smiles. But she didn't think of Francis much, which astonished her. Greywell as a physical presence was much more real than the poet had ever been.

Elspeth took to studying her husband. When he was in the stableyard, in his shirtsleeves, she watched the strength and gentleness with which he handled the more obstreperous horses. In the nursery there was something of the same quality in the way he handled his son, waiting patiently for complete confidence to come, as it inevitably would. On Andrew's birthday she insisted he be the one to present the rocking horse.

"It's from both of us," he said, ruefully winking at her over his son's enchanted head.

"Your Papa chose it for you," she insisted, but it made her feel wonderful when Andrew hugged each of them, his eyes shining with delight.

"He's a natural rider," Greywell said when his small son quickly mastered the unfamiliar toy. "But we'll put pillows down if you think it's necessary."

"I don't suppose it is."

And she watched him in the evenings, when he sat reading opposite her in the Saloon, his dark head bent over some leather-bound volume from the library. His concentration was so deep she often longed to ask him what it was he read, but she didn't have the courage. Once, when he looked up and caught her looking at him, instead of working at the tambour frame she had set in front of her, he asked, "Can I get you a book, my dear?

Your fingers must be stiff from all that handwork." What she had wished was that he would offer to read to her while she worked, but she merely smiled briefly and answered, "No, thank you. My fingers are fine. I'm hoping to finish this tonight."

Most revealing of all, perhaps, were the social occasions. He had been away for a long time and felt he must invite all the neighbors to dine over the first weeks after his return. So every three or four days they had someone with them in the evenings—the Mardens, Abigail Waltham, the Treyfords (without Francis, who was visiting elsewhere), Dr. Wellow, Mr. Clevedon, the vicar. These occasions were exceedingly pleasant, except for one circumstance. Greywell answered their questions about Vienna and Waterloo.

And he had still never gone into any depth on either subject with her. It somehow hurt her feelings that he would open up to them when he wouldn't to her. Naturally, he didn't describe the grimmer aspects of the latter or the great frustrations of the former at a dinner party, nor did he really make "tales" of either of them. Still, he told these people, relative strangers to her, a good deal more than he'd ever vouchsafed to *her*. Elspeth did not mention this to him. She played cards with a smiling face, and enjoyed the company of her neighbors, and said goodnight to him, when the time came, with polite, if distant, courtesy.

If Greywell noticed her reaction, he gave no sign. Far from avoiding her society, he sought her out almost every day to suggest a ride. And while they rode, they talked on any number of subjects—farming, the weather, the harvest, the horses, Andrew, the household staff, the local people and politics. He was perfectly willing to give her his opinions on each of these issues, and not above seeking hers. Sometimes, just to see if she could shake him out of his careless equanimity, Elspeth expressed some outrageous opinion. He would laugh and squeeze her arm affectionately, or laughingly scold her for teasing him. Which may, in actuality, have been why she did it in the first place.

It may also have been the reason she frequently suggested they descend from their horses, the fact that he held her as she climbed down. His hands felt so strong at her sides. Occasionally she even allowed her bonnet to become disarranged, because he would retie it under her chin, his fingers so casually adept as they brushed her skin. He never suggested that they lie side by side in the sun-baked meadow or on the dappled ground of the wooded areas. They sat uneasily, not quite looking at one another, and he would often tell of his ancestors, or of some ancient happening in the village, but seldom of his boyhood years. Impatient, discouraged, Elspeth would eventually climb to her feet and say she was ready to continue their ride. What else was there to do if he wouldn't speak of anything personal? Had he shared all that information with Caroline, and now felt it a betrayal to confide in her?

Greywell would regard her turned back, stiff with indignation, as a decidedly good sign. His wife, in spite of her protestation of loving Francis Treyford, seemed to him to have entirely forgotten the poet in an astonishingly short time. Of course, he knew it might be an act she resorted to in order to convince him of her good faith, but he didn't think Elspeth quite so consummate an actress. No, he felt almost sure her irritation with him was an indication of her wish to have him be more open with her, and he could only count that as a victory. Women in the throes of love weren't particularly interested in acquiring close friendships with other people, in his experience. Lovers tended to seal themselves off from the rest of the world, not seek to include it in their special emotional hideaway.

This increasing tension she felt was confusing to Elspeth, and set her nerves a little on edge. One morning she found herself in the Miniature Room, looking at the tiny portrait of Caroline. She had intended, while Greywell was away, to commission a painter to do a full portrait from it, as a gift to him on his return. He could have kept it in his study, so she wouldn't necessarily have to come across it in the course of her daily route. He had never invited her into his study, and she could think of no possible reason for interrupting him there. Now the thought of a full portrait of his late wife hanging where his eyes would meet it constantly gave her a sinking feeling. But it might be the best thing to do. After all, Andrew should have a picture of his mother to remind him, and Greywell might appreciate the gesture, coming as it did after her own lack of consideration for him. She had just replaced the miniature on the wall when Greywell himself entered the room.

He was surprised to find her there, and immediately thought her presence had something to do with the snuffboxes. It never occurred to him she might be studying his first wife's miniature. He had himself come to look at it, because he found his memory of her already dimming and he wanted to refresh it, if for his son's sake as much as his own. Absently he straightened the miniature on the wall before he turned his gaze to Elspeth. "Are you still worried about the snuffboxes? Did you want me to put them somewhere else?"

She had no intention of telling him why she was there. "No, no, I've become quite fascinated by them. Would you . . . tell me a little about them?"

His expression was quizzical, but affectionate. "I never thought I'd see the day," he laughed. Selecting one of the oblong boxes with a rural landscape, he held it out to her. "This one is from the York House factory. The plant at Battersea lasted only three years before Jansson went bankrupt in 1756. Henry Delamain managed the plant, and John Brooks was the designer and engraver. This is one of the best of the English enamels with transfer-printed decoration. They cover an engraved copperplate with printer's ink that will sink into the engraved lines and can be wiped off the remaining surface. Then a piece of paper is placed on the copperplate and pressed with a hand roller, and the inked lines are transferred to the paper. Next the paper is fitted to the enameled surface to be decorated and placed in a muffle kiln until the design has again been transferred and fused on the enamel. The paper burns away."

"It's beautiful." Elspeth ran a finger gently across the gleaming surface. "Do you know that much about all of them?"

"Most of them," he admitted, a rueful smile tugging at the corners of his lips. "I've always been fascinated by the craftsmanship. As to the snuff itself, well, I'm not the expert Petersham is on that. He's made an art of mixing, moistening, and blending his congue and Pekoe and Souchong. I simply buy mine from George Berry and let him do all the work. Petersham swears he has a different snuffbox for every day of the year, and I wouldn't be surprised if he did. I only carry half a dozen or so of them. Not all at once! The rest I keep as artifacts."

"Tell me about this one," she said, lifting an oblong box with rounded corners, slightly convex lid and *bombé* sides. A metal foot rim was simulated by a row of gilt dots painted around the bottom edge of the box, and the cover and sides were painted in a midnight blue shading to purple. Reserved against the ground was a painted scene with the underside left white.

"That's a Staffordshire box. They're hard to date because of their consistency of style. More often than not they have a scene of a lady and two gentlemen fishing, or a couple walking in a park, or a bullfinch perched on an overturned basket of fruit, engraved by Hancock."

"How did you find this one?"

"That's an interesting story." He glanced up as Selsey arrived at the doorway to announce that luncheon was served. "I'll tell you over our meal."

And thus began Elspeth's lessons in snuffboxes.

Chapter Thirteen

Elspeth's original intention in getting Greywell to tell her about the snuffboxes had been to distract his attention, but she soon found herself fascinated by them. Not only did he begin to open up about himself when he was telling her how he'd acquired a particular box, but her interest in his collection won his instant approval. She was sure of it, because he spent a great deal of time with her, paying serious attention to her requests for information, even finding her some books which would be informative on the subject.

What was perhaps most rewarding about these sessions with him was the contact they promoted. Elspeth grew to love the way he handed a box to her, carefully placing it in her hands, his fingers brushing hers. And the way his eyes were so intent on hers, willing her to understand and appreciate the beauty of the delicate little boxes. In the evening he would draw his chair beside hers, so close their arms touched as they examined a porcelain box from Nymphenburg or a silver box from Paris. Now, too, he began to give her some account, in sketchy details at first, of his recent travels. As the evenings passed, however, he became more informative not only on the externals, but on his thoughts about his various occupations. Elspeth liked the way his mind worked, optimistic but practical, always taking into account the realities of a given situation. She doubted if Francis would have had the least interest in the complexities of the issues Greywell patiently explained to her.

At first Greywell didn't bring out the more risqué of the boxes, but a time came when they had considered each of the others. Elspeth was aware of his hesitation, and she herself gathered three of those with naked nymphs to present to him in the evening for his usual lecture. The one she handed him first was one of the Battersea boxes of Paris awarding the apple to Hibernia. Paris was, of course, clothed, and there was a female warrior behind a shield, but Hibernia stood with her garments well below the bustline.

"This one was engraved by Simon-François Ravenet after James Gwim. It's one of the Battersea boxes, with the monochrome transfer-printed decoration." He flipped the lid open to reveal a portrait of the Countess of Coventry attributed to John Brooks after a painting by Francis Cotes. "As you can see, this isn't in as good condition as some of them. Surprisingly, the outside seems less affected than the inside." But he held it open, nonetheless, where the perfectly uninspiring portrait stared up at them.

Elspeth took it from his unresisting hand and closed the lid, staring down at Hibernia's high, full breasts. "Do you suppose she really accepted her prize that way?"

"I doubt it," he said with a chuckle. "And I think it would be very uncomfortable for her to play that lyre in her uncovered state."

"Do you . . . admire that kind of figure in a woman?"

Greywell considered Hibernia's body, with its long, rather muscular legs, as though the artist had accidentally used a male model for the lower half of her. "Not her legs, particularly, though she would probably ride rather well."

His answer was not at all what Elspeth was getting at. Her own legs, she felt sure, were unexceptionable, but her breasts were much smaller than Hibernia's, and not nearly so high. Well, really, who did have breasts that high, after all? They were almost up to the woman's shoulders!

Instead of pressing him for a more satisfactory answer, she presented him with another snuffbox, this one of a group of nymphs disporting themselves in an idealized woodland clearing. It reminded her of another woodland clearing, but she firmly put that occasion from her mind. The box had a diamond thumbpiece, on which Greywell concentrated.

"This one is German," he said, "with a particularly fine diamond, the original, I feel sure. The gold is good, but the enameling hasn't stood up as well as it should have. Probably from the early 1760s."

The women were round and pink, and again full-breasted. "Do you like that kind of figure?" Elspeth asked, tapping the box with one finger.

"It's a little full-blown for my taste." The lamp between their chairs flickered, the flame falling and rising again, making it look as though the figures moved. Greywell grinned. "But I wouldn't mind seeing a bevy of naked women dancing about in the woodlands. There's something quite enchanting about the idea."

"Humph." Elspeth passed him the last box, which was gold set with Sèvres porcelain plaques. The man and woman were partially draped, with a cupid above and to the left, arrow in bow aimed at them. The man's hand was on the woman's breast. It was an oval-shaped box with plaques of cherubs or cupids around the sides. Elspeth made no comment as she watched Greywell turn the box over in his hands.

"Paris, about 1763, I'd say. A friend of mine gave me this one, a few years ago." He handed it back to her. "Part of the body of the box is a replacement by P. F. Drais in the '70s. The rim is engraved 'Madame Du Barry au Bien-Aimé.' I don't know how he came by it, but he thought it would be a special addition to my collection."

On second thought, perhaps the man's hand was not on the woman's breast, but only appeared that way because he was pointing to something off to her left. Elspeth felt slightly flushed as she set all three boxes on the table beside her. There was an undertone of amusement in Greywell's voice when he spoke.

"You don't have to bring out all the boxes, you know, Elspeth. You could probably identify most of the workmanship on them by now."

"But I want you to tell me about every one of them," she protested. And then, a little hesitantly, "Even the ones in your study."

"When you undertake a task, you do it thoroughly, don't you?

Well, tomorrow, come to my study and I'll tell you about the ones I keep there."

Elspeth dropped her eyes before his curious gaze. He reached across and took her hand, pressing it gently. "I'm not making fun of you," he said. "Your interest pleases me. You have a quick and retentive mind. I had thought you scornful of my hobby, my collection." His seriousness evaporated as his lips spread in a wide grin. "But then, I had thought a lot of obviously incorrect things about you. For instance, that you had no interest in fashion. Your taste in finery hasn't escaped me, you know. Perhaps I must congratulate Emily Marden for getting you to the shops, but I think I have your own choices before me each day. And they're delightful." He touched the puff of figured muslin at her shoulder, running a finger along her bare throat to the locket that hung down close to her breasts.

His touch made her tingle, but she repressed the delicious shudder. "I have a miniature of my mother in the locket," she said breathlessly. "Have I ever shown it to you?"

"No." He opened the locket where it hung, being careful not to brush his sleeve against her bosom. "She was a lovely woman. You greatly resemble her."

Elspeth laughed a choked little laugh. "Not so very much, I'm afraid. On me her features are not so delicate."

"How can you say so?" His fingers followed the course of his catalogue. "Your eyebrows are perfectly arched. Your eyes are magnificently wide and your cheekbones high. No one could ask for a more aristocratic nose, and if the chin is a little pronounced, well, I like it that way. It rather indicates your determination, I think. Now, your lips . . ." He shook his head, staring at her lips. "They don't quite fit with the rest of you, somehow. The rest of your features are rather cool and exquisitely self-contained. But your lips are full, almost sensuous. When a woman has such a wide mouth, you expect her to be . . . hedonistic, for want of a better word. Still, on some it is merely a sign of geniality, isn't it?"

She swallowed with some difficulty. "I don't think anyone would describe me as above the average in geniality," she confessed.

"Ah, well." He shrugged. "You are perfectly genial with everyone I know. Our neighbors are enchanted with you; our household admires you. No one ever said that such an indication as sensuous lips was an infallible indication of personality."

"In what way would it be an indication?"

Greywell made a dismissive gesture with one hand, the hand that was not running along the length of her lips. "Women with generous lips are often generous with their bodies. Not in a vulgar way, necessarily. They're just more giving, more receptive of physical pleasure." He found no difficulty at all in making up the argument as he went along. "They enjoy giving quite as well as receiving, which of course is a very Christian sort of thing to do, isn't it?"

"Yes," she mumbled.

The way her eyes became sultry intrigued him, and he removed one hand to each of her shoulders so he could better observe her. The lips he had so recently touched were slightly parted, almost in invitation. He resisted the temptation, with a certain effort. In fact, he was finding the effort entirely too much and he released her to sit well back in his chair. "I'm sure you come by your lips quite legitimately," he said, in a teasing voice meant to break her spell over him. "Would you ring for tea, my dear?"

In something of a daze Elspeth tugged the bell rope. She was unable to sit still, however, when she had done it, and got up to pace across the Axminster carpet to the windows. Her body felt somehow swollen and achy, from the lips that had thrilled to his touch to the very core of her, where everything was chaotic. Elspeth felt as ripe as the moon that beamed down on her through the slightly rippled glass, and as heady as the evening fragrance from the flowers in the garden beyond.

This was not, of course, a completely new sensation to her, but the fact that Greywell inspired it in her was confusing. She tried to concentrate on Francis for a moment, but found the thought of him left her cold. It was only Greywell she wanted to fill her mind, with his nearness, and his gentle fingers, and his warm eyes. She wanted the sound of his voice in her ears, whispering of . . . what? Telling her he desired her? But of course he didn't, with his memories of Caroline. Telling her he admired her, that he had come to love her? Is that what she really wanted, or did she merely want to join her body with his, to feel again that glowing sensation she had felt, only more so? She wanted to run her hands over his body, to feel the strength of his shoulders and the softness of his skin. Her longing made her feel giddy.

"I think, if you don't mind," she said, not turning to look at him, "that I'll go to bed now."

His voice was full of concern. "Aren't you feeling well, Elspeth? It's early."

"I know, but I'm a little tired."

A footman entered to her previous summons and she directed him to bring tea for Greywell. When he had left she turned almost, but not quite, in Greywell's direction and bid him goodnight before hastening from the room. Greywell watched her departure with a thoughtful expression, then slipped the neglected snuffboxes in his pocket.

The next day a message arrived from Sir Edward announcing that he intended to arrive at Ashfield on the following day. Elspeth was very put out with him, and apologized to Greywell for this abrupt and unsolicited visit.

Greywell laughed. "Abigail told us he was coming, my dear. We should have believed her. I have no objection to his visit. Far from it. I shall be happy to see him again."

"He could have given us a little more notice," Elspeth said crossly. "There's just time enough to have a room prepared for him. And if it's like the last time, he'll stay forever."

"Ashfield is quite large enough to accommodate all of us without infringing on one another." He regarded her for a moment, his head slightly to one side. "What is it you're really concerned about?"

Elspeth looked down at the sheet of paper in her hands and sighed. "I wouldn't be surprised if he spent a great deal of time with Abigail."

"I see. Well, that's his business, and I don't think we need worry about it."

"It can't do your consequence any good to have a guest who spends his evenings—sometimes until the middle of the night—with a woman neighbor on her own."

"My consequence, dear Elspeth, won't suffer in the least. I'm not responsible for your father." He considered her frowning face. "And you aren't either. Please bear that in mind."

They were sitting alone at the breakfast table, their meal finished. Greywell had been reading a paper, but he set it aside, next to the silver coffee pot. "Your father insists on being a law unto himself. You aren't going to change him, and if you try, you will only cause tension between the two of you. I promise you his activities won't affect me, and they won't reflect on you. In many ways you've inherited his stubbornness and determination, my dear, so you of all people should realize the hopelessness of trying to change him."

"Are you saying you've found it hopeless to change me?" she asked, uncertain.

"Not at all. I admit there were some things I worried about in the beginning, but I shouldn't have. You're a sensible woman, and I apologize if I made things difficult for you. I can only offer my distraught frame of mind as an extenuating circumstance. No, my dear, I'm quite pleased with you just as you are. I hope that doesn't sound patronizing; I don't mean it that way."

"No, of course not. Thank you."

"Perhaps I should inquire if there are things about me—habits, mannerisms, opinions—that you find offensive. I would do my best to correct them."

Elspeth glanced sharply at him to see whether he was mocking her, but his countenance was perfectly serious. There was even a touch of apprehension about him, she thought, as though he expected her to find some unacceptable fault. "You're quite the nicest man I've ever met," she mumbled.

His features relaxed into a smile. "And you are by far too generous. But I shan't quibble. Shall we take Andrew out into the garden this morning?"

The way he smiled at her had the odd effect of making her feel as though butterflies had gotten loose in her stomach.

Greywell had brought Andrew's rocking horse out into the garden with them, and the child was joyfully galloping along on it, burbling as he rode. Elspeth had stopped to speak with Bates, who had decided to take a new position, since Andrew no longer needed her. The child took one of his hands off the handle to wave to her and very nearly fell off in the process, but Greywell steadied him, saying, "Perhaps we should put pillows around after all."

"Oh, he's all right, aren't you, Andrew?"

The child continued to babble happily, and Elspeth came to stand beside Greywell. "I talked to Bates. She wants to go to the

Monroes. I'll miss her." She shaded the sun from her eyes with one hand, since she'd forgotten to put on a bonnet before she came out. "Bates says Lucy can handle the nursery without any difficulty. I'm inclined to agree with her."

"You manage everything so efficiently," he teased, stroking her sunwarmed hair.

How was she supposed to ignore the way his fingers twined in her tresses and absently massaged the back of her neck? "You might wish to be involved in decisions that affect Andrew."

"I appreciate your consideration, my dear, truly I do, but I have the utmost faith in your ability to handle such matters." He removed his hand to assist Andrew from the rocking horse. The little boy had spied an abandoned toy under a bush and was wobbling in his first steps toward it.

Elspeth's eyes glowed with excitement, and she unconsciously grasped Greywell's hand to call his attention to the stunning event. She didn't look up at him, because her eyes were trained on Andrew, so she didn't see the double delight on his face, but she felt him squeeze her fingers. When Andrew inevitably fell, looking astonished that such a thing could happen, she quickly withdrew her hand and went to the child, laughing down at him with an abundance of good humor. "And what did you expect, love?" she teased when his face puckered. "It takes practice. Lots of practice. Upsy daisy." She set him on his feet again and watched him toddle toward the toy, feeling as though she herself had accomplished something quite astonishing. But alongside the strong maternal feelings there was another, heady sensation, and she glanced under her lashes at Greywell.

He was, of course, watching his son, and gave no indication that he had even noticed her unusual action in grabbing his hand. Probably he had pressed hers just as absently. Well, she was glad to know he thought nothing of it. Andrew had claimed the little rubber ball and was now attempting to gnaw on it.

Elspeth took it away from him, and he pouted. "We'll have to wash it, first. You don't want a mouthful of dust, sweetheart. Come along now. We'll take it inside with us." She picked the child up, smiling at him, and turned toward the house. Greywell followed, up the many stairs, with the rocking horse. "You should have had a footman carry it," she scolded as they left the nursery together.

"Probably," he said, and smiled at her, "but I wanted to show you how strong I am."

"Whatever for?"

He looked at her for a moment without speaking. "My vanity, I suppose. Pay no attention to my whimsies, Elspeth. They're of no account."

But the incident bothered her. When they had parted, he to go to one of the farms and she to check on the room they were preparing for her father, she could not clear her mind of her reflections on it. Such a remarkable thing for him to say—or do. Why would it matter to him if she credited him with strength or not? Actually, she was very well aware of his strength, and his masculinity. Too well aware of it, perhaps. When he was in a room with her, she felt an almost physical tug in his direction. Her body became wholely aware of his presence, and she longed for his touch. Not that she put it precisely that way to herself. When he stroked her hair or touched her cheek, she felt a warmth invade her flesh that made her glow with happiness. Most of the time she was given to crediting this response to her appreciation that he had come to accept her.

At other times she faintly acknowledged to herself that it was more. Elspeth stood at the window, gazing absently out over the lawn to the wood beyond, where she and Francis had lain on the ground. But she wasn't thinking of Francis, any more than with a slight shudder at how close she had come to behaving too foolishly to be forgiven. How ridiculous she had been to think herself above human frailty! Obviously she was all *too* frail when it came to her body's desires. Had she inherited her father's proclivities? It certainly seemed so. Standing there, her forehead pressed to the glass, she admitted that she wanted to be held in Greywell's arms, she wanted to feel his hands on her naked body, she wanted to touch him and explore the mysteries of his sun-browned person. Most of all she wanted to know the full experience of making love, with him, to share that exotic passion that joined men and women, that released and bound at the same time.

Drat her father! Why did he have to come to Ashfield at such a time? Just when she and Greywell might have worked something out between them. Well, she thought, straightening and taking a deep breath, she had one night before he arrived.

* * *

There was one gown that Elspeth had not yet worn since her husband's return. Emily Marden had absolutely insisted she have it made up when they had seen a picture of it in Ackermann's Repository. The top was cut very low and square around the bust, and was tight to its shape. White crepe covered a white sarsnet slip which followed the lines of Elspeth's trim figure with astonishing fidelity. The fashion plate had dictated rather broad scallops, to which Elspeth had agreed, but she had refused the fancy trimming and the embroidery of crepe roses, thinking them too elaborate for wear in the country. Perhaps in London, she had said, but not at Ashfield.

As she donned the dress she wondered if it hadn't been a mistake not to leave on the roses. Greywell was no doubt used to ladies who dressed much more elaborately. Why, if Caroline's gowns were any indication, he quite admired such an effect. But many of them had been purchased in London, and were no doubt only worn there, she reminded herself. Elspeth allowed her maid to arrange her hair so it was parted on the forehead and worked into light loose ringlets which fell over each ear. The back hair was braided and brought around her head so it formed a sort of crown. She wore a strand of pearls she'd inherited from her mother around her neck, but no other jewelry, save her wedding ring.

Elspeth was still wondering if the dress were a little too special for an evening at home alone with her husband when she made her way to the North Drawing Room, where they always met before dinner. Greywell was already there, lounging comfortably against the mantel, his biscuit-colored coat fitting perfectly to his wide-shouldered frame. He looked incredibly handsome to Elspeth, his straight brown hair coaxed onto his forehead and face after the fashion of the day, and his gray eyes widening with appreciation as she entered. She liked the fact that he never wore his cravats as high or as elaborate as Francis did, that he always looked relaxed in the most elegant clothes.

"You look wonderful," he said now, coming forward to take her hand and lift it to his lips. "I'm sure I haven't seen this dress before. Is it new?"

"This is the first time I've worn it." A smile came and went from her lips. "I thought perhaps it wasn't quite right for a simple family dinner."

"You could wear it every night, and I would only applaud

your decision." He released her hand and touched the pearls at her throat. "Were these your mother's?"

Elspeth nodded, feeling choked at the touch of his fingers.

"What you need is an emerald necklace to bring out the green in your eyes. There is one of my mother's, but the setting is too old-fashioned to appeal to you, I'm afraid. Even I find it far too heavy and ornate. Let me have it reset for you. I can send it to London and have it back in a matter of weeks."

"I . . . Thank you. It's not necessary."

"No, I don't suppose it's necessary," he drawled, "but I'd very much like to do it. You wouldn't refuse, would you?"

His eyes were very close to hers. She was sure she could see the affection in them, and something more. Elspeth swallowed before nervously wetting her lips. "No, I wouldn't refuse."

"Excellent. I'll send them tomorrow." He rearranged the shawl about her shoulders so its gossamer threads did not conceal so much of the bosom her dress exposed. "You probably don't need this tonight, it's so warm."

"I bought it to go with the dress."

"Well, there is always something of a draft in the dining room, so perhaps you're wise to wear it." He turned toward the tray Selsey had left on the sidetable. "Can I pour you a small glass of sherry?"

Though two glasses were always set out there, Elspeth consistently refused to partake of anything before dinner. Tonight, however, she thought she could do with just a little, and agreed. When she had seated herself on the sofa, he handed her a half-filled glass of the lovely amber liquid and sat down beside her.

"We should celebrate tonight," he said, "since your father comes tomorrow and we won't have quite as much opportunity to be alone together."

Elspeth was mesmerized by the way his eyes caressed her face. "Well, he wasn't around all that much the last time he was here. I never knew whether to plan on his being in for dinner. But then it was much as it had been at Lyndhurst." She took a small sip of the sherry and held the glass tightly in both hands.

"Perhaps we should invite Abigail to join us for dinner tomorrow night so we'll be sure to have his company on his first day."

"I hadn't thought of it. First thing in the morning I'll send an invitation over to her."

"Better yet, why don't we deliver it this evening? We could take a drive in the curricle. It's going to be a perfect night, you know, with a full moon and a warm breeze. I promise I'll drive carefully. I've never taken you out for a drive."

It was true. They walked or they rode horseback, but he'd never taken her in the curricle. Had he done that with Caroline? Elspeth didn't want to think about the possibility. Driving at night was a little hazardous, but she had heard nothing but praise of his handling of the ribbons, and the night promised, as he said, to be perfect. The thought of driving over country lanes with him, seated close at his side, was too appealing to even think of rejecting. "I'd love to go," she admitted just as Selsey arrived to announce dinner.

Greywell had a pair of matched grays to draw the curricle. During his long absence, the coachman had exercised them regularly, but it seemed to Elspeth that they were exceedingly high-spirited animals, whose energy wasn't in the least dissipated by even the longest excursion. Her husband handed her into the carriage as the animals stomped restlessly, Greywell's groom at their heads. She was relieved when Greywell told the boy he wouldn't be needed.

Pale white moonlight streamed over the landscape, turning the familiar countryside into a magic setting. Greywell kept the horses to an even, slow pace, chatting about his recollections of previous summers at Ashfield. He had become much more willing to speak of his youth and young manhood, to share insights into himself and his family. Elspeth listened eagerly, interposing questions as he went along. She was disappointed to have these reflections interrupted by their arrival at Abigail's.

They were shown into a small room at the back of the house. Abigail was seated in a mammoth chair that dwarfed her small figure. Two cats, one orange and one gray, were lolling on her lap, and she didn't bother to get up when they entered, because, she said, she didn't want to disturb them.

"We won't take a minute," Greywell assured her, noting that for a change she was dressed almost presentably. "We wanted to let you know, in case you hadn't heard, that Sir Edward will be arriving tomorrow, and to invite you to dine."

"That's kind of you," she said regally as she stroked the gray cat. "Of course, I knew Edward was coming. He assured me he would be here to visit me shortly after his arrival. Now he may escort me to Ashfield to dine. That seems a perfect solution. I'd not want to draw him away from your table on his first day."

Elspeth and Greywell exchanged an amused glance but declined Abigail's offer to join her for a cup of tea. "We're going to drive around for a bit to enjoy the summer evening," Greywell explained.

The older woman eyed them intently for a moment, taking in Elspeth's low-cut gown, and then nodded her head in approval. "A fine idea," she said. "Take her to the Ridge Wood, Greywell. The view from there is not to be missed on a summer's eve."

He ducked his head in acknowledgment and bade her good evening. Elspeth added her farewell before preceding Greywell from the room. She was not surprised when her husband turned the horses' heads toward the spot Abigail had suggested, but she grinned at him all the same. "Who would have thought her such a romantic?" she asked.

For it was indeed one of the loveliest spots in the area, even in daylight. Willows drooped their feathery branches down toward a stream where water babbled gently over moss-covered rocks. From the bank one had a view down over most of Ashfield, and it was a beautiful sight. Greywell tied the reins to a tree and led her to where they could seat themselves comfortably on the rug he brought from the curricle. Lights twinkled in several windows of the house and stars shone above, but mostly the night felt velvety black, silent, luxuriously warm.

Greywell seated himself beside her and put his arm about her waist, but he made no attempt to say anything. They sat in silence observing the scene before them, taking in its beauty. But Elspeth could not for long concentrate on the view; she was too aware of the warmth of his hand at her side, the length of his body along hers. She turned her head to look up at him, a shy smile curving her lips. "It's beautiful," she said.

Her lips were slightly parted, her eyes darkly glowing. Greywell tilted her chin up with one finger. "So are you," he murmured, gently pressing a kiss on her waiting mouth. Then he drew back to regard her tenderly. There had been no time for her to respond; he hadn't expected her to. She blinked rapidly under his keen observation, her long lashes brushing her creamy cheeks. "I want you to know, Elspeth, that I'm very glad you agreed to marry me. You've given me more than I can hope to repay:

Andrew's health and happiness, the efficient running of Ashfield, a calm and capable woman for my wife. I never thought to be so fortunate."

"It is I who am fortunate," she whispered. She lifted a hand tentatively to touch his face, to trace the firm line of his jaw, to lay a finger against his lips. When he kissed her finger and grasped her hand in his, she turned more toward him, pressing forward a little so her breasts almost touched the front of his coat. Both of his arms went around her to draw her against his chest, where he tucked her head under his chin and hugged her. It was less than she had hoped for.

"We'll do very well together," he said, his voice slightly constrained. "At least, I think so. You won't mind growing old with me?"

"No, there's no one I'd rather be with," she confessed, feeling a little forward, but not caring. She put her hands around his waist, letting her fingers play along his back as his were on hers. Still he made no move to kiss her again. She was very conscious of her breasts pressed against his chest. His fingers came up to stroke the back of her neck.

"I want you to be happy, my dear," he said. "I want you to feel as comfortable at Ashfield as you ever did at Lyndhurst . . . or more so. This is your home now. If there are things you want to do in the community that you haven't because you thought I'd disapprove, please don't hesitate to act on your conscience. I wouldn't feel right restraining you from doing what you thought best. You have a free reign, Elspeth."

"I don't deserve one," she said, with a muffled sob, burying her head more deeply against his shoulder. "I was always so *sure* I knew what was right for everyone, and I couldn't even exert a proper control over myself."

"That's in the past. It wasn't a bad lesson to learn, that we're all fallible." He held her slightly away from him, to see if she was actually crying. But her eyes, though brilliant with moisture, had not overflowed, and he smiled down at her, stroking the hair from her face. "You're a remarkable woman, so strong and yet vulnerable. That's the kind of woman I'd most like to depend on, Elspeth. I wouldn't have it any other way." And he bent to kiss her.

This time she responded immediately, so he didn't have an opportunity to draw away without recognizing her willingness to accept his caress. The pressure of his lips increased tentatively. Elspeth welcomed it eagerly, bold now, herself, in plying him with kisses, quick, excited little assurances of her affection. And then her mouth was slightly open and she felt his tongue explore the moist, warm recesses. They had edged themselves down until they were lying on the carriage rug, their bodies touching at almost every point.

His thumbs rubbed softly under her earlobes, his mouth still joined with hers. For what seemed an eternity, or only the length of time a lightning bolt took to flash, they lay that way, their kisses savored with a sort of timeless wonder. Then Greywell drew back, smiling apologetically. "You're going to catch a chill."

"Oh, no," she assured him. "I'm perfectly warm."

But he only shook his head and sat up, carefully studying her in the ghostly moonlight. She continued to lie on the rug, consternation plain on her face. "I didn't mean to alarm you," he said.

"You didn't alarm me! Really!"

Though he nodded, he made no move toward her, but wrapped his hands around his bent knees and gazed off toward the distant lights at Ashfield. Elspeth hadn't the first idea what he was thinking. He seemed to be frowning, but from her vantage point she couldn't quite tell. Hesitantly she said, "I wouldn't mind if you kissed me again."

Greywell turned to smile down at her. "Then I will, but it's getting cooler, Elspeth. That shawl doesn't provide you much protection."

"When you were lying beside me, I couldn't even feel the breeze."

Gallantly he lowered himself to afford her a shield from the evening cool. His arms enveloped her, hugging her to him, and his lips once again met hers. Elspeth resisted the need to shudder under his touch; he would only think she was cold, when she was actually becoming increasingly warm. Or he would think she disliked the way his hands stroked her sides, getting caught in the gauzy overdress. As his kiss deepened again, she longed for him to touch her aching breasts, but he steadfastly kept his hands some distance from them.

Desperate for more contact, she whispered, "I wouldn't mind

if you warmed my bosom with your hands. It's a little . . . exposed."

Actually, it was as exposed as she could make it by surreptitiously tugging down the bodice with one hand. There was a great expanse of white now visible, and he covered it with his warm fingers, his mouth still on hers. For a moment his hands remained unmoving, but there was something too tempting about the soft mounds for him to resist their attractions. Slowly he began to move his fingers, first over only those parts of the breasts which were uncovered, but when he encountered no resistance, he slid his fingers under the material. Elspeth sighed.

His fingers stilled, but when she continued to run her tongue along his lips, he resumed his exploration. The touch on her sensitive nipples was almost electric, sending bolts of delicious sensations through her body. Impatient with the constriction of her gown, she pushed the material down over her breasts and watched, with some trepidation, his reaction. "I'm not so . . . large as those women on the snuffboxes," she confessed.

"No," he agreed, his gray eyes appearing almost black in the darkness. "That doesn't matter, you know. You're lovely. Do you mind my touching you?"

"It feels wonderful."

"Would you like me to kiss your breasts?"

Her eyes were wide and unblinking. "Yes, please."

Elspeth wasn't sure she could stand the ecstasy his mouth produced. Every nerve in her body seemed to come alive. She found her fingers woven in his dark hair, holding on as though she might be swept away. The moisture from his tongue, the suction from his lips, connected with that part deep within her that craved satisfaction. "Oh, David, I can't bear it," she whispered.

Confused as to her meaning, he lifted his head to look into her eyes. They were sultry with desire, shining in the moonlight like two new stars. He touched her quivering lips with a gentle finger. "Do you want me to stop now?"

"No. Yes. Could we go home and . . ."

Without another word he slipped the gown back over her breasts and rose to help her to her feet. Elspeth's knees felt slightly weak, and she clung to him for a moment before she was able to walk to the curricle. To her surprise, she found she was very nervous now. The tension in her body refused to abate, and she wasn't sure, from his silence, that he had understood what she meant. He was as gentle, as solicitous, as he ever was with her, driving now with a necessary concentration on the dark road.

"David?"

"Yes, my dear?"

"I meant, when we get back, that, if you wanted to, you could come to my room."

"Yes, I thought that was what you meant."

"Would you want to do that?"

He turned to smile at her. "Very much. But perhaps this is as good a time as any to mention our original agreement. I will certainly abide by it if you prefer that, Elspeth. If there is any reason, other than your own desire to consummate our marriage, that's leading you to this step, I don't think you should take it."

"What kind of reason?"

"I don't know. Guilt. Sympathy. Duty. Any number of things might be influencing you. I don't want you to do something you'll regret."

"I won't regret it," she said firmly, clutching her hands together in her lap. "It's what I want."

He shifted the reins to one hand and reached over to touch her cheek. "I'm glad."

As he swept the curricle down the carriage drive she noticed the lamp was still burning on the second floor in the nursery. And when he handed her down at the front door, Bates came scurrying out to inform her that Andrew wasn't feeling well and had been crying for her. Forgetting everything else, Elspeth hurried into the house and up to the child.

Chapter Fourteen

The child had a fever and was fretful, but his condition didn't seem to warrant sending for Dr. Wellow. Elspeth sat with him, putting cold, wet cloths on his forehead to make him more comfortable. When Greywell came in, she looked up at him and said, "He'll be fine, but he doesn't want me to leave. I'll just stay here with him, if you don't mind."

"Of course I don't mind. Shall I stay, too?"

Elspeth didn't know how to respond to the question in his eyes. If they stayed together until the child fell asleep, they could go down together to one of their rooms. But Elspeth had already decided she would spend the night in Andrew's room, sleeping in the chair in case he should need her during the night. "No," she said finally. "One of us should get a good night's rest."

He nodded and went over to lay a hand softly on his son's head. Then he bent and gently kissed Elspeth goodnight before walking quickly from the room. Elspeth watched him go with a certain misgiving. Would he resent her defection? She couldn't imagine he'd mind her sitting up with his sick child, but perhaps he would think it unnecessary and would assume she had actually changed her mind. Well, she could straighten him out on that. But with her father coming . . . Elspeth sighed and leaned her head back against the chair.

When she woke it was morning. A weak gray light was filtering through the space between the draperies, and Elspeth could hear soft movements in Bates' room. Andrew was sleeping peacefully; when Elspeth reached over to touch his forehead it was cool again. She stretched her aching shoulders and rose from the chair. There was no reason to stay longer. When Andrew woke, which would probably not be for another hour, he wouldn't likely even remember he'd been ill the previous evening. Childhood ailments often came and went quickly.

Elspeth still wore the lovely dress from the night before, and as she drew the fragile shawl about her shoulders a daring possibility occurred to her. She could go to Greywell's room—now. He would be asleep, of course, but he wouldn't mind being awakened, would he? She had never seen him asleep, didn't know if he lay sprawled across the bed or curled in one small space. She suddenly had an urgent need to find out.

It was too early for him to be awake, not yet seven, she supposed. Some of the servants were already up and about, no doubt. Would Clemson be? Elspeth didn't wish to run into the valet as she made her way to Greywell's room, so she proceeded cautiously, peering around corners as though she didn't belong in the house at all. At his door she hesitated, having second thoughts, and feeling tremendously nervous. Just because she wanted to be there didn't mean he would want her to come. What if he was inordinately grouchy in the morning? She'd never noticed such a thing, but it was always possible.

The door was unlocked, as she had assumed it would be. It was also well oiled, and made no sound as she cautiously pushed it open. Heavy draperies obscured any light that was gracing the early morning outside. In the gloom she could barely make out the bed at first. There was a monstrous concoction of valances and hangings on it, so that he was completely shut off from the rest of the room. Elspeth wondered that he didn't suffocate in there.

She felt a little foolish sneaking over to his bed on tiptoe and nervously pushing back the heavy maroon velvet hangings. Her eyes had accustomed to the gloom and she could see him lying there, one hand flung out over the sheet. His face was partially hidden in the fluffy pillow, and his hair adorably disarranged, standing up in a cowlick at the back. There were no blankets covering him, and the sheet came only to his waist. From what she could see, it seemed likely he was wearing nothing at all, which was not surprising in the stuffy enclosure. Tendrils of hair clung moistly to his forehead.

"David?" she said softly.

His eyes opened instantly, full of alarm. "Is Andrew worse?"

"No, no! He's quite well this morning. At least, he isn't awake yet, but his forehead felt perfectly cool. Bates was already up; I could hear her. So I thought there was no need for me to stay longer."

He reached for her hand, and his face relaxed into a smile. "Did you sleep in the chair all night, my dear? How very uncomfortable."

"No more uncomfortable than your sleeping in this airless closet," she said dryly. "How can you bear it?"

"I did it for you," he said, taking hold of the other hand and pulling her down to sit on the bed. "I thought to myself, 'If Elspeth should come to me I will want to have the hangings closed, in case Clemson should wander in in the morning without knocking.' He does sometimes, you know, since I'm here by myself."

"It would have been simpler to lock the door against him," she retorted, a faint flush rising to her cheeks.

"Why, so it would. I should have consulted you."

"You really thought I might come?"

"I hoped you would, but it didn't seem likely. And yet here you are."

She stared at her wrinkled gown. "I couldn't be sure you would want me to come."

"Of course you could." He made to sit up and thought better of it. "Why don't you lock the door now, my sweet. Then we can tie back this stifling material and have a little fresh air." He pushed the damp hair from his forehead as he spoke.

"Very well," she said, a little stiffly. "Don't bother to get up! I'll get the hangings, too."

Elspeth didn't notice his twinkling eyes as she scurried off to lock both doors, open the window a bit, and then tie back the maroon velvet. He had moved over to the opposite side of the bed when she was finished, and he patted the side nearest her. "Join me," he invited, arranging himself in a sitting position against one of the pillows.

It was an enormously large bed, and she found it was a little awkward climbing onto it. Sitting on the side, she kicked off her shoes and positioned herself against the pillow he had placed for her at the head of the bed. Greywell immediately took hold of her hand and brought it to his lips. "You look a bit pale," he said. "Are you feeling all right?"

"Yes, I'm fine."

"Let me take your shawl," he suggested. "You really don't need it."

Elspeth shifted slightly so he could remove it from her shoulders, and watched as he folded it carefully and placed it on the floor beside the bed. Her nervousness was increasing by the minute. "Do you want me to ring for your morning tea?" she asked.

There was a trace of amusement in his voice when he said, "Thank you, no. Unless, of course, you yourself are impatient for yours."

"I drink hot chocolate," she reminded him, her fingers unconsciously playing with a fold of the sheet. She hastened to add, "And I don't want any now."

"Good." He had turned to face her and was now gently removing the pins from her hair and running his fingers through it to unbraid her long tresses. "I particularly liked this hairstyle," he told her as he ruined it. "I hope you'll wear it again soon."

"Yes, I . . . I will."

"And your gown. I dare say your maid won't have any difficulty getting out the wrinkles, but I should have thought to send her up with your dressing gown. I'm sorry."

"It doesn't matter."

"No, but perhaps we should remove it now so that it doesn't get any more wrinkled. Would you mind if I helped you out of it, Elspeth?"

He was running a finger along the hollow of her throat and could feel her swallow convulsively, but he smiled encouragement, and she nodded. There were dozens of tiny covered buttons down the back of the dress. He undid each one with unhesitating, patient fingers while her back was turned to him and her arms folded protectively over her breasts.

Elspeth allowed him to slip the dress down her arms and then under her bottom and down her legs. The muslin chemise was thick enough not to be transparent, though just barely. He draped the dress over a nightstand beside the bed. Then he moved over to put his arm around her shoulders. "There. You'll be more comfortable now," he said.

"Thank you."

"We expect your father about midafternoon, don't we?"

"Sometime before dinner, yes."

He was rubbing his fingers through the hair that rested on her shoulders. "You have beautiful hair, Elspeth. And your maid is very clever in dressing it. Are you satisfied with her, your maid?"

"Oh, yes, she's excellent. Emily Marden recommended her."

Elspeth was having a little difficulty meeting his eyes, but her shyness was diminishing as he continued to talk and caress her shoulder. It disappeared altogether when he kissed her, his warm, eager lips against hers. This was not a tentative kiss at all, but one born of desire, though carefully controlled so as not to frighten her. She responded to the longing pressure, parting her lips so his tongue could enter. He tasted a little different than he had the night before, more like autumn walnuts than summer fruit. She loved the taste of him.

They had been sitting, but she found they were now lying against one another, and she could feel his naked hardness through the thin coating of her muslin pantalettes. She moved her hands to feel the firm skin on his back, to run them down to his waist. And still her lips were joined with his in a continuing, delicious exploration that had no object but their pleasure. His hands moved gradually from her back to her sides, where they slid under the chemise, stroking her tenderly on the silky unexposed flesh.

They heard the doorknob rattle, and Greywell grinned at her. "I won't need you this morning," he called to Clemson, whose "Very good, milord" sounded more than a little put-out. Elspeth blinked at her husband in the growing light, disliking even the small interruption. Greywell brushed back her hair and kissed her forehead and eyelids, his hands beginning a cautious journey up her body under the chemise. When he touched the swell of her breasts, he was gazing into her eyes. Her lips trembled, but not with fear or even surprise. "I love to touch you," he said.

"I love having you touch me," she whispered. His hands gently cupped her breasts, finding and fingering the already prominent nipples.

"Let's take off your chemise," he suggested.

Elspeth struggled eagerly from the offending garment with his help, sitting up to toss it off the bed. Greywell clasped her to him, his arms tight around her in an affectionate hug. "You're a real treasure," he murmured.

Then he kissed her gently on the lips before lowering his head to her breast. As on the evening before, the sensations he produced made Elspeth's body tingle with desire. Each movement of his lips, his tongue, sent a riot of messages throughout her. When his hand came to stroke her gently between her thighs, she thought she would burst with wanting him, but he was not yet satisfied that she was ready. Or he was not himself ready to culminate the delightful rising passion in himself. Elspeth didn't mind. If possible, she wanted this glorious headiness to last forever.

He had pushed down the pantalettes, and his fingers were doing excruciatingly erotic things to her. She gasped. "It will hurt a little the first time, Elspeth. There's a bit of tissue that has to be broken for me to enter you."

"It doesn't matter," she said breathlessly. "Only don't wait any longer."

He laughed and kissed her before removing the pantalettes entirely. Then he positioned himself over her and began to let nature take its course, though thrusting slowly, patiently forcing her maidenhead. She made only one murmur of pained surprise before the waves of ecstasy rolled over her. She clung to him as he came, feverishly kneading at his buttocks, drawing him into her as far as she could. Her eyes shone with wonder as they lay together, spent. He continued to stroke her, whispering unrecognizable phrases in her ear.

Their bodies cooled gradually, and he lifted himself up on his elbows to ask, "Are you all right, my dear?"

"I've never felt better in my life," she said, purring like a kitten.

Greywell laughed and kissed the tip of her nose. "And this is the woman who wanted nothing to do with pleasures of the flesh. I'll be eternally grateful you changed your mind, Elspeth." A slight frown creased his forehead. "I hope you won't regret the decision."

"I promise I won't."

"No, I don't think you will. Shall I have your maid come to you here?"

"I'd rather go back to my room, if you'll lend me a dressing gown."

Greywell disentangled himself from her and hopped off the bed. Elspeth watched him walk unselfconsciously across the room to where his dressing gown lay across a chair. She was even more fascinated when he walked back toward her. "You may be a little sore today," he said.

"I don't mind." She climbed out of bed, determined to be as easy in her nakedness as he was in his, and allowed him to help her into the dressing gown.

Greywell shook his head, bemused. "You never cease to amaze me, Elspeth. Shall I come with you?"

"Good heavens, no! I have a thousand things to do before my father comes. Andrew will be awake now, and I'll want to check on him, and there are flowers to cut, and the menu to be gone over, and . . ."

"Yes, well, I can see I'd only be in the way," he conceded as he opened the door. "Don't be so busy I don't see you all day."

"I won't," she called back over her shoulder as she marched down the corridor, her head held high, her body regally erect.

Greywell watched until she disappeared from sight around a corner. He was remembering the last time he had thought how she held her body differently. Decidedly she had become aware of her sexuality then, because of Francis. But this was not the same. Even if he hadn't had the proof of her virginity, he would have seen the distinction. This time there was not only an awareness, but a glorying in her body, in its power and its pleasure. The curiosity had given way to knowledge, and there was a pride in the knowledge, an acceptance in the experience. Elspeth had never felt more a woman, and the excitement radiated from her.

Greywell felt an odd stirring of his emotions, and realized, with some regret but mostly with thankfulness, that he had come to love this unusual woman. He promised himself he would always reserve a special place in his heart for the memory of Caroline, but accepted that time passed, and wounds healed, and that he had been exceedingly fortunate to have stumbled across Elspeth, the prudish spinster of Lyndhurst.

The only thing that disturbed this understanding was his uncertainty as to her own emotions. Oh, he didn't doubt that she had enjoyed their lovemaking as much as he had, but he questioned whether she was as deeply involved emotionally as he was. After all, it was only a few weeks ago she had told him she loved Francis.

Sir Edward arrived in the early afternoon. This time he came with only a modicum of luggage; it was too soon for fox-hunting, unless he intended to stay for several months. Elspeth, of course, had no idea as to his intentions, since he had neglected to advise her of them. When she inquired as to his health, he said, "Tolerable, very tolerable, for a man my age."

"You look wonderful," she agreed, taking his arm and leading him to the North Drawing Room. Greywell was just coming out of his study to join them.

The baronet paused in the hall to look down at his daughter. One brow lowered and the other rose as he attempted to pinpoint the change in her. "It's not your hair or your dress," he muttered, still puzzled. "You were already fixing yourself up the last time I was here. It's the way you carry yourself. By God, you've—"

"Welcome to Ashfield," Greywell interjected smoothly as a flush worked its way up Elspeth's cheeks. "We're delighted to have you come for a visit, Sir Edward. Will you be able to make it a long stay?"

"Can't say yet." The baronet turned to him, after one more quizzical look at Elspeth, and extended his hand. "Congratulations," he said. "I wasn't at all sure it could be accomplished, you know, making a real woman of her."

"Elspeth has always been a real woman." But Greywell refused to take offense, knowing Sir Edward's peculiarities too well. "How was your journey?"

"No worse than any other I've made," he conceded as he followed Greywell and Elspeth into the drawing room. "I could use a little something to work the dust of the road out of my throat."

Elspeth gave a vigorous tug to the bell rope before seating herself on the sofa. Greywell sat down beside her, his shoulder touching hers. "We've invited Abigail to dine with us tonight," he said. "We thought you would like to bring her here yourself."

Sir Edward grumbled something that sounded like approval, but he refused to meet Elspeth's eyes. "You'll want to know what's been going on around Lyndhurst, I dare say. The big news is that Blockley's getting married. Little slip of a girl, ugly as sin. Can't think for the life of me why she'd have him. Quite a pair they'll make. He's pursued several of the ladies since you left, Elspeth, but they had as much sense as you did. This one probably thinks it's the only chance she'll have. Poor child."

Since Elspeth couldn't think quite how to respond to this information, it was fortunate Selsey arrived just then in answer to her ring. She ordered refreshments, which included Madeira for her father, and then turned back to him to inquire after others in the neighborhood. They sat chatting pleasantly until after he had downed a glass of Greywell's finest brandy, when he rose abruptly and announced he must change for his call on Abigail.

He was gone with such suddenness that Elspeth sat staring at the door after he left. "Well! I don't know what can have possessed him to leave so quickly," she said, a little embarrassed for his precipitateness. "It's still several hours until dinner."

Greywell looked thoughtful but said only, "I imagine he's eager to see her. Shall we take Andrew out in the garden?"

On no occasion had Elspeth seen Abigail dressed as she was that evening. True, the night before she had looked entirely presentable, but when she arrived on Sir Edward's arm for dinner at Ashfield she was so elegant as to be almost unrecognizable. Her dress, though long out of fashion, was striking in its suitability to her. Full folds of emerald satin flowed about her, and a high-standing collar graced a surprisingly simple but effective hairstyle. Elspeth was shaken by her appearance and turned to Greywell with a half-fearful question in her eyes. She felt him press her hand before addressing Abigail.

"You look magnificent," he said. "Quite like the old days."

But Abigail was paying no attention to his flattery. Her gaze was on Elspeth, those small, sharp eyes assessing her so omnisciently that Elspeth squirmed beneath the scrutiny. Finally she turned to Sir Edward and smiled. "You're right," she said. "It was a near thing. If he'd come home a week later . . ."

Elspeth would have succumbed to a fit of the vapors if she'd had the capability. But such maidenly ploys had always been denied her, and she met Greywell's gently probing eyes with a lifted chin. How dare any of them discuss her this way, as though she weren't even there? She had been sorry for what happened, and she'd told him about it—well, a little about it—when he'd questioned her. There had seemed no sense in going into details, and what, after all, did Abigail know about the matter, anyhow? Surely she hadn't been bird-watching in the woods that night! No, of course she hadn't. She simply wished to seem all-knowing about Elspeth's affairs, though they certainly didn't concern her in the least. Elspeth offered the chair nearest the fireplace to Abigail, though there was no blaze on the hearth.

She heard Greywell offer the older woman a glass of brandy, but Abigail refused, in a very genteel, chiding voice, saying, "Sherry before dinner, my dear Greywell. I would accept a glass of sherry were you to press me."

Greywell pressed her, and Elspeth, who dearly needed the distraction and the courage the beverage provided. Were they going to ask her when Greywell had finally succeeded in seducing her? Really, her father and Abigail made the most astonishing . . . couple. Oh, my God, she thought suddenly, he's going to marry her! That's why he's come, and dressed in such a pompous, formal style. Her eyes flew to Greywell's, and her husband nodded, acknowledging he, too, had guessed their ill-kept secret. He seemed half amused, half pleased by the turn events had taken. Elspeth felt somehow betrayed.

Sir Edward waited until dinner was almost finished before making the announcement. By that time Elspeth had gotten her rebellious emotions somewhat under control. This had nothing to do with her mother. As far as Elspeth was concerned, there was not one way in which Abigail could compare with her mother. They were two entirely different types of people, and if Sir Edward thought he could be happy with her, so much the better. Perhaps it would end his gallivanting in the neighborhood around Lyndhurst.

"I want you to wish me happy, Elspeth," is what Sir Edward was saying. "Abigail has consented to be my wife."

"How . . . how lovely," Elspeth managed, turning to Abigail on her other side and smiling. "David, perhaps we could toast them with a bottle of champagne. Have you set a date, Abigail?"

"We'll have the banns read, of course," said the older woman self-righteously. "Edward suggested a special license, but I want no hint of havey-cavey business about it. So it will be several weeks, I imagine. Then I shall move with him to Lyndhurst. If

Greywell would be so kind, we thought he might find a tenant for my property, and keep an eye on it."

"I'd be delighted," he said. He had already spoken to a footman about the champagne and now turned to his wife. "I'm sure Elspeth would like to have the wedding breakfast here, if you would allow us. You'll not want to have that burden when you're getting ready to leave for Lyndhurst."

Elspeth wished she were close enough to Greywell to kick him under the table. "Of course you must let us have it here," she echoed, in what she considered an exemplary tone of voice.

"If you insist," Abigail said.

"That's kind of you," Sir Edward said.

Elspeth wondered if they had planned on it all along.

Her husband sat smiling at the head of the table. When the champagne came he made a delightful toast to the betrothed couple. Elspeth said she hoped they would be very happy. They moved back to the drawing room and talked of Lyndhurst and the wedding and plans for the future. Abigail drank a little too much, which kept Elspeth from doing it, but Sir Edward merely looked enchanted with his chipper bride-to-be.

"I'm going to take this young lady home," he announced after what seemed an eternity to Elspeth. She had never seen a man his age so besotted. "Don't wait up for me."

"We won't," she said, with sublime indifference. Greywell pinched her little finger, and she smiled benignly on the departing couple. From the drawing room they heard the front door close, and she said, "He's lost his mind."

Greywell laughed and kissed her cheek. "They're perfect for each other, my dear."

"I can't believe he'd *marry* her!" Elspeth saw the disappointment in his eyes, but she was too upset to heed it. "My mother wasn't at all like that. She was sweet and kind and beautiful and sympathetic. She wasn't crazy like Abigail. Why would he want to marry her? They'll make such a spectacle of themselves at Lyndhurst."

"You won't be there to see it."

His cool words had the desired effect of bringing her up short. She stood for a minute, not looking at him, and then said, "I have a bit of a headache. I think I'll go to bed now."

As she took a step away from him he said, "Elspeth."

Though she stayed where she was, she didn't answer.

"I know it's not easy to accept that your father wishes to remarry, but I don't think that's what's really bothering you."

"What else would be bothering me?" she asked crossly. "Isn't it enough that my father plans to marry a dotty neighbor of yours?"

"Of *ours*."

"Yes, well, of ours, then."

"Don't you think they'll be happy?"

She shrugged. "I suppose they will."

"Isn't that what you want for your father?"

Elspeth didn't answer. She stood with her back to him, making it perfectly clear she wished to leave the room. Greywell came to stand beside her, lifting her face with a gentle finger. "Just don't let it settle in your mind that their marriage is what has entirely discomposed you, my dear. You are surprised, and a little unhappy about someone replacing your mother in Sir Edward's affections, but you know it's a suitable arrangement. More than suitable, really. It will make both of their lives more pleasant. It will keep your father at home and give Abigail someone on whom to lavish all that pent-up care she has. After the initial shock, the people around Lyndhurst will think nothing of them—they'll be enchanted to have such a quaint pair in their midst. You know that's how it will be, Elspeth."

Her eyelids flickered rapidly under his unswerving gaze. "Probably."

"What has really upset you was what Abigail said earlier, wasn't it?"

She was tempted to pretend she didn't know what he was talking about, but she knew it was useless. There was always the possibility of brazening it out. "Well, it was a very uncivil thing to say, which only goes to show what a strange old woman she is."

Greywell abruptly removed his finger and stepped back from her. "Very well, Elspeth. Why don't you run along to bed? Sleep well."

His forebearance infuriated her. And the certainty that he wouldn't come to her, that he wouldn't expect her to come to him, made her feel desolate. "You said we didn't have to talk about it again."

"That's true, I did. And we won't . . . if you don't want to."

Elspeth knew he was backing her against a wall. "Why would

I want to talk about it? It's embarrassing to me. I've told you I'm sorry about all that."

If she hadn't used the same phrase again, "all that," he might have been able to let it go. But now he was truly curious as to how much "all that" was. She had been a virgin that morning, so it couldn't be so very much, could it? Why wouldn't she tell him and get it behind them? But he *had* promised to let it be. "I think we're both tired. I did promise not to press you. I'll see you to your room."

"But you won't come to me later, will you?" Elspeth moistened her lips. "What she said has upset you and made you think all sorts of things about me, hasn't it? Oh, I could throttle her! And how dare they discuss me in that way? Well, she's right. I'm a wanton, David. All he had to do was kiss me and I was nearly ready to . . . to . . . to jump into bed with him. Only there wasn't really any bed we could use, which made it more difficult."

Elspeth dropped onto the nearest chair and tapped her fingers against the arms. Her face was a confused mixture of shame and remorse and fear. "I didn't know how easily I could be tempted. Francis was very sweet to me. He wrote all these poems about me and he told me he adored me. Well, *you* didn't adore me. You left here being very annoyed with me, and your letters weren't much of an improvement, were they? I'm not trying to excuse myself. Well, yes, I suppose I am, actually. You have to understand, David, I'd never been in a position like that before. My purpose in being here, to see that Andrew got well, had been accomplished. Emily Marden was preoccupied with her new baby. The only visits Abigail made were these strange calls—she would pop up in the house somewhere and start talking to me practically in the middle of a sentence. You had written that you were going to join Wellington's staff, and I felt quite put out with you about that, thinking you would probably just get yourself killed."

She made a dismissive gesture with one hand and allowed it to fall listlessly on her lap. It was impossible to read his expression. He hadn't seated himself, but stood there watching her without changing position or allowing his eyes to register anything more than polite interest. Elspeth let out a long, shaking breath. "So one night we took a walk to the woods over there." She indicated with one quivering finger and continued. "It was the day before I got your valet's letter, so Abigail is right, in a way, about what might have happened if I hadn't heard from you when I did. But I'd heard about Waterloo and I was upset and I let Francis comfort me. I'd let him kiss me a few times before, and the sensations were quite pleasurable. That night I let him . . . touch me.

"I had my gown on!" she insisted, flushing and not meeting his eyes. "But I might have let . . . everything happen if it hadn't been for remembering my father and how I'd been so upset with him for what he did. Still, I started to understand *why* he had done it. The desire is stronger than I'd understood."

"Yes," he agreed, "it's very strong. I wouldn't have liked you to sleep with another man, Elspeth. I probably wouldn't have cast you out, as you were determined to think I would, but I would have suffered. No man likes to think of himself as a cuckold. I realize I didn't give you any special reason to be faithful to me, but I expected it of you."

She studied the hand lying in her lap. "Yes, I know."

"Do you think it will be difficult for you to remain faithful to me in future?"

"Oh, no, I shouldn't think so."

He smiled and came to take her hand. "Shall I come to your room tonight, or do you prefer mine?"

"It doesn't make the least difference," she murmured as his lips met hers.

Chapter Fifteen

During the two weeks before the wedding, Elspeth saw very little of her father, unless Abigail came to dine at Ashfield. Sir Edward was gruffly good-humored with his daughter, strikingly easy with Greywell, and totally oblivious to little Andrew. Under Greywell's watchful eye, Elspeth behaved as though the match were the best idea since the seed drill. Actually, she didn't mind it, once she became accustomed to the reality, but she liked pretending that it was only Greywell's constant attendance on her which guided her behavior. That way she saw a great deal of him, which made her days as inordinately pleasing as her nights were dazzling.

Greywell never let on that he understood this little ploy. It was a game they played, and he was perfectly willing to participate. His intention was to consolidate the gains he'd made, before putting them to the test. He had already devised a scheme for bringing matters to a head, but it would have to wait until the marriage was safely performed and Sir Edward headed to Lyndhurst with his new bride.

Of course, Greywell could simply have told his wife he loved her and asked if she'd changed her mind about Francis, but Elspeth was not quite the same woman he'd married. When he looked back at that time he'd spent at Lyndhurst, he remembered how easy it had been to read every emotion in her face. In those days she could not have dissimulated if she'd wanted to, but the past months had affected her. She had become more cautious, and with her caution had come the ability to dissemble. Hadn't she withheld from him the gravity of her involvement with Francis? She had purposely let him believe it had been little more than a harmless flirtation. And it had certainly been more than that.

And yet he found it difficult to believe that Elspeth loved Francis, that deep inside her she maintained a secret desire to be with him. Greywell was not convinced that his assumption wasn't wishful thinking, or even unsuspected arrogance, but he could not believe Elspeth was so thoroughly attuned now to artifice that she could behave toward him as she did if her affections weren't wholly attached. But there was the nagging doubt which would not leave him alone. He wanted this matter settled once and for all.

The morning of Sir Edward's wedding dawned hot and still, with a promise of suffocating heat later in the day. Elspeth and her father were already at the breakfast table when Greywell arrived. They both looked lethargic and were taking desultory bites of food around a few uninteresting comments such as "I think everything is ready for the wedding breakfast" and "This is going to be the damnedest heat to travel in." Greywell didn't feel any more energetic than either of them, but he smiled cheerfully as he seated himself, saying, "It's a good thing we decided to have the meal outside under the trees where there will be a little shade."

"What we'll need is a bit of a breeze if everyone isn't to expire on the spot," Elspeth sighed. "Even with the wedding as early as planned, we're going to have people eating at the very heat of the day. If we didn't need all the servants to pass the food and drinks, I think I would devise some of those enormous fans you see in the Eastern drawings, where the slaves stand about waving them to cool some overindulgent potentate."

Sir Edward regarded her speculatively. "I believe you would. You know, Elspeth, you've become almost frivolous since the last time I saw you, and it's very becoming. Don't you think so, Greywell?"

"I think Elspeth is charming," her husband agreed, smiling

across the table at her. She accepted the compliment with a demure lowering of her lashes. That was the sort of thing he wondered about. When he had first met her she had had none of those little feminine tricks; she had been all bald frankness. Who had taught her that, if not Francis? And where she had been capable of blushing at any hint of intimacy she was now almost coquettish. Well, perhaps not that, but certainly warmly affectionate. Not that he minded! Unless it was part of an act to disguise her true feelings. . . .

"Well," Sir Edward continued, "she has more of a taste for finery than I would ever have imagined, and I for one am pleased to see it. With Abigail I don't mind in the least that she dresses a little oddly now and again, but Elspeth is too young to be so eccentric. And Abigail has a flair for wearing the most outrageous outfits. I quite like them on her. Elspeth, on the other hand, used to look like a scalped rabbit the way she wore her hair, and she dressed as though she were companion to the bishop's widow."

Greywell chuckled as he helped himself to another slice of toast. "She looks very much the fashion plate these days," he teased.

"Don't you like it?" she asked, anxious. "I thought you wanted me to dress as befits your wife."

"Of course I do. I'm delighted with the transformation. Though I can't say I ever remember your looking like a scalped rabbit, some of your more unflattering dresses might have been fit for wearing with the bishop's widow. Perhaps you should confess you don't do it just to please me, though."

Elspeth looked puzzled. "Who else would I do it for?"

"For yourself, my dear," he said gently. "I think Sir Edward is right. You have a taste for finery that you didn't previously acknowledge."

"Oh, that." She lifted her shoulders negligently. "Emily Marden showed me what was fashionable, and I found I like pretty clothes. Now I even subscribe to some of the magazines to see what they're wearing in London. If we were to go there one day, I wouldn't want to be thought a complete dowd."

Greywell was strangely silent after these remarks, Elspeth thought. She had rather hoped he would take her hint and ask her if she'd like to go to London for a visit. It needn't be a long visit. She would just like to see the metropolis, with him. But it would probably be painful for him to introduce her to his friends. She was not, after all, the beautiful, vivacious Caroline with whom he'd left London some years ago.

A hot gust of air ruffled the curtains behind the baronet, and he mopped his forehead with a linen handkerchief. "I guess I'd better be getting ready," he said as he stuffed the cloth back in his pocket and rose. "This is an important day for me. One of the most important in my life."

A small murmur of protest escaped Elspeth's lips before she could stop it. Sir Edward laid a hand on her shoulder in passing and said, "I haven't forgotten your mother, Elspeth. I won't ever forget her. She was a very special woman. But I'm fond of Abigail, and I think we'll get along together very well. We need each other." And then he straightened his shoulders and walked briskly from the room.

Elspeth bit her lip and kept her eyes on the napkin she was twisting in her lap. "I'm sorry," she said to Greywell. "I didn't mean to do that, honestly. I'll make up for it at the service and at the breakfast."

"You needn't apologize. Your father understood how you felt. I dare say he's remembering your mother a great deal today."

She wondered if he'd remembered Caroline a great deal on the day he'd married *her*. Well, of course he had. He'd been cross with her the whole of their drive to Ashfield, but she hadn't understood that it was because she wasn't Caroline. Elspeth didn't think her father would be like that at all, but then her mother had been dead for ten years. Greywell hadn't married Elspeth because he wanted another wife, but because he needed someone to take care of Andrew. He still needed her for that. A footman rushed to help her as she pushed back her chair. "I should be getting ready now, too," she said, giving him a brief smile. "There are a few last-minute things I should see to."

"Of course," he said, rising politely. There, she was doing it again. How had she so quickly learned the art of masking her face that way? Greywell had far preferred it when her countenance was an open book.

Mr. Clevedon performed the wedding ceremony with great aplomb. The vicar was genuinely fond of Abigail Waltham, and he had no reason to think anything but the best of Sir Edward, since he wasn't one to listen to gossip of a man's past, and, in truth, very little of Sir Edward's notorious past had followed him into this distant county. Certainly Elspeth had never mentioned his propensities at home, and since Abigail herself knew of them, from his own mouth, that was all that could be expected.

The wedding breakfast was the largest function Elspeth had handled during her stay at Ashfield, and she was slightly on edge about everything coming off well. Aside from the indecently hot weather, however, there was hardly a hitch. She had remembered, from that long-ago afternoon at Lyndhurst, the idea of serving ices, and they were a special treat on such an intolerably scorching day. In fact, the only thing that arose to disturb her complete satisfaction was the arrival of Francis Treyford with Sir Markham and Lady Treyford.

Elspeth had not been aware of his return to the neighborhood. And she had no way of knowing that Greywell had insidiously worked the matter out himself, by declaring to Lady Treyford one afternoon, when he happened to come upon her in the village store, that he was sure Abigail would be devastated if Francis didn't attend the celebration. "He is, after all, one of her young protégés," he had said. Though Lady Treyford was not aware Abigail *had* any protégés, she had immediately sent an express off to her son insisting on the necessity of his being there for the wedding.

This summons had come as something of a surprise to Francis. He was still mooning over Elspeth and writing florid poetry about her, which he scrupulously avoided showing to the friend with whom he was staying. But the more he thought about the matter, the more he was sure Elspeth herself must have spoken with his mother and pressed for her allegiance in getting him to return to the area. This was, of course, very flattering to Francis, but he wasn't particularly comfortable with the idea of courting her (or whatever it would amount to) under Greywell's nose. Therefore, he was delighted when, during the course of the wedding feast, Greywell happened to mention to him that he was off that very afternoon for London. What could be more propitious?

No word of this plan leaked to Elspeth during the final flurry of activity. Sir Edward and his bride were safely stowed away into his traveling carriage, and departed in a fine spray of dust. The guests gradually took their leave, discreetly patting at their damp foreheads and holding their arms tightly to their sides.

Elspeth was disturbed at the way Francis pressed her hand at leavetaking and murmured something about seeing her soon, but she forgot it a moment later when she entered the house on her husband's arm. Andrew wobbled before them, overtired from the excitement, and she prepared to take him up to the nursery.

"Before you go, my dear," Greywell said, in his most languid voice, "I should tell you I'm about to be off for London."

Elspeth regarded him with astonishment. "London? In this heat? Why didn't you tell me sooner? Is there some emergency?"

"No, no. It is merely an auction of personal effects that I'm particularly anxious to attend. Several excellent snuffboxes in the collection. I didn't wish to interrupt your preparations for the wedding by mentioning it before this. Clemson has taken care of all the details. I shan't be gone more than a week."

"But I . . ." Elspeth didn't finish the sentence. He must have known she wished to go to London; she had as good as said so that morning. So it was evident he didn't wish to take her, and she wouldn't put herself in a position of begging him, or even allowing her disappointment to show. If disappointment was a strong enough word. Elspeth felt crushed by the weight of his rejection. Scooping Andrew up into her arms, she said to the child, "Kiss your papa goodbye, Andrew, love. He must go on a short trip, but he'll be back soon."

Greywell very nearly backed down at the child's pathetically puckered face, and Elspeth's own suddenly paled complexion. But, dammit, a week wasn't all that long, and it had come to seem vital that he know the extent of Elspeth's involvement with Francis. He searched her face for some sign of relief at his departure, and could find nothing but stony acceptance. "If you would prefer I stayed here . . . ?" he said.

"Certainly not," she replied, her chin lifted. "You will of course do exactly as you see fit, my dear Greywell. It's not every day that particularly fine snuffboxes are auctioned off. How fortunate that my father was married in time for you to go. I hope there is time." She allowed a questioning note to creep into her voice. "You would not, I trust, have missed the auction on his account."

"There's plenty of time," he assured her. He refused to grab the bait she dangled so attractively before him. He was in no mood to quarrel with her or anyone else. Already his plan seemed a little foolish and overly dramatic. Why couldn't he just tell her he loved her, and trust her to tell him the truth about the state of her own heart? But their eyes were locked in stubborn refusal to compromise, and he merely ruffled Andrew's hair, being careful not to brush her breast. "I'll bring you a toy from London," he told the boy. "They have wonderful toys there."

This seemed to satisfy the child, and he smiled sleepily as Greywell placed a chaste kiss on Elspeth's forehead. "Perhaps I could be back sooner," he offered.

"Please don't hurry on my account."

Miffed, but whether with her or himself he would have been at a loss to say, Greywell sketched a bow in her direction before taking the stairs two at a time to change to his traveling clothes. She didn't come to see him off. He couldn't even make out her figure in the nursery as his carriage bowled down the drive and away from Ashfield.

When Francis called that evening she had Selsey tell him she was worn out from the festivities and could not see him. After that, she felt a little better. At least Francis wanted to see her. Apparently Greywell didn't. Who ever heard a flimsier excuse than going to London to purchase snuffboxes? He who already had so many he didn't know where to put all of them.

Elspeth assumed he was tired of her already, that their lovemaking was not enough to hold him. She had thought their lovemaking quite spectacular, but she supposed, as a man, he was more accustomed to it and thought no more of it than he did of his daily meals. And perhaps Caroline had somehow been better at it than she was, though Elspeth could not imagine how. Certainly Greywell had seemed very pleased with her, as she was with him, but she had to confess to herself that she had long been naive, and a few weeks of physical intimacy with her husband had probably made her no more sophisticated than a newborn babe.

It was almost too hot to sleep that night, and as the stifling air closed in on her like a physical presence, she tossed on the bed, baffled and hurt by Greywell's defection. Only last night he had come to her here, stroked her body into an iridescent flame that burned so fiercely she had felt herself almost out of control, delirious with the shattering culmination of their lovemaking. And he had experienced the soaring heights, too; he had told her, his lips whispering softly in her loosened hair. Why had he gone away?

Well, perhaps the lovemaking wasn't enough. Elspeth had never assumed it would be, until she had experienced it. Then she had thought possibly it was. She had thought she might survive with even this sort of intimacy, if she had to. She didn't want to have to. Oh, God, how she wanted to believe his displays of affection were love. How she wanted to be cherished by him, just as though he'd never loved another woman, had no memories to stand between them. She didn't want to believe he was merely making the best of a bad situation, having married her for his son's sake.

How did you know when someone loved you? Elspeth rolled over on the bed and stared at the ornamented plaster ceiling. There must be as many different kinds of love as there were people to do the loving. Look at her father. He loved Abigail, but in a different way than he had loved her mother. And Francis. He said he loved her, but Elspeth had long ago realized that he loved the idea of being in love, he loved the excitement it generated, the poetry it inspired in him. Anyone would do as an object of his devotion. Not that it wasn't pleasant being such an object. But it was a hollow thing, puffed up out of hot air and wholly insubstantial. Was there ever a love that was substantial enough?

Elspeth wondered if her mother had ever doubted her father's love. And whether she would mind, now, that he loved someone else, in this different way. She wondered, too, whether Caroline would have minded Greywell's loving someone else . . . if he did. But did he? Elspeth could list a whole page of her own faults, and in the sultry night they seemed to exclude the possibility of his loving someone with all those flaws. It was easy to love him; he had so few flaws. She wished he had more, so she could love him anyhow, and make it more fair for him to love her in return.

Well, she would try to be better. She would try to make herself more lovable, if he would give her a chance. And she would take her courage in her hands, forgetting her pride, and tell him she loved him, that she had never really loved Francis, which he must know very well. Who in her right mind could love someone like Francis? Especially when there was someone like Greywell there with whom to compare him. She finally fell asleep thinking of the way her husband treated his son, and his wife, with such infinite kindness.

Francis came the next morning. When the footman told Elspeth he was there, she was tempted to put him off again, but decided against it. Instead she took Andrew with her to the North Drawing Room as a precaution. Francis was standing by the sofa, one hand elegantly resting on its back. He was dressed in his usual careless style, which had endeared him to her in the past, but now simply made her feel a little impatient. It was a studied kind of carelessness, the kind of look he thought a poet should have. His head came up sharply when he heard the door open.

"Elspeth! How I've longed to see you alone!"

At that moment Elspeth stood back to let Andrew toddle into the room in front of her. "It's good to see you again, Francis. I thought you would wish to see Andrew. He's started walking since you went away."

Francis was too startled to speak for several seconds. He regarded the small boy as he might have a soaking wet dog about to shake all over him. Finally he said, "Um, that's nice. He hasn't quite got the knack of it, has he?" This to Andrew's sudden fall to the floor, where he scowled at Francis, as though the young man had tripped him.

"Oh, he's coming along beautifully. They take tumbles all the time at first, you know."

"I didn't know," he assured her, looking as if he would rather not have learned. "Doesn't the nursery girl take him outside to play?"

"Sometimes," Elspeth said, seating herself on the sofa. "But I like to have him around me as much as possible, he's such a love."

Francis gazed at her tenderly. "Speaking of love . . ."

"No," she said, her tone firm, "we won't speak of love."

"But he's too young to understand," Francis protested. He threw himself down on the sofa beside her and grabbed for her hands, which she obstinately refused to allow him to hold. "This is our chance, Elspeth, with Greywell away. He'll probably be gone for a week, maybe more. Don't be shy now that I'm here. I know you sent for me."

"Sent for you?" Little frown lines developed between her brows. "What are you talking about? I never sent for you."

"Well, not directly, of course, but I knew. My mother would never have insisted on my coming if you hadn't pressed her."

Elspeth gave a tsk of annoyance. "I never spoke to your mother at all, Francis. I'm afraid you've completely misread the situation." But she wondered who *had* spoken to Lady Treyford.

He rushed on before she could settle this point in her mind. "It doesn't matter," he said, obviously not believing her but willing to accept that she wouldn't confess to such an action. "I'm here now. That's all that matters."

As he inched himself closer to her on the sofa, she worked her way in the opposite direction. Finally, when he had her up against the arm, she rose, exasperated, and glowered down at him. "What we did was wrong, Francis. I'm not interested in continuing any sort of dalliance with you. Oh, I'm saying it all wrong. You're a very sweet fellow, and I'm fond of you, but I've . . . well, I've fallen in love with my husband. Which is all to the good, as you must realize. What happened before was entirely my fault; I should never have allowed it. I don't want to question your sincerity, or your motives, Francis, but I can't really believe you love me, either. It was inspiration you were looking for, not a lasting love. Why, you had hardly met me before you were declaring your eternal devotion. There wasn't really time for such a strong feeling to develop."

He sat unblinking on the sofa, thunderstruck. "But that's the way I am. I know instantly when I love a woman. And if it's not possible to recognize one's emotional state so quickly, how does it come that you're declaring yourself in love with Greywell? He hasn't been home all that long."

"Long enough," she said with a smile, reaching down to pick up Andrew, who had his arms stretched out to her. "I told him about us, Francis. Not everything, at first." His alarmed look made her say hurriedly, "He didn't seem particularly upset with you, but he said he wouldn't have liked to be cuckolded. I feel terrible that I never even thought about that. Did you, Francis? Did you think about him at all?"

Her would-be lover was attempting to loosen his cravat and failed to meet her eyes. "That's not something we should discuss, Elspeth."

"How ludicrous! You don't think we should discuss such matters, but you were willing to have me."

In his own defense, Francis blurted, "Well, he didn't care about you, did he? He went off and stayed all that time, leaving you here to take care of his heir. He may even have been with other women when he was there. Did you think about that? Have you thought that he might have gone to London to be with someone? He was quite the eligible *parti* before he married the first time, you know. You may be sure there are plenty of women who would welcome him as a lover. It wasn't possible for me to think about him, when it was only you I had engraved on my mind, Elspeth." He hopped to his feet and ran long, thin fingers through his hair. "I won't bother you with my declarations again, if they are offensive to you," he said stiffly. "I never would have if you hadn't seemed to welcome them."

Elspeth placed a hand gently on his sleeve. The baby bounced up and down in her arms, making it difficult for her to present a dignified front, and she sighed. "You were there when I needed you, Francis. Thank you for that. Thank you for caring about me, and please don't be angry. I was a little confused; perhaps I'm still a little confused. But I do know we mustn't think of continuing that ill-advised flirtation, and I don't want to. Greywell has been very good to me; I wouldn't want to do anything to hurt him. He's suffered quite enough."

Francis gave an embarrassed shrug. "Yes, well, I suppose he has, but he's also had every advantage, Elspeth. Wealth, title, understanding. He's had everything he ever wanted, from the time we were children. He was even older than I was! And now he has you, too."

"I'm not sure that's an advantage."

"Of course it is! You're not at all the sort of woman anyone would have expected him to marry, and yet there you are, transformed into the perfect wife and mother to his child. And he'll get all the credit, though I honestly think I had a good deal to do with it. Didn't I, Elspeth?" he pressed, eager for some commendation.

"Yes," she said softly, standing on tiptoe to brush his cheek with her lips. He squared his shoulders then, and gave her a bleak smile before bowing formally and excusing himself. Elspeth watched him go with a heavy heart, not because she regretted ending their association but because he had given her several things to think about. Such as her not being the kind of woman Greywell would have been expected to marry. And the possibility that he would see some other woman in London. They were both rather disheartening thoughts, and she was only stopped from immersing herself in their diverse implications by Andrew's insistence on her undivided attention.

The days stretched out empty before her. A whole week, perhaps longer. He could so easily have taken her with him. That he hadn't made her prey to grave doubts. *Was* he going to see some other woman? It seemed to Elspeth that no sane man would leave for London in such heat for the sole purpose of purchasing a snuffbox, even if he was as avid a collector as Greywell was. One more box, more or less, could hardly matter that much to him. There had to be some other reason.

It was several days before she realized what that purpose was, and then she was furious with him. He had deliberately left her and Francis together to see what would develop between them in his absence. The wretch! How could he devise such a pernicious plot? Elspeth was sorely tempted to send a note to Francis on the spot. But the idea repelled her. Not even for revenge would she do such a thing. And how did Greywell think he would establish whether she and Francis had been up to no good, anyhow? Did he have the servants spying on her? He had taken his valet, and no one else in the household had seemed to pay the least attention to Francis' visit.

When she had come to the conclusion that Greywell meant only to *ask* her about Francis on his return, she softened toward him again. He really did place a great deal of confidence in her. Or in his own ability to judge whether or not she was lying. Either way, she waited impatiently for his return, planning her days to keep her as busy as possible. She had refused his offer to return early, but she held some small hope that he would be as eager to rejoin her as she was to have him back. Did he think—could he possibly think—it would take her a whole week to decide whether it was Francis or himself that she really loved? He could not possibly be that thick-headed!

So on the fifth day, and on the sixth, she dressed with special care and sat in the garden in the afternoons with Andrew toddling about the paths. And she listened for the arrival of his traveling carriage, starting at the least sound on the distant road. Several times neighbors came to visit, and she welcomed the diversion, but she began to wonder if he would even be back on the seventh day. Everyone counted a week differently, after all. Had he meant from one Tuesday to the next, or on the seventh day? She had assumed the latter, but when he hadn't arrived by ten in the evening she went wearily to her room and allowed her maid to undress her, trying to prepare herself mentally for an even later return than the following day.

The weather had cooled considerably, and a light breeze wafted over her from the slightly open window as she slept. There was a bright moon, but she had turned her back on it before going to bed. What good was a beautiful moon if her husband wasn't there to share it with her? She slept soundly.

The sleep of the virtuous, Greywell thought with a rueful smile as he stood gazing down on her. The moonlight made her skin look luminous and turned her hair into an unlikely halo about her face. He sat down on the edge of her bed.

"Elspeth?" he said softly.

Her eyelids flickered open. "David?" She hastily brushed back the tangled mane of hair that had caught about her cheeks. "And here I've spent the last three days sitting around the garden looking as nice as I could make myself. I might have known you'd arrive in the middle of the night when I was a wreck." But she turned her face up to him, smiling, for his kiss. "Did you have a good trip?"

"Very successful. Sit up and I'll show you what I got." He plumped the pillows, and while she raised herself against them he lit the branch of candles on her mantel and moved it over to the bedside table. Only as he returned was he aware that she had on the lacy nightdress the staff at Lyndhurst had given her as a wedding present. "You weren't totally unprepared for me," he teased.

"Well, I did rather *hope* . . ." she began, and then she frowned at him. "David, you went away to see if I would resume my . . . attachment to Francis, didn't you?"

"Yes," he admitted, looking slightly shame-faced.

"And you made sure he would be here, didn't you?"

"Yes."

Elspeth was taken aback by how readily he confessed to his treacherous behavior. "Well," she said, trying to sound angry, "it was very mean-spirited of you."

"Odious," he agreed as he seated himself once more on the side of her bed.

"Then why did you do it?"

"Because, my dear, I had to know. You will recall that the last time we talked about Francis you said you loved him."

"Surely you're mistaken! I couldn't have said such a thing, because it simply isn't true."

Greywell smiled at her and took her hand. "I'm glad to hear it. And to be perfectly correct, I think it was the first time we talked about Francis, and what you said was that you 'supposed' you loved him."

His wife grimaced. "I didn't know what love was then, David," she said shyly.

"Do you now?"

Elspeth reached out her free hand to touch his face, tracing the lines of his brow and cheeks and chin. "Yes, I know what it is now. And I don't mean just in bed. That's only a part of it. I thought you would simply know that I loved you. It never occurred to me that I would have to put it in words when it fairly radiated from me." She covered his lips with her fingers when he tried to speak. "No, let me say this first. Because of how I feel about you, I can understand how you felt about Caroline. I don't expect to replace her, David. You've let me know that you're fond of me. You've been kind, and thoughtful, and yes, even loving. I was thinking yesterday about my father and Abigail. They needed each other, and I believe you . . . need me now, too. That's a form of devotion I won't sneer at again. In its own way it's as important as any other kind of emotion . . . isn't it?"

"I'm sure it is." He kissed the fingers she'd removed from his lips. "But it's not exactly the sum total of how I feel about you, Elspeth. I don't think my affection can be compared with Sir Edward's. Or maybe his is stronger than I think. What I'm trying to say is that I've never felt a stronger attachment for a woman than I feel for you, my love. Loving Caroline was like loving sunlight and the sound of laughter. It was a glorious sensation, but it was based on something fleeting and ethereal. Since I've known you I've wondered how we would have weathered the years together, Caroline and I. I hope that doesn't sound unkind of me; she was a delightful woman. But she hadn't your substance, or your perseverance, or whatever it is that makes you what you are."

"She was still very young," Elspeth said. "And what I am is not always what I should be."

"That's what makes you so incredibly dear to me," he said, drawing her to him in a fierce hug. "You're always striving. You're always questioning and changing, even while you go about your everyday life. Do you have any idea how rare that is?"

Elspeth looked surprised. "No, but I'm glad you like it, because that's one part of me I don't think I could change, for you or anyone else. It's just . . . me."

He released her in order to dig in his pocket. The snuffbox he withdrew was a beautiful gold-and-enamel one, the cover set with a portrait miniature. "Do you know who this is?" he asked.

"Why, it's my great-grandmother! We had a painting of her at Lyndhurst. She was a countess, you know."

Greywell smiled and touched her cheek. "Yes, my love, I know. When I heard the snuffbox was for sale, I thought you would particularly like to have it. Which was another reason I went to London."

Elspeth took it from him and ran her finger along the cover. For a moment she thought she might disgrace herself and weep, but she blinked back the tears that threatened and smiled tremulously at him. "Thank you. You're so incredibly good to me, David."

"Do you think so?" He laughed and buried his face in her hair. "And I thought it was you who were good to me, and for me, my dear. I've had the house in London opened, so we can go whenever you wish. We probably shouldn't put it off too long. The weather is fine now, but it will turn rainy later. Andrew is certainly strong enough to go now, and I want you to have a chance to buy some frivolous gowns."

"I'd like that," she said, "but I'm not sure I should buy any frivolous gowns."

"Why not? I thought you'd developed an excellent taste in finery."

"Well, there's . . . That is, I haven't . . ." Elspeth met his eyes with a wistful gaze. "It seems I may be with child, David."

His puzzled brow cleared instantly, and an enormous grin enveloped his face. "Nothing would please me more. But surely it's too soon to be certain. Perhaps we should . . ." His hands moved to caress her breasts through the delicate lace. "Just to be on the safe side."

Elspeth lifted her lips for his kiss. "Nothing would please me more," she said.

About the Author

Laura Matthews was born and raised in Pittsburgh, Pennsylvania, but after attending Brown University she moved to San Francisco. Before she sat down to write her first novel, she worked for a spice company, an architecture office and a psychology research project, lived in England for three years, had two children, and sold real estate. Her husband, Paul, has his own architectural practice, and they both work from their home in the Upper Haight Ashbury of San Francisco. Ms. Matthews' favorite pursuits are traveling and scrounging in old bookstores for research material.